D0959595

DE ANIMA(L)

Joe Costanzo

Scripture taken from the King James Version of the Bible.

ISBN: 978-1-4834-9293-3 (sc)
ISBN: 978-1-4834-9294-0 (e)

Library of Congress Control Number: 2018912704

Lulu Publishing Services rev. date: 10/30/2018

CHAPTER 1

"Jumpin' Jack's gone."

It took Edward a few seconds to figure out what Dean Walters was talking about, and then he waited a few seconds more for everyone to burst into guffaws or at least the indulgent smiles they sometimes tried to stifle when discussing student mischief. But there was neither. Dean Walters, Coach Jespperson, Pastor Bartholomew and even Judith Scott stood there just as solemn as they'd been when they first filed into his classroom, though Judith let slip a perceptible twitch of her lips.

"Jumpin' Jack's gone?"

Jumpin' Jack was the school's mascot, a jittery, overweight black-tailed jackrabbit with huge ears that was kept in a pen in the foyer of the women's dorm. He was carted out to the gym or the stadium for all the home games. There, he cowered under the Gatorade table or hopped around nervously as far as his harness and leash allowed until he was corralled by the cheerleaders and raised over their heads like a trophy whenever the Gennesaret Jacks scored or an opponent was thwarted. In the stadium, the student body would always leap to its feet en masse and do a half-dozen jumpin' jacks after every touchdown. In the more confined bleachers of the gym, the jumpin' was tasked to the cheerleaders, who set up and jumped behind the basket whenever an opposing player was at the free-throw line. It was a surprisingly effective tactic, and with every missed shot, Jumpin' Jack would be cheered like a champ. Edward's introduction to the ritual came while sitting between Pastor Bartholomew and Judith Scott at the first football game of the season at the beginning of the fall semester, his first at Gennesaret Christian College.

"Oh c'mon, Eddie, your dignity can take a little hit," Judith had said when he tried to get away with just standing without the jumpin'.

No one ever called him Eddie. Even to his parents and his friends, he was and always had been Edward or, rarely, Ed. Never mind his last name – Stathakis – which his schoolmates spat out like one of Daffy Duck's lispy grievances. Yes, he may have been an unusually earnest child and reserved as an adult, but he didn't like to think of himself as a stuffed shirt, a stick-in-the-mud, a wet blanket, someone too sober for a sobriquet.

He had read somewhere that a person's name, or what he or she is called, had a measurable influence on how that person was perceived by others, and, by reflection, how that person perceived himself or herself. The researchers had offered up a list of names to a cohort of children and asked them to select which ones they would want for friends. They invariably picked the likes of Morts and Maggies over the Mortimers and Margarets. And a similar test revealed that adults would rather have a beer with those grown-up Morts and Maggies than the Mortimers and Margarets. So, the Morts and Maggies of the world were more likely to grow up with more pals, become more outgoing, and continue to have more close friends as adults than the Mortimers, Margarets and Edwards of the world. But that got Edward wondering whether everyone called him Edward because he was earnest and reserved, or did he end up being earnest and reserved because no one had called him Eddie? And more to the point, why had Judith? And what if he were to call her Judy?"

He wouldn't yet admit to himself that he was attracted to Judith Scott, but she was definitely attractive. Tall and athletic, she regularly won the local charity tennis tournaments and 5K races in her age group, forty to fifty, and she still held the record for the women's 500-yard freestyle at the Seven Sisters intercollegiate swim meet. She sported a healthy, natural tan even in winter. Her tastes in fashion leaned toward the expensively tailored casual, which she wore as well as any fashion model. Her hair was an unruly amber-blonde, which she seldom bothered to tame, even after stepping out of her convertible. And her eyes, a soft blue, were anything but soft. She was not one to bat her eyelashes or demurely look away when speaking to men. She had a voice that was crisp, mature, sonorous, the grown-up woman's voice from his mother's and grandmother's generations.

He was willing to admit that he liked Judith Scott, and had done so whenever her name came up during conversations with colleagues, who liked to remind him that, though twice divorced, she was way out of his league. Be that as it may, she was always attentive to him whenever she spotted him standing alone at a campus social function, and she even dropped in on him in his classroom a few times just to say hello and ask him how he was doing. At the moment, standing off to one side of the three men with her arms folded and her head tilted to one side, hers was the only reassuring presence. She seemed to be more of an observer than a participant in whatever was going on.

"Yes, he's gone," Dean Walters said.

"You mean he's dead?" Edward asked. From the looks on their faces, he just assumed.

"No, damn it!" Coach Jespperson said as if scolding a player for a fumble. "Somebody took him away or let him out. We want to know who it was, and we want to know pretty damn quick."

With Gennesaret Christian facing Riverbend Community College in the NJCAA regional basketball semi-finals Saturday afternoon, Edward could appreciate the urgency. While Jumpin' Jack was little more than a prop in the cheerleader hijinks, his absence might dampen some of the distractive enthusiasm.

"Yes, of course," he said. "How can I help?"

"We thought you might have some idea where he is, and who took him," Dean Walters said.

"No. I mean, I have no idea. My guess would be somebody from Riverbend. A college prank. Isn't that what students do: kidnap each other's mascots before the big games? I remember it happened once with the hawk at my university. They returned it the day after the game."

Coach Jespperson, who made it known to everyone, and not only his players, that they were reckoning with a former U.S. Marine, ran his fingers over his silver buzz-cut and shook his jarhead in a fit of exasperation.

Edward felt as if he were about to be benched. "What does this have to do with me?"

"Whoever took Jumpin' Jack apparently left us a clue," Dean Walters said.

He removed a yellow Post-it Note from an envelope and handed it to Edward.

"Lamija found it on the floor next to the cage. She said she saw that same thing, that L whatever it is, up on your whiteboard when she was cleaning your room the other day."

Anyone else finding a crumpled scrap of paper with nothing on it but an L in parentheses – (L) – would have simply tossed it into the trash. But Lamija, a Bosnian refugee who had been hired as a custodian a few weeks earlier, never threw away anything that might be important to somebody. When in doubt, she'd check. That's what she had been told to do, and that's what she did.

"Ah!" Edward remarked. There was little doubt that it was his (L) that someone had drawn with a green felt-tip marker in the center of the yellow Post-it Note.

"We think someone stuck it on the cage and that it probably fell off, and then it was trampled underfoot during all the commotion," Dean Walters said.

Given the circumstances, Edward agreed with the dean's hypothesis. It wasn't likely that somebody had heedlessly dropped an unrelated doodle of a parenthetical L near Jumpin' Jack's cage on the same day time that Jumpin' Jack went missing. Nevertheless, he continued to examine the note, front and back, playing for time to formulate his response. He sensed that he was not only under suspicion but that he would bear a share of the responsibility if and when the actual culprit was identified. As the new man on campus, his job security was tenuous at best.

Pastor Bartholomew hooked a finger over his banded collar as if to stretch it out, even though it was at least a full size larger than his pencil neck. Edward's stall hadn't fooled anybody. They knew more about it than they had let on.

"My friend, Edward, we're not accusing you of anything," the pastor said. "We've come in good faith not only because of the connection between the note and what Lamija saw on your whiteboard but additionally because one of your students confided in me regarding the derivation of the symbol. Your lecture, you see, apparently caused him and perhaps some of the other students a degree of discomfort and confusion that might reveal a motive."

"Oh?" Edward was surprised that his lecture had had such an effect and also disappointed that the student hadn't come to him with his concerns.

"Look, I'm not saying you did it – you tell me – but if you didn't, then it looks to me like you probably inspired the person who did," Coach Jespperson said. "So, if you know who that might be, tell us so we can get back to work. I have a team to coach."

The coach came across as intimidating even under the most collegial of circumstances. He tended to thrust his head forward and clench his fists in a combative stance regardless of the topic. Even his tight dome of a beer belly was menacing, like the bronze shield of a Roman gladiator. He may have surrendered his gut to time, but the coach had held on to his bull neck and the massive musculature of his shoulders, arms and legs.

Edward had heard some of the jocks joking that their coach could lift weights with his eyebrows.

"I really have no idea," Edward said to him.

"It must have been one of the girls," the pastor surmised. "The boys aren't allowed in their dorm."

Edward saw Judith rolling her eyes, and he smiled in spite of himself.

"For God's sake," she said. "Aren't we all taking this a little bit too seriously? Edward didn't take the rabbit. If one of his students got carried away by one of his lectures, good for Edward. It means he's getting through to them. What's the big deal, anyway?"

The others looked to the dean to respond. As the Board of Trustees' liaison to the college, Judith Scott was afforded a certain degree of deference among the administrators, faculty and staff. However, as the daughter of Franklin Scott, the billionaire benefactor of the institution, she exerted a measure of influence that far exceeded her official capacity. Edward had never seen her consciously play the "Franklin Scott card," but he knew she held it.

"No, you're absolutely right, Judith," Dean Walters replied. "Perhaps we are making too much of this."

A graduate of the Harvard Divinity School, Dean Earl Walters was a thoughtful and well-meaning administrator. He was awkward among the students, collaborative with the faculty, a bit too perfunctory with the staff, and amicable but boring in social settings, all shop and small talk. He always wore a dark blue or charcoal gray suit with a vest and a bow tie, even at the school's sporting events. Edward respected the dean's administrative skill but otherwise held no strong opinions about the man, good or bad.

Judith once told him that Dean Walters' greatest attribute was his ability to get out of the way of trouble, even when it had him in its sights. For example, years ago he had persuaded the Board of Trustees to drop the school's beloved Christian Crusader mascot, citing a cultural sensitivity stemming from the historical re-assessment of the Crusades in recent years. Moreover, he did it just ahead of the college's seventy-fifth anniversary, no less, when commemorative "Christian Crusader 75" sweatshirts, posters and pennants were already selling like hotcakes. Judith suspected it had something to do with the dean's irrational fear of a fatwā like the one that had just been placed on Salmon Rushdie, but it proved to be the right call regardless. The dean did, however, brave the ensuing outrage and the scorn that was heaped upon him by so many of the proud Genneserat Christian Crusaders past and present, and, ironically, he won accolades for his courage. According to Judith, if it hadn't been for her father's intercession on his behalf, the dean might have had more to fear from those boosters than from an ayatollah.

"So you've got Earl Walters to thank that you're a crazy rabbit instead of a marauding Christian soldier," Judith had said.

"I have a lot of confidence in the coach and his team, and I'm sure they'll do just fine without Jumpin' Jack on Saturday, if it comes to that," Dean Walters said.

"Damn right," Coach Jespperson said.

"However, Judith, there are other considerations," Dean Walters continued. "As insignificant as it may seem, the student body, our alumni, everybody at the game, even the Riberbend crowd, will be wondering the same thing: Where's Jumpin' Jack? And you know how those sports writers are. They'll blow it up out of proportion. And at some point, we'll have to have an answer. If it is a prank that will resolve itself, then fine, let's find out. We'll let everybody in on it, announce it at the game, have a good laugh. If there's something more to it, if it was some sort of misguided protest or an altogether illegal act, then we need to address that as well. But we can do neither until we identify the responsible party. Believe me, it was certainly not my intention to overstate the seriousness of this or to make more of it than it is. I'm sure you have more important matters to attend to, Judith, but I asked you to join us so as to avoid any misapprehensions that might arise among the trustees."

"Well, I, for one, don't know what to make of it," Judith replied. "I wish someone would tell me why the four of us are standing here facing Edward like a firing squad. What exactly did you say to your class, Edward? What is this L thing?"

"I was attempting to stimulate the students' critical thinking," Edward explained. "You see, we were engaged in a kind of Socratic dialogue on the topic of a life's relative value. It's a standard topic in ethics classes."

His was not an advanced philosophy class; it was Introduction to Ethics, which he always introduced to his students with the joke: "If this is your introduction to ethics, I'm assuming you just got out on parole."

Facing what suddenly did strike him as his firing squad, he continued, "I'm sure you've heard this sort of question posed in ethical considerations: Say you're driving down the road and you suddenly have to choose between running over two careless teenage jaywalkers who knowingly took a risk or swerving and killing an innocent old man on the sidewalk. The class picked it up from there, which is the way it's supposed to work.

"At one point, Marty, Marty Engerbretsen introduced a different scenario. What if it's a blind man and his seeing eye dog in the middle of the road and two innocent teenagers on the sidewalk? In this example, everybody's innocent, but does the dog enter the equation? Susan Paxton brought up the Pastor's blessing of the animals last fall and argued that if animals merit God's blessing, they also merit the same right to life as us."

"That's not ..." Pastor Bartholomew blurted, but just as abruptly stopped himself.

Although clergy and congregations from throughout the community were involved in the annual blessing of the animals on the Feast of St. Francis of Assisi the first week of October, it was always held on the Gennesaret campus commons because its vast grassy quad could better accommodate all the creatures "of God and King." Jumpin' Jack had the honor of being the first to be sprinkled with the holy water. Waiting their turns were all breeds of dogs, cats of every stripe, horses, cows, goats and their kids, sheep and lambs, pigs, chickens and roosters, ferrets and minks in cages, exotic fish in bowls, a couple of llamas, a foul-mouthed cockatoo, and even a tortoise and a few reptiles. Seeing one young man with a huge snake wrapped around his neck like one of Liberace's boas, Edward remembered thinking that it very well could have been a boa. He had never before witnessed such an amazing gathering of humans and animals in one place. It seemed to him at the time like some kind of an interspecific convention, where the delegates addressed each other in unintelligible languages as they mingled in common cause upon the earth they shared.

"JJ, you know, the rancher's boy, Jon Herriman, Jr.?" he resumed. Of course they knew. Jon Herriman Sr. was chairman of the Trustees. "JJ brought up that passage in the Bible about God giving man dominion over all his creatures. He argued that in God's eyes animals were inferior to man."

"Genesis 1:26," Pastor Bartholomew offered, expounding, "'Then God said, 'Let us make man in our image, after our likeness. And let them have dominion over the fish of the sea and over the birds of the heavens and over the livestock and over all the earth and over every creeping thing that creeps on the earth.' And 1:27. 'So God created man in his own image, in the image of God he created him, male and female he created them.'"

"Right," said Edward before the pastor could delve further into Genesis. "JJ took it to mean that since only man was created in God's image, only man has a soul. Animals were set apart for a reason."

Turning to the whiteboard behind him, Edward picked up his marker, and said as he was writing, "That's when I introduced the class to Aristotle's *De Anima.* I explained the distinction that he, for one, drew between the soul, or psychē, as he called it, of plants, animals and humans."

He underlined it as he had before:

DE ANIMA

"What does that mean?" the coach asked.

"Anima is Latin for soul," Pastor Bartholomew explained. "*De Anima – On the Soul* - is Aristotle's treatise on the special nature of the human soul. Our immortality."

"Well, I guess that depends on one's interpretation," Edward said. "Aristotle apparently also believed, as many of us do as well, that animals are capable of experiencing the world beyond just their instincts and the gratification of their physical needs and pain. He considered the possibility that they may actually have memories, imaginations, dreams and some of the same subtle emotions that we humans claim for ourselves."

He turned back to the whiteboard and added the incriminating L:

DE ANIMA(L)

Coach Jespperson shook his head. "Is that supposed to be clever? A soul with an L equals animal? Like that ridiculous God spelled backwards shit?"

"No, I wasn't trying to be funny," Edward said, if a little too defensively. "I just thought that seeing the word 'soul' there inside of 'animal' would help stimulate a deeper examination of JJ's distinction between animals and humans. It seemed to have that effect, anyway. For the rest of the hour, that's all the students talked about. Did animals have souls? What did it mean to be made in God's image? Didn't animals have eyes and ears and tongues and hearts and lungs? Didn't they feel pain, fear, sadness, anticipation, even hope? What about self-awareness?

"Peter Huelander said his dog Molly bows her head in shame whenever he scolds her, which to him signified a kind of self-awareness. Colin MacPherson said he watched a documentary about elephants that convinced him that they had souls that were maybe even purer than ours. He said they seemed totally selfless. Sofia March-Trevethian said she wished she knew what her cat was thinking when it stares into her eyes because it was obvious to her that it was thinking something. Everybody had a story. Even JJ recalled that when they were children, he and his brothers set out to name the newest calves on the family's ranch. More than a hundred of them. And they would have done it, too, if their father hadn't found out and stopped them. He said he couldn't understand at the time why his father was so angry but he later realized that he didn't want his sons anthropomorphizing animals that were destined for slaughter. It was for their own good.

"AnaLise Chen thought that in his innocence as a child, JJ must have perceived the cows' individual personalities, a manifestation of their souls. She suggested that he couldn't acknowledge it now without also acknowledging that his family has made millions slaughtering sentient creatures that valued their lives as much as he valued his.

"I know, that was harsh," Edward said, noting the disapproving glance from the dean and the bowed head of the pastor. "I pointed out that until we arrive at a universal set of ethical standards, we're going to have to consider the possibility that our own set may not be the only valid one out there. Either that or we live in perpetual conflict.

"I said the farmers I met at the Feast of St. Francis, for example, clearly cared for and even loved their animals, and yet they intended to kill them some day for their meat or hides. So, I asked, how was it possible to reconcile the one with the other? Was it possible to love lions and giraffes and elephants and yet confine them to cages in zoos for the rest of their unnatural lives? Was it possible to love those primates that look like us and yet subject them to medical experiments and inject them with toxic chemicals that we'd never test on ourselves? You know, science has barely scratched the surface of the animal mind. We're just beginning to discover that animals may have a complex emotional existence that may be different from ours but perhaps just as meaningful. Who knows, future generations may look back with horror at our treatment of these creatures, souls or not."

Sensing that he was getting carried away, a tendency that often served him well in the student evaluations he received but which seemed to be testing the patience of his colleagues, he paused and concluded, "Well, anyway, that's what we talked about. All in all, I thought it was an intellectually provocative discussion, not inflammatory."

"Well, obviously one of them was fired up," the coach said. "When I'm trying to motivate my players, I can usually tell which ones I'm winding up. How about it? Which one of the snowflakes did you rile up?"

"They were all engaged, and some of them were more passionate than others, but I don't think anybody was riled up."

"How did Jumpin' Jack enter into it?" Dean Walters asked.

Well, there it was, Edward thought. Assuming they already knew the answer, he'd have to come clean even at the risk of incriminating himself,

"I brought it up," he admitted. "I mentioned that it was difficult for me to watch Jumpin' Jack crouching in his cage or straining to escape from his harness because of an experience I had as a child.

"My grandfather on my mother's side was an Italian immigrant who brought some of his Old World ways to the New World. In the village where he grew up, having chickens, goats, pigs and even rabbits was considered a great achievement. The meat was special, a blessing, a gift to the family. So for his own family here in America, he had a chicken coop and a rabbit hutch and a pen for a couple of goats. When I was a child, maybe six or seven, I was with him one day when he pulled one of the rabbits out of the hutch by its ears and then hung it up from a tree branch by its hind legs. Before I knew what was happening, he grabbed a steel pipe about a foot long and whacked the rabbit on the back of its head. The rabbit started screaming like a child, like a human child screaming in unbearable terror and pain. I didn't know that rabbits could even make a sound let alone shriek like that. He hit the rabbit two more times before it stopped writhing and screaming. You could hear its skull crack. I've never forgotten that."

"God!" Judith said.

"Yeah, maybe I should have held that story back from the class," he conceded, recalling the stunned look on his students' faces, especially JJ's and that of Audrey Davenport, a timid girl who had seldom expressed herself in class.

"Look, if you ask me," Coach Jespperson said to the others, "I say let's send him out to talk to his students. The culprit's more likely to fess up to him. It's his play. He's the one who got the ball rolling."

"Would you be willing to do that?" Dean Walters asked.

Edward took that as an assignment, not a request. "Yes, of course," he said.

"Great, now I can get back to the gym," the coach said,

"Keep me apprised," the dean said, hurrying away as well.

Pastor Bartholomew asked Edward to meet with him sometime soon to discuss the inadvisability of introducing theological principles into the philosophical curriculum, and then he, too, walked out.

"I'm really embarrassed about all this," Edward said to Judith.

"So now what? Are you're going to beat a confession out of one of your students and march them into the principal's office?"

"No, I'll talk to them. If I find out who did it I'll encourage them to own up to it, but I won't force them to. If nothing else, maybe I can get them to hand the rabbit over to me and let me return it anonymously."

"That's not going to happen, Edward. Whoever took Jumpin' Jack isn't going to send him back to his cage. That rabbit is long gone. He's probably hopping along through the fields outside of town oblivious to the coyotes and hawks and weasels and owls and badgers and kids with .22s that are hot on his trail."

Edward might have felt a little more hopeful about his prospects, both for finding the rabbit and keeping his job, if she had called him Eddie again.

"I'm sure you're right," he said, glumly.

She smiled and said, "I'm guessing you're vegan or vegetarian."

"Semi-vegetarian. I can't seem to give up eggs and cheese. Why?"

"I thought I'd treat you to lunch or a last supper or whatever. There's this place in town that serves a primo spinach omelet. I like mine with a side of bacon, but to each his own."

"Thank you, but I've got to chase down my students before the game. There's not much time."

"Maybe I can help. I was a psych major before I switched to marketing.

They're a lot alike, by the way. Talking about your suspects with me could help you pull some of them out of the lineup. How many are there?"

"Just eleven," he answered sheepishly. "The marketing class across the hall has twenty-eight."

"Ah, don't worry," she laughed. "Your class was just added to the curriculum last semester. I'm sure it'll catch on. Philosophy is making a comeback."

"They've been saying that ever since Socrates drank the hemlock."

Chapter 2

As they were hurtling down the winding road from Gennesaret in Judith Scott's convertible Mercedes-Benz, Edward felt a little like Cary Grant sitting beside Grace Kelly as she drove along the Cōte d'Azur in the movie *To Catch a Thief*, except he was no Cary Grant. Oh, he was gripping his knees while trying to get a grip on his nerves the way Cary Grant did whenever Grace Kelly calmly took another curve at breakneck speed, but that's about where the similarity ended. He was neither suave nor rich, and while he was occasionally complimented on his full head of brown hair with nary a strand of gray even as he approached middle age, he harbored no illusions about his looks. With his lifetime gym membership and compulsive three-mile jog each morning he managed to stave off the paunch and sags that were common to men of his age but he was nowhere near buff. Sandra, his ex-wife, once told him that she had been attracted to him by his seriousness and kindness, which she later found to be tedious and maddening.

"A handsome boy like you won't have any trouble finding someone new," his mother had assured him after his divorce. In fact, looking back on it, he really was still a boy at the time, only twenty-six after his three years of marriage. Twenty years on and he had yet to find the someone new that his mother had promised him. He hadn't even had a date since his arrival at Gennesaret. And even before then, his dates were few and far between and invariably went nowhere. Bouncing around from one adjunct job to another, he hadn't been in any one place long enough to get to know very many women outside of the confined spaces of JC academe. And inside that arena, an adjunct professor of philosophy far off the tenure track was not much of a prospect. A few of his female students had flirted with him along the way but he had too many scruples to resort to predation. He practiced what he preached in his ethics classes.

"You look worried," Judith said loud enough to be heard above the wind whooshing through his full head of hair. "Is it my driving or the rabbit?"

He thought he had been masking it as well as Cary Grant, but maybe she had noticed his fingernails digging into his knees after that last hair-pin curve. There was no reason to worry, he told himself. She obviously knew the road very well, and her S-class supercar seemed capable of handling it safely at any speed. A car like this, a diamond white beauty with tan leather seats and the technology of a starship, had probably set her back more than he earned in three or four years.

"It's my default expression," he said.

She laughed and shook her head. "Really, there's nothing to worry about."

"Okay," he smiled, but he was not altogether surprised – and maybe even a little relieved – when he heard a siren wailing and turned and saw the flashing red and blue lights coming up fast behind them.

"Oh shit!" Judith said into the rearview mirror. She pulled over and waited for the patrol car. "I'm sorry, Eddie, I'll plead guilty, apologize, sign the damn ticket and get us out of here as fast as I can."

But when the officer stepped up to her car, it was he who apologized, tipping his visor and saying, "I'm sorry to stop you like this, Miss Scott, but there's an emergency and we couldn't get through to you on your phone."

He was a young man with a trim mustache and a breast pocket tag that identified him as "Sgt. Marchant." One of Edward's students was named Marchant, Riley Marchant. He had been one of the more pragmatic participants during his apparently incendiary lecture, opining that the driver of the hypothetical car was unlikely to have time to choose one person's death over another's. It wouldn't have been a conscious choice, Riley insisted. Just a "kneejerk reaction" that said nothing about intent. And that's all he had said. Edward doubted Riley would have been among the suspects that he and Judith would have pulled out of the line-up, despite the tiger head tattoo prowling beneath his left sleeve. If he had been driving, he might have asked Sgt. Marchant if Riley was a relative, just to make the kind of personal connection that can sometimes mitigate a tense interaction, and maybe get away with just a warning.

"I always turn it off when I'm driving," Judith was explaining. "No multi-tasking behind the wheel. It's something ..."

Sgt. Marchant raised his hand to stop her and said, "Ma'am, your father's lodge is on fire."

"My God!" Judith cried, turning away from the officer and looking past Edward to the plume of black smoke billowing from the hilltop across the river from Gennesaret. She slipped off her dark glasses and repeated, "My God!"

"We got ahold of Mister Scott in Chicago, and he told us to find you and have you take charge of the situation."

"Of course."

"I'll run escort for you if you like," Sgt. Marchant offered.

"Not necessary," Judith said.

Sgt. Marchant stepped back and smiled as he appraised a car that could have lapped his SUV without taxing the tach. "I guess not," he said. "I'll meet you there."

Her car spewed out a torrent of dust and gravel as it spun around and then shot back up the road they had just traveled, only this time even faster.

"I'm sorry, Edward," she said once again.

"It's fine, Judith, I understand. Don't worry about me."

He could worry about himself. And riding a torpedo back toward Gennesaret was not necessarily a bad thing, as it would actually save him the time he would have squandered, however enjoyably, over a primo spinach omelet. He hadn't taken Judith's offer of help seriously, considering the lunch more a gesture of sympathy on her part. Evaluating his eleven students' propensities for crime with her was unlikely to have resulted in a breakthrough, whatever her marketing insights. Assuming she'd drop him off at the college on her way to the fire, he nursed his glass half full until the car suddenly veered to the right, hurdled over a culvert, and plowed onto a dirt road. If he had actually been holding a glass, it would have now been imbedded in his forehead.

"A short-cut to the lodge," she said. "It's a little rough, but a lot faster."

"Great," he said, though probably not loud enough to be heard.

They ended the jarring ride over the river and through the woods at the ornate, arched iron gate of her father's lodge, arriving just behind a water tender, a ladder truck, and a TV FourNews crew. Here, the air was thick with smoke mixed with flakes of ash, and they could see flames above the screen of pines. Loud popping and crashing sounds, the buzz of chain saws, shouts and radio chatter could be heard above the rumbling of engines. An officer posted at the gate waved the arriving fire trucks through but stopped the TV news van. He shouted to the driver of the van to "get the hell away from the gate," and then he waved Judith through as well without asked her business.

The courtyard in front of the lodge was filled with fire-fighting equipment, police vehicles and a couple of ambulances. Both the fire chief and the sheriff were there, attesting to the importance of this conflagration, which at the moment had pretty much engulfed the central three-story section of the lodge and appeared to be spreading through both of the two-story wings. Ladder trucks were pouring water through windows and into caved-in sections of the roof. Seen through the billowing smoke and from a distance, firefighters clad in oversized hazmat helmets and fluorescent orange rubber suits looked like sci-fi cyborgs as their fearsome saws ripped holes into sections of the roof that were still intact.

Edward had never seen anything like it except on the news and in movies. "Hellish," was the description that came to mind as he was taking it all in. Judith, too, seemed momentarily stunned, but then she quickly turned away from it and approached the fire chief, who was standing nearby shouting into a walkie-talkie. She waited until the chief holstered the radio and then asked him if anyone had been hurt.

"No, no, at least not yet. I just ordered those hotdogs off the roof," the chief said, pointing up at the cyborgs.

"How did this happen?"

"Your housecleaning staff discovered the fire when they arrived this morning. It was spreading fast and there was nothing they could do. They called us right away, but it was pretty hopeless by the time we got here."

"Shit, Nate!" Judith said.

"I know," the chief said.

Easy going and good looking, Chief Nate Hammond had a reputation as a ladies' man. He had unusually dark eyebrows and a trim beard and looked as if he had been poured into his dazzling white shirt, which was somehow deflecting the ash and mist that saturated the air around them. Reflections of red and yellow flames danced over the polished silver shield on his breast pocket. Edward had met him recently at an alumni banquet, where Hammond, wearing that same dazzling white shirt, seemed to spend most of his time chatting with cheerleaders, until Judith Scott arrived.

"What caused it?" she asked again.

"Don't know, yet. Maybe the fireplace. We won't know until we can get in there, maybe tomorrow."

"Daddy loves this place. The great room was his heaven on earth."

"Yeah, I know, Judith, I visited with him in that room a couple of times. At least all of his trophies are safe."

"What? You were able to get them out?"

"No, no, they were already out. They're all safe in the garage."

"Who put them there?"

"Well, I guess Mister Scott had them in there for some reason. I don't know."

Judith sighed and walked away, shaking her head. Edward stayed behind and greeted Hammond, who said he remembered him from the alumni banquet.

"You're new here," the chief said.

"Yes, well, it's been a few months now."

"What are you doing here?"

"I'm teaching a class in philosophy."

"No, I mean here at the fire."

"Oh, I was with Judith when she was notified, so I came along."

"Yeah?" Hammond said, eyeing him suspiciously.

"What kinds of trophies?" Edward asked. It was either change the subject or follow Judith, and she looked as if she didn't want anyone around her at the moment.

The chief shrugged. "The usual big game. Bear, moose, elk, antelope, mountain lion, even a buffalo. This beautiful white bearded bighorn is my favorite. I'd like to see one of those in the wild. The ones old Scott was really proud of, though, were the ones he bagged during his safaris, especially the leopard. Oh, and the wildebeest and the gazelle. He said they were the toughest shots; they're so damn fast. A spectacular collection. Funny they were in the garage."

"Yeah," Edward said.

Summoned by his walkie-talkie, the chief turned his back to Edward, who took the opportunity to slip away and look around. A light breeze was blowing most of the smoke away from the courtyard, but enough of it lingered close to the ground to sting his eyes. The noise from the fire engines and the roaring blaze itself was deafening. The area near the large detached garage was the least congested and almost smokeless. He decided to wait there for Judith. The sheriff had apparently discovered that sweet spot as well. He was leaning against one of the six garage doors while talking to one of his men, who had been photographing the scene.

When the deputy resumed his work, Edward stepped up to the sheriff and introduced himself.

"We met at that game a few months ago," the sheriff reminded him. "Westminster kicked the shit out of the Jacks."

It was the sheriff's words rather than his face that reminded him of their meeting. Sitting in the bleachers in front of him, the sheriff had turned to him after the game and said, "They kicked the shit out of us." The sheriff hadn't been in uniform and hadn't introduced himself, but Edward recognized him from the election posters plastered all over town: "Re-elect Sheriff Dallas Ortega – A Job Well Done." He had replied to the sheriff's summary of the game with only a laugh and shrug, and so he was surprised by the sheriff's recollection, attributing it to the man's professional powers of observation. It was a sheriff's job, he supposed, to know his citizenry.

"I came up here with Judith Scott," Edward thought it necessary to explain.

"I know. My sergeant tracked you down."

"This is quite a place."

"In a couple of hours, you'll be saying this *was* quite a place. All log construction and no sprinkler system. It's a goner."

"Except for this garage, I guess, and the trophies."

"Yeah, and the cars," Ortega nodded. He scratched his cheek and lifted his cap off his shaved head. "There's a Bentley and a '62 Vette in there alongside your more pedestrian Rovers and Humvees, so I suppose other than the ten million dollar lodge, it's not a total loss."

Edward wasn't sure if the sheriff was trying to be funny or sarcastic, but he smiled just in case.

As they stood in silence watching the reinforcing fire crews begin their attack on the north wing, the deputy with the camera returned and handed it to the sheriff, saying, "What do you make of this?"

Ortega studied the photo for a good thirty seconds before asking, "Where is it?"

"The double doors out back."

Taking the camera with him, the sheriff walked across the courtyard to Judith and showed it to her. She immediately glanced at Edward with a shocked look on her face and walked quickly toward him with the sheriff in tow.

"Look at this," she said to Edward.

Edward studied the digital picture in the camera's viewer for about as long as he had the incriminating Post-it Note that Dean Walters had showed him earlier that morning. But there was no point in stalling for time this time; it was his (L) alright, two of them in bright yellow, this time apparently spray-painted on double doors behind the garage.

"Christ," he said beneath his breath. The day had just gone from bad to catastrophic.

"What do you know about this?" Ortega asked him.

"It's a long story," Edward said.

"Give me the Cliff Notes for now."

Edward briefed him on the kidnapping of Jumpin' Jack and its suspected connection to his lecture, leaving out the philosophical details and any hint of the passion he had exhibited earlier.

Saying nothing to what he had just heard, the sheriff walked away and disappeared behind the garage. His deputy took back his camera and quickly followed him.

"My God, Edward, I can't believe this has anything to do with it," Judith said. "I mean, taking a rabbit is one thing, but setting fire to Daddy's lodge?"

Edward hoped she was right. Maybe the fire was unrelated. An accident. A coincidence. But it seemed too much of a stretch, unless, of course, Judith's father had had the trophies moved into the garage. Otherwise, they almost certainly had been placed there by whoever had spray painted the yellow (L)s on the garage doors. And those two symbols would link him to a $10 million arson just as surely as the Post-it Note had linked him to the theft of a jittery, overweight jackrabbit.

Hoping against hope, he asked, "Do you have any reason to think it was your father who had the trophies moved into the garage?"

She pulled her cellphone out of her purse and within a few seconds was describing the scene to her father with all the pessimism it warranted.

"Listen, Daddy, they found all your trophies in the garage…Yes…I don't know…Yes, all of them, I think. I'm not sure. Is there any reason?…I don't know, Daddy, to have them cleaned or something? I'm asking you…I don't know…I'll have to ask Dallas…That's right…No, nothing, just theories…No doubt about it, it's definitely suspicious…I know, Daddy, I'm so sorry…I know…I know, and Mother's absolutely right; you should… Yes…Give her my love…No, I haven't. She said she was going camping with some friends…She didn't say…No…I will…No, don't bother with that, I'll call your agent myself…Yes…Yes…OK, good-bye Daddy. Love you."

Edward didn't have to ask. The link was forged. Whoever had moved the animal heads into the garage had done so for reasons related to his (L) and in the process they had made him their unwitting accomplice, the instigator.

Ortega and his deputy returned and stood facing Edward with almost identical icy squints.

"Where were you going when we caught up with you?" the sheriff asked.

"We were going into town for lunch. Why?"

"And the first you heard of the fire was from my sergeant?"

"That's right. Why?"

Judith intervened, saying, "Oh, for God's sake, Dallas, not every arsonist hangs out at their fires."

"A lot of them do."

"Well, Edward's here by chance, not design. He had the bad luck to accept my invitation to lunch. He's not your arsonist," she said with the same conviction as her earlier, "He didn't take the rabbit."

He wasn't and he hadn't, but how could she be so sure? Edward wondered. They hardly knew each other. Either she was a good judge of men, which failed to explain her two divorces, or she was too trusting, which might explain her two divorces. The sheriff's suspicions were more logical, even if they were unfounded.

"If this turns out to have been arson – and my money's on it – I'll have a few more questions for you," Ortega said to Edward. "I'd like you to come in to my office first thing tomorrow, and bring along a list of your students."

"Of course," Edward replied as the sheriff was already walking away. It clearly hadn't been a request.

The sheriff suddenly stopped and turned back. "Another thing. There's a reporter down by the gate. I don't want any of this information here getting out to her or anyone else. Do I make myself clear?"

"Of course," Edward repeated.

Judith, however, just rolled her eyes at the sheriff, who left it at that. After Ortega was gone, she told Edward that she was sorry but that she wouldn't be able to drive him back to Gennesaret. He was welcome to borrow any of the cars in the garage, except the Corvette. Edward could see the college's clock tower on the hilltop across the river and figured it was just a couple of miles away, as the crow flies.

"I'd really rather walk, Judith. It will help clear my head. There's a lot to take in."

"Listen, there's a trailhead about a half mile down the road. Just follow it over the foot bridge to where it forks and then take the south fork. It's shorter than the main road, and it's also a lovely hike. I'd go with you if I could. My head could use some clearing as well." She smiled sympathetically. "Don't get lost. I'll be in touch."

"Thank you." He started to leave but then paused, saying, "I'm sorry. I feel I'm responsible for all of this – your father's lodge, Jumpin' Jack…"

"You worry too much. It's not your fault. You couldn't have foreseen it. Some kids are just dangerously impressionable. Anyway, believe me, I know my father; he'll have his construction crews out here within a week. This place will be rebuilt by the time hunting season comes around. Only this time, I'll make sure he installs some good security and sprinkler systems."

She left him there and was soon climbing into the fire chief's car with the chief at the wheel and the windows closed against the maelstrom.

Edward took a deep breath and began his lovely hike back to Gennesaret, grateful that he had worn his comfortable trail runners that day. As he was walking through the gate, he noticed that the TV news crew had its camera trained on him.

"Hey there, mind if I ask you a question?" shouted a young woman standing behind the cameraman.

Edward stopped, but before he could respond she said, "We saw you arrive with Judith Scott. Are you family?"

"No, I just happened to be meeting with her when…" he gestured vaguely toward the burning lodge.

The reporter signaled a cut to the cameraman, who nodded and turned off his equipment. Her name was Mindy Dumont. Edward recognized her from watching the local news, which he did only rarely. About the same age as his students, she was much shorter and thinner in person but just as chipper and wearing the same disconcerting smile he had noted once while she was recounting the discovery of a dead homeless man in the public library's A/V room.

"Is Franklin Scott up there?"

"No, I don't think so," Edward replied.

"Whoever did it sure hit him where it hurts," she said.

Taken aback, Edward blurted, "What do you mean? They don't know what caused it."

"Oh, it was arson," she said with her on-screen cheerfulness. "We got an email from someone claiming to have done it, and it's pretty credible. If this officer here would just let us through, I'd show it to the sheriff."

She had said it loud enough for the officer to hear, and he answered, "I told you, Mindy, I notified the sheriff and he'll come down here shortly."

"OK, Dave," she said, "I'm just yanking your chain."

Edward would have liked to hang around to hear the details of the email, but he had no excuse to do so. Also, he was afraid he might call further attention to himself if the sheriff spotted him rubber-necking the interview. After all, wasn't that what arsonists did?

As Ortega had pointed out, "A lot of them do."

Chapter 3

He was not one to shy away from introspection, no matter how difficult or unpleasant. In fact, he believed it was imperative to a comprehension of his existence. He had been prone to introspection even as a child, when he had few friends to take his mind off his mind. Not self-absorbed, he would insist, but rather contemplative. Throughout his life, he tended to peer inward while exploring the world outside of himself, as if viewing life through the internal mirror of a reflective telescope. He thus avoided the direct observation that he feared might distort the reality of what he saw. Reality, he believed, is filtered through one's perceptions, and one's perceptions are focused through introspection. He had come to believe this even before he began the study of philosophy, though it was philosophy that had clarified this belief in his mind and enabled him to put it into words.

Introspection is why he had majored in philosophy in the first place and also why he was always dwelling on his failure to make a career of it. All he had ever done with his PhD was hang it on the wall of whichever institution required his temporary services. Nothing more published after his thesis, no further research, no tenure. A peripatetic adjunct for life. A temp. His lack of ambition was one of his greatest sources of wonderment. Another was his tendency to feel guilty whenever anything that he did, or thought that he did, or someone else thought that he did, caused difficulties.

So, it came as no surprise to him that he was feeling guilty about the fire at Franklin Scott's lodge as well as Jumpin' Jack's disappearance. He felt like the guy who throws a match out of a car window and starts a forest fire. He hadn't meant for it to happen, but he had been careless, and, therefore, he was responsible. As Judith with her marketing degree had so astutely observed, some kids are dangerously impressionable. They'll buy just about anything. He knew that. He should have known that when he was selling them on the souls of animals.

Though raised a Catholic, he himself had stopped believing even in human souls, his own included, not long after his Confirmation. To him, the word "soul" meant the living, breathing essence of a being, its "being." Like everything else, he had arrived at this belief through introspection and contemplation, methodologies that lay somewhere between meditation and pathological obsession along the spectrum of concentrated thought.

Whether all "beings" were equal, was a question he had yet to resolve for himself. Whenever the question came up, as it had in his classroom, he tended to arrive at a tentative equivalency through a kind of philosophical mathematics. Where humans and animals were the coefficients and the constant was death, the only variable was cruelty. Animals, he believed, killed without cruelty. He could not prove it, but he believed it. The fox who kills Jumpin' Jack would get a pass in his book; the kid who shoots him with his .22 would not.

What about Franklin Scott? Did he kill animals for sport, i.e., fun, or out of cruelty? Again, the constant was death, but was the variable mitigated by the intent? Did the enjoyment of the hunt let him off the hook? Perhaps someone who is unintentionally cruel when he snatches a buffalo away from its calf and proudly hangs its decapitated head on the wall is like the guy who unintentionally starts a forest fire; blameworthy but not necessarily evil. Maybe the billionaire was the real king of beasts. He was the lion king who had the capacity to kill even when he was not hungry, nor afraid, nor protective of his pride, and he could kill without cruelty. He had dominion over the "beings" of the sea, the heavens and the earth, and "every creeping thing that creeps on the earth." He was the Supreme Being.

Or was it more likely that cruelty and pleasure had found some way to coexist in the fertile psyches of morally damaged individuals? Perhaps the cruel streak in the hunter whose veins throb with adrenalin as he watches a majestic giraffe writhe with pain and terror as it topples dying to earth is cancelled out by the thrill of the kill. Perhaps the Supreme Being had more in common with a serial killer than the king of beasts. Perhaps the pleasure he felt was derived from cruelty, the gratification of the lust for cruelty, rather than the satisfaction of any basic instinctual imperative.

On the other hand, Edward believed, wanted to believe that his grandfather had derived no pleasure in cracking the skull of a gentle rabbit save for that of serving it *a la cacciatore* to his cubs. But how could he square that with his belief in the "being" of animals? Try as he might, he couldn't seem to erase the (L) from his mental whiteboard.

Trudging along the trail, he found himself inching closer to pathological obsession and thought it best to nudge his ruminations back to the solid footing of the moment. It actually was a lovely hike through a beautiful forest of spruces laced with aspen, an old-growth forest that had obviously been spared from any culling fire for decades. Some of the spruces were as thick as whiskey barrels, and the aspens that had been toppled by old age were rotting naturally and were now nurturing mushrooms and harboring varmints. The undergrowth was dense, but the trail was clear. He passed several camp sites with identical circular fire pits and log benches before arriving at the foot bridge over the river, which was swift and high from the spring runoff.

On the other side, he spotted another camp site through a screen of spruces. Hearing what sounded like the rattling of aluminum cans, he decided to take the detour to greet whoever was sharing his restorative experience of the forest. In the clearing, he saw a woman with her back to him dropping a beer can into her nearly full black plastic garbage bag.

"Good morning," he said.

The woman spun around, spilling half the contents of her garbage bag, and cried, "Jesus Christ, professor, you scared the shit out of me!"

"AnaLise? God, I'm sorry," Edward said to his student. "It was thoughtless of me to come up on you like that."

"Yeah, Jesus," she said, sweeping a tangled mess of hair away from her eyes. "I just woke up, so I'm still a little groggy and, you know, jumpy. A hangover, to tell you the truth."

He smiled indulgently and was about to say he had been young once himself but she beat him to the punch.

"You know how it is. Camping out with a bunch of friends, too much beer, some weed…" She stopped herself at the grim expression on his face. "You know how it is."

He didn't, which was the reason for the dark look that she had misinterpreted as disapproval. He had never had a wild night out with friends while in college, or before, or after, and he had never smoked a joint, though he kept promising himself he'd try it someday.

"Yes, well it's a beautiful spot for it," he replied with a reassuring smile. Glancing around at the fast food wrappers, beer cans and even some items of clothing – a Gennesaret Jack sweatshirt, a sock, and the thong underwear that abruptly ended his survey of the camp site – he asked, "Where are the others?"

"I guess they took off before I woke up. You'd think they would have helped clean up this mess." She shook her head. "God, what a mess!"

"Let me help you," he offered. He began by scooping up some Styrofoam cups farthest away from the underwear and he pretended not to notice when AnaLise discreetly and gingerly discarded a condom.

"It's a nice day for a hike, I guess," she said, looking up at the sunlight filtering through the film of clouds and the verdant canopy. "Do you usually take this trail?"

AnaLise Chen was one of his favorite students. She was well-read in the classics, intellectually curious, and a fearsome defender of her principles and beliefs. She was not easily moved, as he found out when he attempted to redirect her away from her harsh criticism of JJ. She was fluent in the Chinese language of her father as well as her mother's French. A JC champion gymnast, she was compact, erect and graceful.

"No, actually there's been a fire up at Franklin Scott's lodge. I've just come from there. It's pretty much a total loss."

"Wow, really? Jesus, I wonder if Kat has heard about it. She was here with us last night."

"Kat? Katrina Morrison?" Another one of his students, she was the only person called Kat that he knew of at the school.

"Yeah, she's his granddaughter."

"Franklin Scott's granddaughter? I didn't know that."

"She doesn't advertise it, but I thought everybody knew it. Judith Scott's her mother."

He was surprised, almost shocked that Judith hadn't mentioned it to him. But then why would she if she had assumed, as AnaLise had, that everybody knew it? Maybe it was Judith who was surprised that he hadn't mentioned her daughter. He would have if he had known, if only to note that Katrina was a good student and pretty low on his list of suspects. During his lecture, she had suggested that the driver should have run over the blind man and his seeing eye dog and then turned around and run over the teenagers on the sidewalk as well so as to spare himself not only from the agony of having to choose one life over another but also from the possibility that he would later regret his choice.

"Let's see; apple pie or cherry pie? Apple pie or cherry pie? I'll take apple. No, wait, I'll be sorry if I don't have the cherry. No, I'll take apple.

No, cherry. Oh, what the hell, I'd better take both," she had performed to the laughter of her classmates.

Edward had laughed along with his students, although in the context of the Socratic method, he had found it to be a not altogether absurd argument.

"Well, I'm still new around here, so I haven't made all the connections."

"It shouldn't take very long. This is a small town."

Rather than try to further excuse his ignorance of the community's relationships, he thought he could make better use of the encounter by crossing her name off the list of students that he was planning to interrogate regarding Jumpin' Jack. Interrogate, though, was too strong a word. Question, or maybe just talk to each one of them, feel them out. And not about the fire. He couldn't bring the fire into it without mentioning the (L)s on the garage, and the sheriff had made himself perfectly clear on that point. So his only job was to try to find the rabbit, with the emphasis on *try*, which is all that he had promised to do. As Judith Scott had noted, there was little chance that he'd succeed.

"Hey, AnaLise, you've heard about Jumpin' Jack, haven't you?"

"Oh, sure. I thought it was actually pretty funny."

He told her about the Post-It Note with his (L) on it and tried to discern from her expression whether she already knew about it or not. A good detective might have been able to read something into her knitted brow and pursed lips, but he drew a blank.

"You didn't take him, did you?" she asked, squinting at him as the sheriff and his deputy had done.

"No, no, of course not," he said, caught off guard by the question.

"I mean if you did do it, I wouldn't blame you after that story you told us about your grandfather's rabbit. That was horrible. And seeing Jumpin' Jack terrorized the way he is, I can see why you'd want to. I feel as passionately about animals as you do. They're so innocent and so much at our mercy. They deserve our help."

"Yes, I do understand why someone might have taken him, but I can't condone it. I would have suggested instead starting a dialogue about it with the student body and the administration. You and others who feel as you do I'm sure could have accomplished the same thing through your powers of persuasion."

"You really are new here," she said. "They'd never agree to free Jumpin' Jack. He's their mascot. I'm sorry, professor, but I for one hope whoever did it gets away with it. They'd get a medal if it were up to me."

He wanted to agree with her, but as he was playing the adult, he knew he couldn't, so he simply nodded and went back to picking up the trash. AnaLise did likewise, and when they had finished she declined his invitation to join him on the hike back to the college, saying she wanted to get some more rest.

"Thanks for the help," she yelled just before he disappeared into the forest.

Back on the trail, he took stock of his interaction with AnaLise and concluded that his first foray into sleuthing had failed to identify any suspect except himself. However, it suddenly dawned on him that he'd probably be taken off the case anyway. As much as Dean Walters might fret at the prospect of a criminal investigation and its attendant negative publicity descending upon Gennesaret Christian, he would recognize that it was no longer an internal matter. That would be fine with him. He hadn't asked for the assignment and he would be happy to drop it. But at the same time, he worried that whichever one of his students was responsible for misappropriating his (L) might soon be confronted by someone much less sympathetic than him. There was a new sheriff in town.

Upon arriving at the campus, Edward debated whether to go directly to the dean's office and confess the new and much more serious disaster linked to his (L) or leave it to the professionals. He took the coward's way out and headed instead for the parking lot. What he wanted right now was to wash the smell of smoke off his body and out of his clothes. Then he'd sit down at his kitchen counter with a salad and a hearty loaf of seven-grain bread that he'd pick up straight from the oven of Babe's Bakery, and wash it all down with a glass or two of wine from the box beneath his sink. Afterward, he'd get started on his by now all too familiar online search for a college adjunct job. Where the applications asked, "When can you start?" he'd answer, "Immediately." Attach updated resume, hit submit, and then repeat as many times as necessary to score an interview. He might have survived the missing rabbit, at least through what was left of the academic year, but not the fire.

As he was driving back toward town, he began to feel sorry for himself.

He had hoped to keep his job at Gennesaret for at least the three years and possibly even up to the five that the dean had held out to him when he was hired. His previous stint teaching English composition at a for-profit academy in Arizona had lasted two years, but he had been eager to leave it long before that. The place was too hot, the subject too stale, the students indifferent, management somewhere in Houston, and his social life non-existent. At Gennesaret he found himself engaging not only with colleagues but also with the broader community. He hadn't met any of the parents of students, nor any of the alumni, nor boosters – of which there were none – where he last worked. For that matter, he hardly even knew the students, who were not actually required to attend classes. As far as he was concerned, he had been a witting participant in a fraudulent enterprise for which he was well paid. Government loans enriched everyone affiliated with that college except the students, who would be paying for their loans with interest for most of their working lives. The pay cut he had taken to come to Gennesaret had seemed worth it at the time, when he was looking at three-to-five years teaching a subject he loved in an idyllic environment. He would be Aristotle addressing his rapt acolytes as they strolled through Arcadian temple grounds. And maybe after five years, they'd keep him on. His dashed dreams were always better than his reality.

The winding road that Judith had straightened at breakneck speed was not nearly as frightening with him at the wheel of his Subaru Outback. He was as attentive as always and as usual he was driving below the speed limit when suddenly a rabbit hopped out of the woods not more than three or four car lengths in front of him. He slammed on his brakes as the rabbit stood frozen in the middle of the road. He somehow managed to stop in time.

"God damn it!' he muttered.

Only then, as the rabbit calmly continued on its way, did he notice that it looked a lot like Jumpin' Jack. He couldn't be sure – it had already disappeared in a grassy field across the road – but it really could've been Jumpin' Jack. Should he chase after it? What chance would he have to catch it? And if he did catch it, then what? Would he return it to its cage and screamin' fans? He answered each of the questions in his own mind and then slowly drove away, hoping he still had some tread left on his tires.

What if he had run over the rabbit? The irony of it wouldn't have been lost on his students. A few of them would have probably suggested that the ethical thing would have been to swerve off the road rather than kill an innocent creature. That hadn't even occurred to him. Put to the test, Riley Marchant had been right about the kneejerk reaction in such situations, He hadn't had time to rationally choose whether to kill the rabbit or himself. Either of those outcomes would have transpired absent intent.

Taking a deep breath, he checked the time and turned on the radio. The local talk radio station would break for news in a few minutes, "at ten past the hour and as it breaks." There was only a brief mention of the fire, stating only that firefighters from throughout the county had been dispatched to the four-alarm blaze at the billionaire Franklin Scott's lodge and that any additional information would be reported as it became available. He switched to a classical music station playing a blithe Mozart concerto that he could not abide in his present mood. He turned it off altogether and concentrated on his driving. Up ahead lay farmland and ranches followed by an industrial area, where the road curved sometimes sharply alongside the river. Further on were the subdivisions and apartments – including his own in the Connor Park Apartments – leading into the town of Connor.

A couple of crows landed in the road up ahead, but he knew that unlike the jackrabbit they had the good sense to get out of the way before he got too close. As he watched them fly off over a field to his right, he spotted what looked like that same jackrabbit hopping alongside an irrigation ditch. It couldn't possibly be the same one, but it could have been its twin, another Jumpin' Jack look-alike. A few minutes later, he saw another one at the edge of a plowed field on the other side of the road, and then another one after that scurrying across the parking lot of a farm implement and machine shop. From a distance and at 40 miles-per-hour, they all looked like Jumpin' Jack.

He derided himself for thinking this was in any way unusual. He had seen jackrabbits along this road before; he just hadn't taken notice of them. Now, he was seeing them everywhere. It was the Baader-Mienhof Phenomenon, that's all, he said to himself.

His introduction to that so-called "frequency illusion" came during his senior year in high school when, one morning, the vice-principal announced over the PA system that a student's car had been stolen and asked that everyone be on the lookout for a white 1982 Ford Escort. It was not the sort of car that would normally attract the attention of a boy his age, but after school that day, he noticed for the first time that the neighbor across the street drove a blue Escort. Later that evening, he spotted a white Escort station wagon zipping through the shopping mall parking lot. The next day, he came across Escorts while going to and coming home from school. Soon, he was seeing the unremarkable little car everywhere: at service stations, the grocery story, in driveways, on streets. The following Sunday at a family gathering, he realized that his Uncle Fred drove an Escort. All this time, it had been hiding in plain sight.

"You know what that is?" his uncle had said to him when he mentioned his sudden awareness of Ford Escorts. "It's called the Baader-Mienhof Phenomenon."

A barber, his Uncle Fred, passed the time during breaks in business sitting in his comfortable barber's chair and reading the old magazines that his customers dropped off.

"I read about it once in that *Psychology Today* magazine. It's when for some reason you start thinking about something you never gave much thought to before. It could be a word, or a thing, anything. Your brain subconsciously begins looking for it, and sure enough, you start seeing it where you never saw it before, which shouldn't come as a surprise, because it was always there."

The way Uncle Fred explained it didn't make much sense to him at the time. But a couple of years later when he came across the theory again in a college psychology class, he learned that it was simply a matter of selective attention; the subconscious mind looking for and seeing what it wants to see.

Recalling the happy Saturday afternoons that he had spent in his Uncle Fred's barber chair while he was growing up gave him a break from the foreboding that was threatening to overtake him as he drove the rest of the way into town. There had been moments over the past few months when he had allowed himself to believe that Connor might actually become his permanent home. But approaching it now, it began to look like just another one of his Potemkin villages.

Connor sat almost dead center of a broad, fertile valley bordered by forests that climbed over rolling hills and up into the mountains beyond. Though not a resort town in the traditional sense, it did attract legions of fly fishermen and river runners in the summer, hunters in the fall, and snowmobilers and cross-country skiers in the winter. Its two motels and half dozen B&Bs thrived year round. Nor was it a college town in the traditional sense. Gennesaret Christian College was a major source of community pride, to be sure, and the seven hundred or so non-resident students who streamed into town at the end of August contributed heavily to the local eat, drink and be merry economy. But that was a small order of fried potatoes and a beer compared to the big money and jobs generated by the patchwork of corporate farms and ranches that covered the valley and the big logging and mining operations that were hidden away in the distant mountains.

As the county seat, Connor had been built up around an early Twentieth Century courthouse and a county hall that anchored each end of a quaint town square. Over the decades, newer government buildings, including the sheriff's office, jail, fire department and public library, had sprung up between the county hall and courthouse, with small businesses filling the gaps in between them and radiating out along a grid of adjacent side streets. A new elementary and secondary school campus had been constructed at the far end of one of these streets, just beyond the city park and the Connor Medical Center. Edward parked his car at the corner of that street and looked out across the square as if for the last time before entering Babe's Bakery.

Babe, who was busy sliding loaves of bread into the oven, shouted, "Be with you in a minute."

The only other customer in the shop was Jerry Moseley, his neighbor and Gennesaret's star mathematics professor.

"Hey, Edward," Jerry said. "The bread's fresh and the Babe's hot."

"Fuck you, Jerry," Babe yelled with a laugh over her shoulder.

Her plump cheeks were, in fact, as red as apples from the heat of the oven, and the back of her neck beneath her hair net glistened with sweat.

"Hi Jerry," Edward said. "It smells great in here, doesn't it?"

"Yeah, we're probably breathing in some calories," Jerry replied, taking a deep breath and holding it. "I could get high on it."

"A few extra calories would do you some good," Edward remarked.

"They would if Babe would hand them over."

"Oh, for Christ's sake, Jerry," Babe shouted. "You're like a little dog yapping for its bowl."

Jerry was as angular and skinny as a stick figure. His boney legs made his baggy hiking shorts look even baggier, and his feet were so narrow that his sandals slapped against his heels even when they were strapped as tight as they could go. He had no hips to speak of, his butt was flat, and his face was long. He looked like a slender man whose five-foot frame had been stretched like an elastic band to over six feet. But he was also vigorous and sturdy, more hickory stick than twig. He was captain of the faculty basketball team, ran marathons, had a shelf full of golf trophies, hiked and biked and kept a kayak atop his car for quick runs down the river whenever the opportunity presented itself.

Although he was still in his twenties, Jerry was already balding. It didn't seem to bother him, however. In fact, nothing seemed to bother him. He was droll, always cheerful and carefree. At the college, he mostly hung out with students, who were closer to his age and shared the same interests and amusements. His apartment was next door to Jerry's, and the throbbing music that sometimes shook their shared wall was not the kind you'd expect to hear from a Gennesaret professor. He was an odd-ball alright, but apparently a brilliant one. It was common knowledge that Jerry had turned down positions at Stanford, Berkeley and MIT, among others, to take the job at lowly Gennesaret Christian College. Franklin Scott had endowed a chair for this wunderkind with perks and bonuses afforded to no other faculty member. His salary was said to be substantially higher than the dean's.

He had gotten to know Jerry a little bit from the conversations they had while "chillen," as Jerry called it, on their adjacent balconies. He had come to believe that Franklin Scott needn't have paid so much to bag this particular trophy. Jerry had no use for big cities and the back-stabbing of high-stakes academe. And the money didn't seem to matter to him.

"I've got a carbon fiber bike, my kayak, these sandals and those mountains. I'm set to go anywhere I want," he had said to Edward one evening as they watched the sun set from their respective balconies.

Perhaps more to the point, he also had a boyfriend in Connor, though that was not common knowledge. Whiz or no whiz, Jerry thought he'd be forced to quit his job if it were to become widely known that a gay professor was shepherding the precious lambs of the Christian college. Of course, he had been open about it with Franklin Scott and Dean Walters before he was hired, making it clear to them that if they didn't like it they could always hire someone else, as if they stood any chance of hiring anyone else with his kind of credentials. In not so many words, he understood them to say there'd be no problem so long as there was no public scandal attached to it that would cause a stampede among the parents, boosters and alumni. There were other faculty members and people in town who also knew or suspected that he was gay, and all but a few seemed willing to live and let live. The exceptions made their displeasure known by having nothing to do with him, for which he was grateful.

"You heteros can screw each other's wives and seduce the young women in your classes and then slip them a wad of cash for abortions, but God help anyone with a scarlet LBGT or Q on their chest," Jerry noted following the nasty divorce of a colleague who had been caught napping with an unrepentant student.

Edward had been introduced to Jerry's boyfriend, Doc, across their balconies. Doc, Dr. James DiPietro, was an orthopedic surgeon specializing in sports medicine at the Connor Medical Center, which was owned by his father Anthony, a wealthy gastroenterologist. Because he was under contract as well to care for the medical needs of Gennesaret's student athletes, Doc, too, had to be somewhat discrete. As they hardly knew each other, Edward assumed that the only reason Jerry had been open with him about his relationship with Doc was that Jerry wasn't the sort of person who'd subject a man like Doc to the indignity of having to sneak in and out of his apartment. Nor was Doc the sort of person who'd put up with that kind of indignity.

"So what kind of storm are you cooking up tonight," Edward asked him while they waited for Babe.

"We're having stuffed butterfly pork chops, roasted veggies and Babe's crusty baguettes, assuming they're not stale by the time we're served."

"One more word and I'll serve one up the side of your head!" Babe cried.

"We're planning to grill on the balcony," Jerry continued, ignoring the threat, "so you may want to close your windows and cover your face with a wet washcloth if you don't want to smell the burning flesh."

"Cannibals," Edward laughed.

"Are you calling me a pig?"

"How is it you never gain any weight?"

"Elementary. I take the number of calories I consume, cancel half with genes and then I subtract the rest by shooting some hoops with Doc after dinner and biking to work in the morning. The only wild card is the wine. A glass too many and I'll have to add a couple of laps around the track."

"I should have gone into mathematics instead of philosophy. In the best of all possible worlds, I could have been another Leibniz."

"The road not taken," Jerry replied, and then paused as if struck by a thought. "I should have been a fucking poet."

After Babe had finally taken their orders and handed them their warm loaves of bread in paper bags, the two men walked out together.

"Have you heard about the fire up at Franklin Scott's lodge?" Jerry asked him.

"Yes, as a matter of fact, I just came from there."

"No shit? What's the story?"

"It's a long story. I just happened to be with Judith Scott in her car when she was notified, so I ended up going along."

"Shit, that was sooooo fucking long! I thought you'd never wrap it up."

Edward laughed and said, "Listen, Jerry, it really is a long story. I'll tell you all about it sometime if you're interested."

"It's a date, but let's not say anything to Doc, okay. By the way, Doc tells me you're looking for Jumpin' Jack. Professor Edward Stathakis gone rabbit hunting? That's pretty damn funny. Say, if you do catch it, share and we'll have rabbit stew instead of chops."

"News travels fast. How did Doc hear about it?"

"Coach called him in this morning to treat one of his players. Just a twisted ankle, but we can't have a gimpy point guard in there against Riverbend. Doc ribbed him about how they were likely to lose without Jumpin' Jack in the game, and I guess Coach launched into some kind of jeremiad about animal lovers and how that bleeding heart Stathakis had better put down his kale smoothie and find the goddamn rabbit. What the hell did you do?"

Edward smiled lamely and said, "It's actually the first chapter of that long story."

"I can't wait to hear it," Jerry said. "And hey, man, don't let Coach get to you. If they're all like him, we're lucky that there are only a few of the proud and the brave."

Edward would have offered him a lift back to the Connor Park Apartments, but he noticed Jerry's bike leaning against the bakery. The mesh panniers were bulging with groceries and a couple of bottles of expensive wine. The nice thing about having a car, he mused ruefully, was that he could buy his own wine by the five-liter box.

"By the way," Jerry said as he was mounting his bike, "Leibniz was a much better mathematician than he was a philosopher."

"Yeah, Jerry, no kidding."

By the time he reached his apartment, he had lost his appetite for the job search and instead watched a mother and her daughter savagely belittling and insulting each other on *Dr. Phil* while he picked at his salad. He had finished with it and was breaking off one more chunk of the warm bread to have with what was left of his wine when the break at the end of *Dr. Phil* teased "the latest on the big fire everyone's talking about, next on FourNews."

He refilled his wine glass as Mindy Dumont appeared standing where he had left her outside the gate of Franklin Scott's lodge. The fire that had been raging all day had reduced the billionaire's retreat to rubble, she said, but it was now down to just a few hotspots. The live intro then segued to the prepared report. Over video of the fire shot from the bottom of the driveway and other long-range vantage points, the reporter noted with an editorial hint of irritation that the news crew had not been allowed on the property. Her interviews with both the fire chief and the sheriff were conducted at the gate.

He didn't learn anything new from listening to them. In fact, they told Mindy Dumont a lot less than they knew. Nothing, for example, about the trophies in the garage or the spray-painted (L)s on the doors. However, Chief Hammond imparted more information than anyone needed to know about the methods his firefighters employed to extinguish what was essentially "a massive bonfire" because of the log construction. And his men deserved a lot of credit for preventing the fire from jumping the perimeter and spreading into the forest. He said other than the garage, the lodge was a total loss, which he estimated at "north of ten million dollars."

The report then cut back to a live Mindy Dumont, who said FourNews had received an email early that morning, which, "if credible," would indicate that the fire was intentionally set by animal rights activists.

She then read the entire missive as it scrolled down the screen:

"'Franklin Scott and all the other big game hunters masquerading as conservationists must pay a higher price than their pocket change for the "privilege" of squandering this planet's living treasure. To them it's a BIG GAME, but to these innocent ANIMA(L)s, it's their natural lives lost for NO REASON. We have paid our respects to his victims with a funeral pyre worthy of them. May their souls rest in peace.'"

"Oh, shit," Edward moaned.

Mindy Dumont then reappeared with Sheriff Ortega, asking him, "What do you make of that, Sheriff?"

"Until we know the cause of the fire, I can't speculate as to the relevance of the email you received," the sheriff replied. "If it is arson, you can be sure we'll follow the evidence wherever it leads us, and we will identify the person or persons responsible. But at this point, our investigation here is just beginning."

"But doesn't it suggest involvement by a radical animal rights group such as the A.L.F., the Animal Liberation Front? Couldn't that L in parenthesis be a hint?"

"As I said, I can't speculate as to the credibility of the claims in that email. As you know, Mindy, there are certain unstable individuals who step forward and falsely claim credit – if you want to call it that – for these kinds of high visibility events. But again, if there is a connection, we'll get to the bottom of it."

As the sheriff stepped away, Mindy concluded her report with a statement released by Judith Scott, "who expressed, quote, our shock and sadness at the loss of this beautiful lodge, which we have had the honor to share with the community during holidays and other special occasions, unquote. And, Bob, Miss Scott had high praise for the brave firefighters who risked their lives trying to save the lodge."

"As we all do," intoned Bob, the anchorman.

Edward had barely had time to shut down his laptop before his smartphone alerted him to a call from Dean Walters. He let it beep five times, one short of voice mail, before he summoned up the courage to pick up.

"Edward, are you aware of what's happened?"

"Yes, I just saw it on the news."

"I simply cannot believe that one of our students is capable of such an act."

Edward said nothing to that, but rhetorically asked himself, Who does that leave?

"I need to get out in front of this before they tie it to you and by extension to this institution," Dean Walters continued. "I'd like to see you first thing tomorrow in my office."

Edward noted the "I" instead of a "we." He would not be part of the solution; he was the goddamn problem.

"Of course, Dean Walters, but I have an appointment with Sheriff Ortega first thing. Could we make it sometime after that?"

First thing meant different things to different people. To Dean Walters, first thing in the morning was 6:30 a.m., the hour he arrived at the office. To the sheriff, it could mean anything from midnight to noon. Edward felt that the sheriff's invitation offered him the most leeway, but if the dean intended to fire him, why not keep him waiting instead?

After a long pause, the dean replied, "Fine, but absolutely no public comments. If you are contacted by a reporter, it's no comment, and under no circumstances are you to refer anyone to me for comment. Call my office when the sheriff has finished with you."

Right, and then the dean would have at him.

Chapter 4

"I'll let him know you're here," said the deputy behind the counter.

He disappeared down a hallway and was gone at least ten minutes by Edward's watch before he returned behind a briskly stepping woman who held out her hand and introduced herself as Detective Ellison.

"Let's go into the conference room. The sheriff will join us shortly," she said, stepping just as briskly back down the hallway with Edward trailing in her wake.

She waited at the door for Edward to catch up and then invited him to take a seat, anywhere he liked. There were a dozen chairs around the polished walnut table. He chose one in the middle facing the wall of windows that looked out over a parking lot to the gray concrete walls and slot windows of the Connor County Jail. She offered him a cup of coffee, which he accepted, black, and then she excused herself to fetch it.

Edward had arrived at the sheriff's office feeling guilty as charged by no one but himself and had expected a different kind of reception: Sheriff Ortega scowling at him across a card table in a windowless interrogation room, a high intensity lamp blinding him, a glass of tepid water that he would raise to his lips with a trembling hand, and then the thing he dreaded most, being read his rights.

Detective Ellison returned with the coffee and a file folder and sat down across from him. She was dressed in the same black slacks and brown shirt as all the other deputies but the star on her breast pocket was gold rather than silver. And at the moment, anyway, she wasn't wearing a gun belt. She had short brown hair, dark brown eyes and dimples in her cheeks that appeared when she smiled, which she did for the first time when she noticed his hand shaking as he lifted the Styrofoam cup to his lips.

"Stathakis," she said, "is that Greek?"

"Yes."

"Cool! A Greek philosopher." She smiled sheepishly and added, "Sorry, I bet you get that a lot."

"Well, no, not a lot." He wasn't sure why. Either most people didn't make the connection, or they did and thought, as apparently she had after the fact, that it was too lame to mention.

"I'd like to see Greece someday. Have you been?"

"No, I'd like to as well, though."

"Sure, the land of your ancestors. My own heritage is about as bland as American cheese."

"Mine, too, on my father's side. My father, grandfather and great-grandfather were all born here, so we're pretty far removed from Greece. Whenever anybody brings it up with my father, he says it's all Greek to him. My mother though is first generation Italian, so I actually feel a closer affinity to Italy than Greece." He was about to expound on it further but realized from the amused look on her face that he was babbling.

"I've been to Italy," she said. "I loved it."

If she had been trying to put him at ease, she had succeeded. He took another sip of coffee and smiled back at her.

"I've got that list of students the sheriff asked for," he said, reaching into his pocket for the folded sheet of paper. He slid it across the table, still folded.

"Great," she said. "Sheriff Ortega will be here in a minute."

The words were barely out of her mouth when the sheriff entered the room and sat down at the head of the table without greeting either one of them.

"Mister Stathakis," he said, "I asked you to come in for this interview because based on the information we received yesterday, you may be a material witness in a case of arson. You don't have to answer our questions if you don't want to, and if you'd like a lawyer present, we'll reschedule this interview. You can get up and walk out any time you want. If you consent, this interview will be recorded."

"No problem," he replied, glancing around for microphones or cameras that were nowhere in sight. "I'll answer any question I can."

"Fine. I've assigned Detective Ellison to this case," the sheriff said. He then sat back in his chair with his arms folded across his chest.

Detective Ellison removed a small notepad and pen from her pocket and said, "Okay, Edward, let's start with the lecture that featured the L in parentheses. Tell us how that came about."

"So, I was simply trying to engage my students in a Socratic dialogue, a thought exercise, on the topic of a life's relative value. It's a standard topic in ethics classes," he began, launching into the same detailed explanation that he had offered to Dean Walters and the others the day Jumpin' Jack went missing.

The detective interrupted him from time to time to clarify a particular point or to draw a clearer picture of how individual students had reacted to the topic and to what their classmates were saying. As he was answering her questions, she unfolded the sheet of paper he had given her and seemed to be making check marks, dashes, crosses and Os on the list.

At the point where Edward was recounting Katrina Morrison's interaction with the class, it was Sheriff Ortega who interrupted.

"Judith Scott's daughter?" He leaned forward in his chair. "You didn't mention that little detail yesterday. Didn't you think it might be pertinent considering it was her grandfather's lodge that was burning to the ground?"

"I didn't know about it at the time," Edward replied. "I ran into another one of my students, AnaLise Chen, later that day and she told me. She said Katrina herself doesn't bring it up much but that everyone knows she's his granddaughter. Everyone but me, I guess."

"Don Marchant's little brother is in his class as well," Detective Ellison said to the sheriff.

Edward felt she was giving him some cover, as if she were pointing out a failure in their own office. It seemed to have that effect, anyway.

"Riley or Vic?"

"Riley," Detective Ellison said.

"What did he have to say?" the sheriff asked Edward.

Edward recounted Riley's observation that in a real world application a driver would react without thinking. Describing his encounter with the rabbit in the road, he added, "I think he was probably right."

"Law enforcement logic," Sheriff Oretga said with a note of pride. "Their dad's a state trooper. We were in the academy together."

The detective nodded and then asked Edward about the students he hadn't mentioned.

"Let's see; who have I left out?"

Moving her pen down the list, Detective Ellison read the names of Noah Rosten and Audrey Davenport.

"Oh, yeah, well Audrey is very shy. She'll only speak out in class if I call on her, which I don't do very often because I can see how hard it is for her. She becomes flushed and stammers and looks like she might start crying, so I usually leave her alone. But she's a good student, aces all the tests.

"Now, Noah, he's really an interesting kid. His position during our discussion was essentially nihilistic. Every living thing dies and any meaning to its existence dies with it. The only thing that matters is the amount of suffering that precedes death, and even that only matters until death. I think he said something to the effect of 'no suffering, no foul.' AnaLise called it a cop-out and asked about our collective suffering for the suffering and death of others. His answer was the same: our collective suffering ends with our collective extinction. Death renders life meaningless."

"Right," the detective said, drawing the word out. "And do you know if any of your students are active in the animal rights movement?"

"I'm not aware of any, but then I really don't know much about their personal lives."

"I'm sorry, go on."

"There's not much more I can add," he said. "I thought the lecture had gone well, and it came as quite a shock to me when I heard about Jumpin' Jack."

"About that," Detective Ellison said, removing a marked plastic bag containing the Post-It Note that was found at the rabbit's cage. "Do you recall any of your students possessing a pad of yellow Post-It-Notes like this one?"

"Not off-hand, but it's pretty common; I'd say ubiquitous."

"Sure. What about this L? Is the handwriting familiar to you? Similar to something you might have seen before?"

"No, but, you know, it's a block letter. I'd call it a drawing rather than handwriting."

"Okay, let's move on to the fire…"

Other than explaining how he came to be at the fire, Edward had no more information to offer. He had never met Franklin Scott, had never visited the lodge before that day, and hadn't ever heard about the collection of animal trophies. He couldn't say whether any of his students had either, other than Katrina Morrison, of course.

"Franklin Scott has been featured in some popular hunting and gun magazines," Detective Ellison noted. "You've never come across those articles?"

"No, I don't hunt or shoot, so they're not something I'd normally pick up," though he had a few times long ago in his uncle's barber shop.

The detective put down her pen and glanced at the sheriff.

Sheriff Oretga leaned forward and squinted at Edward as he had at the fire. "If you had to guess, which of your students would you say were capable of these acts?"

Edward paused to think before responding. He wanted to be helpful, but he wasn't about to cast suspicion upon any of them with no evidence to back it up.

"If it were just about Jumpin' Jack, I think maybe half of them were capable of it – you know, the sort of thing a college kid might do – but the fire is something else. I can't imagine any of them doing anything so destructive."

"Give it some more thought," the sheriff said. "And think in the plural. It would have taken more than one person to take those heads off the walls."

With that, the sheriff stood and walked out of the room without saying another word.

"Is he always this terse?" Edward asked the detective.

"That was the affable Dallas Ortega that you saw here today," she laughed. "I could tell that he found your answers very helpful. Good details. Once we wrap this up, he'll probably shake your hand and ask for your vote in November."

"Support your local sheriff."

"There you go."

He stood when she did and followed her down the hall to the exit. She thanked him and handed him her card.

"Call me if you have any new information."

"Of course," he said, looking down at the name on the card – Det. Janet Ellison – as she turned and briskly walked away.

Funny, he thought, he had just accomplished with Janet Ellison the virtual suspect line-up that Judith Scott had proposed, and with the results he had expected. Describing each of his students hadn't brought him any closer to identifying who might have done the deeds, but perhaps it had helped the sheriff and the detective, who were experts at that sort of thing. Those check marks, dashes, crosses and Os that Detective Ellison had been jotting down on his list of names must have signified something. However, she and the sheriff both played their cards close to the vest. If they had latched onto something he had said, they hadn't let on.

As he was driving back to the college, it occurred to him that he should have asked them if he was free to leave Connor. Wasn't that something detectives always said to witnesses? "Don't leave town, you hear?" From Dean Walters, he was more likely to hear, "Get out of town."

And he wasn't far off the mark. Sitting like a dunce in the antique, straight-back chair in the corner of the dean's office an hour later, he was informed "with regret" that his contract would not be renewed beyond the academic year. He could finish out the six weeks that remained of the semester unless circumstances caught up with him sooner. Edward nodded sadly. The reprieve was actually more than he had expected. It meant he could leave without the embarrassment of a dismissal. Professor Stathakis won't be returning next year. Oh, well, adjuncts come and go. No surprise there.

Dean Walters paused, took a sip of his coffee. He seemed to be waiting for something more expressive than the nod. A thank you? A protest? Edward would have accepted a cup of coffee, had he been offered one, but amidst his distress, the dean had dispensed with his usual officious brand of hospitality.

"I just got off the phone with Sheriff Ortega," the dean abruptly continued. "He assured me that his office has no intention of divulging the source of that L of yours. In fact, he asked that I discourage any sharing of that information outside the school as it might interfere with their investigation. I assured him that I would do whatever I could to prevent it, but if the news media do get wind of it..."

Edward acknowledged what was left unsaid and found himself in the ironic position of trying to reassure his apprehensive superior. He calmly pointed out that there was no mention of the meaning of the (L) or its source in the email to FourNews because those responsible obviously did not want to call attention to his ethics class, and by extension, to themselves. However, if someone were to tip off the media, he would acknowledge his role and accept the blame for unintentionally inflaming the fervor of an impressionable student or students. And, of course, he would publicly apologize to the Gennesaret Christian College community and resign his position at once.

"Until then," Dean Walters said, as if fully expecting that outcome, "please keep a low profile."

"I try to," Edward said.

The dean stood and held his hand out to him saying, "I'm sorry Edward. You can rest assured that I will do nothing to dissuade any other institution from hiring you."

Which was not quite as assuring as a recommendation, but Edward would take what he could get.

"By the way," the dean added, "you might as well discontinue your efforts regarding Jumpin' Jack. I don't believe the sheriff requires any assistance in that matter."

Relieved of that duty just as he had expected, Edward managed to drive back into town without taking notice of every jackrabbit he saw along the way. Instead, he concentrated on the next phase of his life. While searching for a new job, he could start packing up his possessions. He'd need boxes. He had thrown away the ones he had used for the move to Connor. The lease. Assuming he found a job before the start of the fall semesters, he'd have to break his lease, pay for the unused months. Leave-taking. There wouldn't be much of that. A few good-byes at the college, fewer in town, and he'd be on his way. It didn't seem fair. But one of the benefits of being a philosophy professor was that he could be philosophical about such things. Shit happens.

He set about it as soon as he got back to his apartment, completing two online applications before taking a break for dinner. Neither was very promising and either would take him to places he wouldn't choose if he had a choice. But he was approaching the job search as a beggar. The more desirable schools in the more desirable communities would have already filled their adjunct positions for the next academic calendar. In the kitchen, he stood staring at the can of vegetarian chili in his hand, telling himself that after the day he had just had, he deserved a real break, a meal served on a white table cloth with wine that didn't flow out of box. Before he could make up his mind to go out, however, his hands had of their own accord opened the can and poured the chili into a sauce pan.

The next day, rather than go to the big game as he had intended to do, he holed up in his apartment and continued his job hunt. He didn't find out that Gennesaret had lost until Jerry Moseley got home.

"It was a blow-out," Jerry said from his balcony. "Riverbend made the first basket and never trailed after that. I kept shouting to Coach to put me in the game, but he ignored me. I would have been a hell of a ringer, don't you think?"

"It's too bad," Edward said.

"I wasn't the only one there who thought Jumpin' Jack cost them the game."

"I don't think Coach Jespperson buys into the talisman theory."

"He might after today. The Jacks were worthless at the free-throw line and the RiverRats killed it."

"I'm sorry I missed it."

"I'm sorry I went. I'm going to be pissed all night. We had the better team, goddamn it!"

Edward laughed. "Jerry, it's only a game."

"The semi-finals? Only a game? Maybe Coach was on to something when he told Doc you had something to do with the missing rabbit."

Edward didn't answer, but Jerry caught the look of anguish that had come over him.

"Hey man, I'm just kidding," Jerry said.

"It's okay. I'll plead the Fifth."

"Yeah, I know, it's a long story. Judith Scott said the same thing."

"You spoke to her?"

"She was sitting behind me at the game. Since you weren't very forthcoming, I asked her what she was doing slumming with my neighbor on the day of the fire. By the way, why didn't she know we're neighbors? Are you ashamed of me?"

"It never came up, Jerry. We didn't have that kind of conversation."

"Do I have to spell it out every time I'm kidding?"

"It might be helpful, Jerry. It's hard to tell with you," Edward complained. "So, did she tell you anything?"

"I told you, she said it's a long story. At least you two have got your stories straight."

He wished he could tell the whole story to Jerry. He'd like his take on it if only for the laughs. "A ten million dollar lodge burning to the ground is no laughing matter," he'd say to Jerry. And Jerry would probably say something like, "It is when you have four billion dollars to burn. It's one quarter of one percent of that. To you and me, one quarter of one percent is a nice dinner for two at the Lamplight Restaurant." To Jerry, maybe, but on his adjunct's salary it was a big chunk of change.

By the end of the weekend, he had completed his self-assigned dozen applications. Based on past experience, he expected to receive two or three interviews at the most. There was no telling if any of them would pan out, however, so he planned to complete another dozen applications before the end of the semester. He'd space them out this time, three or four a week.

In class that Monday, he kept to the dean's script and said nothing about the (L) in that email to FourNews. He didn't engage the students at all, devoting the entire hour to a droning lecture on approaches to the allocation of culpability for institutional misbehavior. He occasionally looked up from his notes at the faces of the students, looking for a glimmer of guilt, or the glint of triumph, but saw only bored, sleepy and puzzled faces. He assigned a reading on the 1984 Bhopal disaster to be discussed in class the following week, promising it would all be clearer to them by then. Dismissed, the students shuffled out of the room talking amongst themselves. JJ, however, held back until the others were gone and then returned to the classroom.

"Professor Stathakis, can I talk to you for a minute?" JJ asked from just inside the doorway.

"Sure, JJ, come in." Edward sat against the edge of his desk and gestured toward the nearest chair. "What's up?"

"Thanks," JJ said, but remained standing.

He was a lanky young man, with a square jaw, square shoulders, blue eyes and a mop of blond hair. He looked more like a California surfer than a rancher. His lazy drawl would have fit the surfer persona as well if he had tossed in a "dude" and a dopey chuckle now and then. But that wasn't JJ's style. He had a deliberative manner about him. He was pensive and curious and not afraid to ask what some of the other students might consider a "dumb question." He gave up an easy smile when it fit the occasion, but he was fundamentally a serious young man, bordering on somber.

"I was wondering if I could ask you for some advice about something."

"Well, if I'm able to, sure."

"I have an appointment with a detective this afternoon. Apparently she's interviewing everyone in the class. At least that's what Noah thinks. Someone must have told the cops about your lecture, you know, with the

L in parentheses. Then the TV station gets the email about the fire. I don't know if you saw it. It had your L in parenthesis in the word animal, so I guess we're all suspects."

"I did see it, JJ, and I have to admit I was quite surprised," Edward said. "I hope whoever sent it was just trying to make a point about big game hunting and didn't actually have anything to do with the fire. No one is saying it was arson."

"Yeah, the thing is I've been hearing some talk since Jumpin' Jack disappeared. You know, about how he was liberated. I wouldn't be saying anything now if it were just about the rabbit. I thought, hey, it's no big deal. But there was more of that kind of loose talk after the fire, and I thought, jeez, if they were involved, they're not being very careful blabbing about the L and discussing the fire like that out in the open. The thing is, I'm not sure of anything. Maybe you're right. Maybe they're just trying to make a point about Mister Scott's big game hunting. He's really proud of it, you know, but it really pisses off the animal rights crowd, just like our cattle ranch."

"What kind of talk, JJ? Do you mean they've admitted to starting the fire?"

"Not exactly. It's more like they're admitting that they know something. I'd rather not be too specific because it's not entirely clear to me. Maybe I've got it all wrong. Do you know what I mean?"

"Well, JJ, I don't think the detective is going to ask you to accuse someone of a crime without some evidence. She may ask about any suspicions you may have, and then it will be up to you whether you want to share those suspicions with her. Do you?"

"That's just it. I don't want to involve anybody without knowing anything for sure. I don't know where any of this is headed. I would hate for someone who's totally innocent to be blamed because of me. I feel like I'm caught up in a trap."

"I understand your conflicting emotions, JJ, and all I can suggest is that you go with your gut. If you feel that naming names is justified given the circumstances, then it's justified. If you're harboring too many doubts, then maybe it's not. Keep in mind, though, that sharing a suspicion is not the same thing as accusing someone. And disclosing something you've overheard doesn't even rise to the level of an accusation. I don't think anyone would hold it against you."

"Okay, professor, I guess I'll give it some more thought. But I'm really worried. Like I said, I don't know where this is headed. I just think the way some of them are talking, the things they're saying, they're bound to cause trouble for themselves whether I say anything or not."

"Give them enough rope…" Edward suggested.

"Yeah, exactly. Thanks, professor."

Go with your gut? Really? Thanks for nothing, he said to himself as JJ walked away. He wished that he could have given JJ some useful advice. But how could he when he couldn't make sense of his dilemma? He gathered that JJ was struggling between ratting out his friends and lying to the detective. That much was clear enough. And yet JJ's words, or more so a vague bleakness behind them, betrayed a deeper more personal anguish. With more to go on, he might have been of more help to the boy. Yet anything would have been more helpful than telling him to "go with your gut." He sighed, reproaching himself for sinking to that shallow platitude.

Chapter 5

In the weeks that followed, Edward was not oblivious to the tension that had entered his ethics class. It was evident in the students' interactions with him as well as with each other, among some more than others. The over-lapping chit-chat and prattle about crushing a workout, or bailing on a jerky date, or booking Europe for the summer, all of the of free-spirited interactions that used to occupy the students up to and sometimes beyond the firing of his starter pistol – "Today, class…" – were absent, muted after that first lecture following the fire and gone altogether thereafter. The banter had been replaced with quiet, almost whispered conversations amongst small cliques that always seemed to exclude the same individuals.

At first, he wasn't sure, but after observing these changeable huddles for a couple of weeks, he believed he had identified who was on the outs. Cleary, JJ had been from the start. JJ obviously wanted no part of whatever was going on and maybe he had decided after their talk to "go with his gut" and name names. Edward didn't know if he had because he hadn't followed up. He hadn't bothered to ask JJ about his interview with Detective Ellison. Bothered wasn't the word. He hadn't wanted to ask. He hadn't wanted to put JJ on the spot – did you rat on them or not?

It took a little longer to notice Audrey Davenport's exclusion because hers was not quite as absolute. A few of the students, particularly Katrina Morrison and Noah Rosten, continued to interact with her. Noah was like the kid in elementary school who tugged at a girl's pigtail just to hear her yell, "Stop it!" With Audrey, he teased her with sarcastically sincere questions about the YA romance novels she was always reading just to see her face flush as purple as the prose.

But what surprised him the most was the snubbing of AnaLise Chen. She had struck him as the hub of the social wheel in his class, and now, suddenly, she seemed to be among the ostracized. Katrina had apparently taken over that role. She appeared to be at the center of each of the cliques, which was also surprising. If the tension that had subdued and subdivided the class stemmed from the dustup of the investigation into the fire, as seemed certain, then Katrina should have been the one casting suspicious glances at her classmates, wondering which one of them had destroyed her grandfather's beloved lodge. And then there was Riley Marchant, whose brother worked with Detective Ellison, whose father was a state trooper, who, as the sheriff had noted, possessed "law enforcement logic." No one was dodging him, presumably including whoever was dodging the law. And then, of course, he, himself was among the shunned, which came as no surprise.

Dean Walters had guessed correctly that the sports reporters who covered the big game against Riverbend would take note of Jumpin Jack's absence and have some fun with off-the-wall speculations. "The RiverRats obviously brought along a lucky rabbit's foot," one of the columnists suggested. On TV, the sports guy declared, "What a game! The Christians were thrown to the lions and Jumpin' Jack must have been the appetizer because he was nowhere to be found." However, they were not investigative reporters, and they didn't pursue it. And neither they nor the hard news reporters seemed to have gotten wind of the (L) at the rabbit's empty cage, which would have tied the liberation of Jumpin' Jack and, by extension, Gennesaret Christian College, to the email claiming credit for the willful destruction of Franklin Scott's $10 million lodge.

But Edward's students knew it, and they knew that he knew it, and they had no doubt wondered amongst themselves why their ethics professor said nothing about it. He could have cleared the air from the start. Whoever took Jumpin' Jack had apparently acted in response to his lecture, he could have said. He understood and even sympathized with what he viewed as an impulsive, well-meaning and compassionate act. As for the fire, he could only hope that it was an accident that occurred during a similarly impulsive and well-meaning act. With humans having caused the loss of more than 80 percent of the planet's wild animals, most of them in the last fifty years, it could be argued that a protest against big game hunting was justifiable, even admirable, he could have said.

"We can talk about it, if you like," he could have offered. And if they had chosen not to, if they had chosen to not engage with whoever it was amongst them who was guilty, then he, at least, would have left his door open. Instead, he had allowed the cloak of silence and suspicion to fall over him as well as his class. Nothing would change until the guilty were caught, and he'd likely be gone by then. He'd be following developments and, eventually, the finale from afar. And he was pretty sure that there would be a conclusion, a resolution. There were too few suspects and, based upon what JJ had told him, too much loose talk. Sooner or later it would show up on one of the online alerts that he'd set up: "Christian College

Students Charged With Arson – Mogul's Big Game Passion Apparent Motive." He would take no pleasure from it.

He had lucked out in his job search. A young English PhD who had accepted a position at Upland Community College near the northern Utah city of Ogden had been arrested on a charge of shoplifting. The school then rescinded the job offer that might have rescued the young doctor of English from the penury that drove him to shoplift. "Luck comes in two sizes," Edward's mother used to say to him, "good and bad." Following a perfunctory telephone interview with the college's HR manager, Edward was offered the post if he could relocate in time to teach a summer remedial class. That didn't leave him much time, but he accepted the offer. Upland was only a day's drive away. He would be free to leave Gennesaret upon the expiration of his annual contract in three weeks and could be in Ogden a day or two after that, which would leave him three weeks to settle into an apartment and prepare for his new class. The subject, basic English comp, posed the least of the difficulties ahead. If he had to, he could wing it.

The day after the call from Upland, he hurried through his morning jog, actually jogging instead of walking, and then he began to pack. After he had filled the few boxes he had kept from the move to Connor, he decided to run into town for a few more boxes and then hit the gym and have lunch there while he was at it.

The gym franchise in Connor was small compared to the ones he had frequented in other places along his adjunct circuit but it offered the standard equipment. His routine was always the same: twenty minutes on the spinning bike and then thirty minutes making the rounds of the weight stations. He was pausing between sets at the lat pulldown when someone behind him said, "Hey, it's the Greek philosopher."

Detective Ellison was pushing almost effortlessly at the leg press, which was set at a higher resistance than his usual workout. She stopped and walked over to him.

"I've seen you in here quite often, but of course, at the time I didn't know who you were," she said.

He almost didn't recognize her without her uniform. She was wearing a tight gray tank top, baggy navy blue sweatpants, and red terrycloth sweat bands around her wrists and forehead. If he had seen her in the gym before, he hadn't noticed her, but then he usually didn't notice anyone there except for those who grunted loudly at every rep. He tended to lose himself in the gym as he did while jogging. Exercise seemed to leave his head open to random thought.

"Oh, hello Detective Ellison," he said, and stood up. He didn't offer her his hand as it was considered inappropriate in the gym.

"I'm off-duty; you can call me Janet."

She seemed younger off-duty, even younger than the mid-30s he guessed her age to be. She also held her smile longer as she spoke.

"I even asked Laurie about you a few months ago," she continued. "I thought something was wrong with you, that maybe you were ill. Laurie said you always looked like that."

He was taken aback. Like what? He couldn't remember ever coming to the gym when he was sick. He couldn't remember ever being sick since he arrived in Connor. And to think that not only had a stranger for some reason thought that he looked ill but also that Laurie, the gym manager, thought it was normal!

"I don't understand," he said. "What do you mean I looked ill?"

She laughed at his consternation. "You were sitting at one of the weight benches with a pained expression on your face, just staring up at the ceiling fan. I mean it was one minute, two minutes…I thought, that guy's either totally exhausted or he's just had a stroke, so I mentioned it to Laurie. She told me not to worry. She said you were a college professor and that sometimes you just sat there in a kind of trance. She assumed you were thinking big thoughts. You reminded me of a statue I saw in Rome. What was it called? *The Thinker*?"

Even as he was trying to process what she was saying about him, he couldn't help but be the professor. "*The Thinker* is the one with his chin on his fist. It's by Rodin. It's in Paris."

"Not *The Thinker*, *The Boxer*!" she recalled.

He did sometime pause, lost in thought, during his workout, but he hadn't realized how he looked while doing so or that he held the look for so long that people couldn't help but notice.

"I guess I space out sometimes," he said. "I'm lucky you didn't hit me with the defib paddles that Laurie keeps behind the counter."

"If Laurie hadn't been here, I might have," she said. "Anyway, I think it's admirable of you to exercise your mind and your body at the same time."

He smiled as much in response to her pleasant smile as to the compliment. As they stood facing each other with neither of them speaking, he wanted to ask her how the investigation was going but he thought it would be ill-mannered after she had told him she was off duty. Even police detectives deserved time off.

Instead, he said, "Well, thanks," and was prepared for her and him both to resume their sets.

"Hey, Edward," she said, "I was wondering if we could talk for a few minutes after you're through here. There are a couple of things I'd like to ask you about. Totally off the record."

"Sure, right now if you like."

"No, no excuses for skipping our sets. Let's meet outside in what, twenty minutes? We can talk over a cup of coffee at the café across the street."

He was outside the gym fifteen minutes later, and she in the appointed twenty. She was not nearly as brisk crossing the street with him as she had been in her office, but she reached the door to the café before he did and held it open for him. She chose a corner booth and ordered a café latte' and apple pie, saying it was her reward for the workout. He ordered his coffee black but splurged for the pie.

"We have some pretty good leads," she said to him after their waitress Maggie had served them their coffees. "We may even wrap it up before you leave."

"How did you know I was leaving?" He thought no one except Dean Walters was aware of it.

"Dallas told me."

He chose not to ask how the sheriff had come by the information but figured it could have only come from the dean.

"So, that's less than three weeks," he observed. "That fast?"

"The arrest part of it, yeah. Then the legal process takes over. You'll probably have to come back to testify." She said it cheerfully; as if it were something he'd be looking forward to.

"Oh? Will that be necessary? Couldn't they just take a deposition or something like that?"

"That's up to the D.A., but I'm pretty sure they'll want you on the witness stand to tie your L to the defendants." She smiled sympathetically. "Don't you want to come back?"

"It's not that. I just wish I didn't have to play a role in ruining these kids' lives," he replied, looking down into his coffee.

She sighed deeply and said, "You know, they took it a step too far. And I'm afraid they're not done. They need to be stopped for their own good."

"What do you mean? Has something else happened?"

She took a smartphone out of her gym bag and after a few taps handed it over to him. The screen was stopped on a video on a social networking channel operated under the name "inhumanlees." Edward tapped the start arrow and watched as cows were being led down a chute into an industrial building. At one point, a device of some kind was set against each cow's head. Edward guessed it was the bolt gun he had read about that is used to "brain-kill" the cow ahead of the bleeding process. As the video continued, one of the cows that had just gone through the bolt gun slumped to the ground, wagging its head and kicking its legs as another worker attempted to attach the lifting chains to its hind legs. Its lower jaw was jutting back and forth and its eyes were rolling in terror. When the cow continued to kick, the man picked up a sledge hammer and with both hands brought it down swiftly on its head, once, twice and a third time before the cow finally stopped moving. The video then focused on the name on the tractor trailer that had delivered the cattle to the packing plant: Jon Herriman & Sons. It ended with the note, "This Video Posted by (L)."

"Oh, man," Edward moaned, still staring at the little screen. "They've gone after JJ."

Janet reached for her phone and slipped it back into her bag. Maggie returned with their warm slices of apple pie. The detective started in on hers but Edward had lost his appetite.

He asked her the question he had wanted to ask since they sat down: "Do you know who they are?"

"Not yet, but as I said, we've got some good leads. I wouldn't want you to share this information, but whoever posted that video left their digital fingerprint all over it. We're hoping to trace it to the source."

"It's almost as if they want to be caught," he said.

"Sometimes that's all part of the plan. Get everyone's attention and then make your case in the court of public opinion."

"But why turn on JJ like that?"

"That's one of the things I wanted to ask you about. The first time I interviewed JJ, he knew nothing, saw nothing, heard nothing. It was only after the video was posted that he gave up some information. If it hadn't been for the video, he might have kept his mouth shut and we wouldn't have known that he knew something."

Edward nodded. He could see where she was going with this.

"JJ talked to me about it," he confessed, "but I didn't ask him for names and he didn't offer any."

"I know. He told me that he spoke to you about it, and that's what I wanted to ask you. If you had told me, I would have questioned him and maybe gotten a better read on things a little earlier. Yeah, I know, we got there eventually anyway, but only because of the video. Without the video and without your cooperation, I wouldn't be this close to a wrap."

"I'm sorry, Detective Ellison. I felt that JJ had come to me in confidence for some advice. I didn't want to throw him to the...I didn't want to betray his trust."

"I'm really not a big bad wolf," she said, laughing. "And I'm still off duty, by the way. I just want you to know that you can work with me. I know how to handle these kinds of situations so that no one's betrayed."

"I'm sorry," he repeated, "Janet."

"So, now that we've established that you can trust me, why don't you tell me about your encounter with AnaLise Chen after you left the lodge."

"Wait, I think I did tell you about that," he protested. "Remember? When the sheriff asked me why I hadn't mentioned Judith Scott's daughter, I told him that I only learned of it later when I ran into AnaLise."

Janet nodded. "Sure, but you didn't say where and under what circumstances. She didn't mention any of it either when I interviewed her. I had to hear it from JJ."

So AnaLise and JJ must have been comparing notes. That could explain why they were now among the class outcasts, Edward surmised. But what did his chance encounter with AnaLise at the camp site have to do with anything? He described it to Janet in as much detail as he could recall certain that the detective would be mentally comparing his version with JJ's. And when he was through, he asked her the question.

"I don't know, but I've got some ideas," she replied. "That camp site isn't too far from the lodge, and there were a lot people partying there that night, including some of your students. AnaLise wasn't particularly forthcoming about who exactly was there."

Other than what he had gleaned from the cop dramas he occasionally – rarely – watched on TV, he didn't know much about police work, but it surprised him that someone like AnaLise or JJ could get away with simply clamming up.

"Unfortunately, we can't use the rubber hose or phone book anymore to make people talk if they don't want to," Janet said, perhaps in response to his raised eyebrows. "Other than Katrina Morrison, did she mention anyone else to you?"

"No, she didn't. But, like I said, she seemed embarrassed. Even if I had asked, 'So who else was here for this drunken orgy?' she wouldn't have been forthcoming with me either. Anyway, wouldn't that give everybody there an alibi?"

The detective shrugged and then smiled at him. "I'm glad we talked," she said, "If the sheriff asks, I'll be able to tell him that you provided some good corroborative information."

"So, are you back on duty now?"

"Not yet," she said with the same reassuring cheerfulness that had put him at ease the first time he met her.

He took a bite of his pie and his appetite returned. They spent the rest of their time together explaining to each other how they had come to be where they were. His was simple: Gennesaret was the only school that had offered him a job teaching philosophy. He would have taken it for half the pay of the other places that wanted English or history teachers or a writing coach, positions for which he was qualified but which didn't interest him.

Hers was more complex. She was born in Connor. Her father was the town's mayor during most of her childhood. After high school, she went away to college at her father's alma mater, Sacramento State, to major as he had in public policy and administration. But she tired of it and dropped out after two years. She had learned enough to know that a career in politics or government bureaucracy was not for her. Instead of returning to Connor, she moved to LA with a boyfriend who thought he could be an actor. It didn't work out for him or them.

"He had the looks, but, Jesus, I watched some of his audition tapes and he came across as stiff as a board," she said. "I was honest with him, and he resented me for it."

After they split up, she shared an apartment with a girl everyone called "Trace" who had just graduated from the police academy and was soon working patrol in the LAPD.

"Trace loved it. She talked about her work all the time, about how exciting and rewarding it was. Even the danger thrilled her. Her enthusiasm rubbed off on me."

Her father was less enthusiastic about police work, but he told her that if she was serious about it she should return to Sacramento State and enroll in its prestigious criminal justice and law enforcement program. A degree would offer a wider variety of career opportunities. She ended up with two degrees, undergrad and masters. And then she, too, joined the LAPD working in the Crime Scene Investigations unit. She might have made a career of it except that a few years later, her father began exhibiting the symptoms of Alzheimer's disease and her mother could not cope with it alone. Based upon the prognosis of "a year at the most," she took a leave of absence with the intention of returning to LA at "the end." But her father's living death continued year after year.

"After my year was up, the LAPD cut me loose but they said I'd be welcome to reapply in the future for any available position. In the meantime, I had to do something, and the sheriff at the time was an old friend of my father's. He hired me as the department's one and only detective. He said with my degrees and experience, he couldn't very well have me out there writing parking tickets. Like everyplace else, we were starting to experience more crime around here. Drugs, burglaries, car thefts, fraud, assaults; so it wasn't entirely a charitable call."

Her father had died four years ago, "mercifully for him as well as us," and she was then faced with the hard choice of resuming her promising career in LA or staying in Connor.

"Dallas had just been elected sheriff and he wasn't sure we needed a detective. If he had eliminated the position, it would have made my choice a lot easier. I would have just gone back to LA. But before he could make up his mind, someone stumbled across a couple of bodies that had been dumped in a field outside of town. There hadn't been a homicide in Connor in more than twenty years, let alone a double. Dallas had two choices: He could assign the case to the only person in the department with any CSI experience, or he could swallow his pride and call in the state troopers. The rest, as they say, is history."

"So, did you solve that case?" Edward asked her.

"Sure. They were killed somewhere else and dumped in the field. There were tractor trailer tire tracks alongside the bodies, meth residue in one of their pockets. There was an ATL out of Denver for a trucker who had been robbing drug dealers up and down I-84, and when they caught up with him, we tied it all together in a neat little package."

He regarded her with admiration, which she acknowledged with a modest grin.

"When did you find the time during all of this to go to Italy," he asked.

"Right after that case. I told Dallas that I needed some time away from here to think about my future. He gave me a month off, half of it with pay. Speaking of time," she added, glancing at her watch, "I've got to get going."

He stood up with her and said only half in jest, "I guess I should thank you for not charging me with obstruction of justice."

"This case isn't closed," she laughed. "Hey, Edward, I'll be looking for you at the gym."

She had apparently forgotten that he'd be gone in just two weeks, and the odds of them being at the gym at the same time during that time were slim. He let that slide and simply promised to call her with any new information.

After they parted, he stopped by the grocery store to pick up some discarded produce boxes that he could use for packing and then returned to his apartment and resumed the task. At the back of his mind the whole time was the feeling that he had enjoyed his talk with Janet much more than the circumstances warranted. The tilt of her head as she smiled at him in particular stuck in his mind. Each time he pictured her sitting across from him, he felt like slapping himself and telling himself to snap out of it. And then he'd remember thinking that she hadn't mentioned a husband or children or boyfriend, other than the actor, even when she was talking about the trip to Italy. At that, he felt like slapping himself even harder.

Why did he have to assess every interaction with every attractive woman in terms of possibilities? A couple of weeks ago it was Judith Scott, before that it had been Jerry Moseley's big sister, Alice, who had flirted with him across their balconies the entire week she spent visiting her brother. He would have labeled it a midlife crisis, a fear of growing old alone, except that he had responded to any female who had given him the time of day the same way throughout his life.

Some women outside of his academic world, where his adjunct status wasn't held against him, were easily impressed by the "Professor" by which he was addressed. That wasn't true of Judith Scott or Alice Moseley, of course, but maybe Janet Ellison had allowed it to color her impression of him. Would she have been as open, as warm with him if he had been a traveling salesman peddling snake oil to college kids?

He was still digesting it all when his phone rang with a call from the sheriff's office.

"Hey. Edward," Janet said, "Sorry to bother you again, but I'd like to ask you a favor."

He almost said, "Anything," but caught himself. "Well, sure, if I can."

"AnaLise claims she can't remember which camp site they were at and she's got all kinds of excuses for not going with me to find it. Do you think you could take me to it?"

"I'm not sure. There are a lot of camp sites along the trail, but I might be able to. I'd certainly be willing to try."

"Great, when's a good time for you?"

Anytime. He'd be willing to skip his morning class. He'd go right now if it wasn't so late in the day. "I'm free tomorrow afternoon," he offered.

"Great," she repeated. "I'll meet you at the trailhead at what? Two o'clock?"

"I'll be there."

He was still rolling the prospect of the next day's hike around in his head when his phone rang again, this time with a call from Judith Scott.

CHAPTER 6

Edward had never been in the Connor Heights neighborhood, let alone set foot inside one of the two dozen or so mansions that were hidden from view down long serpentine driveways. This was the exclusive enclave of the county's wealthiest denizens. He knew from talking to Doc that the DiPietro family estate was here, though Doc himself had left it for more modest quarters in town when he returned from his residency. And he knew, now, that this was where Judith Scott lived. Her home was a sprawling faux-Tuscan villa with a stone portico leading to the massive wood and bronze front doors, which Judith herself swung open a good two or three minutes after he rang the bell. He was surprised it took her so long considering she had buzzed him through the gate at the bottom of the driveway.

"Edward!" she said smiling warmly. "Thank you for coming on such short notice."

She took his arm and led him over the ornate Italian quarry tiles of the entryway into what she called the "sitting room," or what in years past would have been known as the parlor. She apologized again for having abandoned him at the fire and then asked him to make himself comfortable while she fetched her father.

The room was sparsely furnished; four leather Queen Anne chairs and a matching couch set around a long coffee table facing a small fireplace, a couple of end tables, a sideboard bar, and Tiffany floor lamps in the corners. He sat down in one of the chairs but then nervously stood up again and circled the room. He paused to admire the large and apparently very old oil painting of a Parisian street scene above the fireplace and then walked over to the mullioned windows that looked out over a tiered fountain in the center of a small cloister. He had just returned to his chair when Judith walked in on the arm of her father as she had with him.

Edward had never met a billionaire before and hadn't known whether to expect someone like Bill Gates or *Rich Uncle Pennybags*. Franklin Scott was like neither. He was a large but not overweight man with a dark, weathered round face fringed with sparse, faded red hair and a rusty stubble over ruddy cheeks. He was an extraordinarily hairy man, bearish, with reddish hair practically sleeving his arm, almost covering his gold wristwatch and spilling out from the V-neck of his t-shirt. He was wearing white sneakers and Chicago Bulls warmup pants. To Edward, he seemed chagrined and even hostile until he held out his hand, and then he smiled broadly like Teddy Roosevelt, like the king of beasts.

"Sorry to keep you waiting," Franklin said, "I was on the treadmill. Staying fit at my age is a full-time job."

Judith laughed and said, "He has a half-dozen full-time jobs. He'd have Einstein scratching his head and wondering how in the hell does he fit thirty-four hours of work into a twenty-four day?"

"Multi-tasking," Franklin said, "Double the work in half the time."

Franklin Scott had made his billions in real estate investment and land development. He had built skyscrapers from Chicago to San Francisco and redeveloped historical buildings throughout the west into the kind of commercial office space coveted by law firms and high tech start-ups. The only reason that Edward could think of for Franklin Scott wanting to meet with him was the (L) that had been spray-painted on the doors of his garage. All Judith would say over the phone was, "I don't know, Edward, he just said he wants to talk to you."

"Take that treadmill, for example," Franklin continued as he and Edward sat in adjacent chairs. "It's got a computer, two screens, voice operation, phone, Bluetooth. The dwarfs whistled while they worked. Me, I walk while I work."

Judith, who had remained standing, stepped over to the bar and said, "Club soda, Daddy?"

Franklin nodded.

"Scotch rocks for me. The sun's setting and I'm over twenty-one," Judith said. "How about you, Edward? A man's drink or soda pop like pop?"

Her father snorted and said, "Hah, I could drink you under a table, Jude, and still be sober enough to do the *Times* crossword."

"Right, with slurred, made-up words."

Edward laughed with them and then said he'd join her in a scotch, neat. "But a small one, please. It'll be dark soon, and those roads aren't very forgiving."

"Two thin fingers," she said, showing them off as she handed him the heavy cut crystal tumbler. She sat on the couch and waited for her father to take over.

Franklin took a sip of soda as if it were hard liquor and smacked his lips. Turning to face Edward, he said, "My own treadmill, the one at my lodge – what was once my lodge – didn't have nearly as many bells and whistles as Judith's. I saw it yesterday, that treadmill, or what was left of it, half buried under a mountain of the burned rubble that they had piled up to haul away. Senseless. Absolutely senseless. Am I right?"

"Yes," Edward said tentatively.

If by senseless, Franklin meant foolish or lacking good sense, then he could agree. However, if he meant it in the sense of lacking purpose, then he was missing the point of the (L) on the garage doors and the message that was sent to the TV station.

"But what?" Franklin said, eyeing him.

"No, of course you're right. I would just say that whoever set fire to your lodge was making a statement. It was an extreme way to do it, an unnecessary way to do it, but to them it must have made sense."

Franklin shook his head and snorted again. "That's why I asked to see you. You're the provocateur who incited this riot. You may not have seen it coming, but you more than anyone know how we got here."

"I wish I did, but I really don't," Edward protested. "I admit that I got it, everybody did, when they took Jumpin' Jack. But to go from what could be characterized as a prank to an act that could end up destroying their own young lives, it's shocking."

"And you don't think they grasp that possibility, or more likely that probability?" Franklin asked.

"Do I think there's a self-destructive element involved? I don't know. Maybe. Or maybe it's a martyrdom mentality, a willingness to sacrifice themselves for a greater good. Just today someone suggested to me that sometimes in these cases the point is to generate a lot of publicity and then get caught and take the message to trial in the court of public opinion. I could see it ending that way."

"And what's the message? That Franklin Scott kills animals for the fun of it? That I murder animals that have souls like our own? That I hang their heads on my walls the way the Romans hung Christians on crosses?"

Edward thought that a pretty good summation of the message, but remained silent. He glanced at Judith, who was watching him with an incipient smile.

"Judith told me about your lecture, the talk that got this started," Franklin said. "Believe it or not, I read Aristotle's *De Anima* when I was in college. It was a long time ago, but as I recall, he was describing biological processes, not souls in the sense of something beyond the body. It wasn't a Christian concept at all."

Edward was impressed with Franklin's grasp of the work. "That's right. Anima, or psychē in Greek, is simply what distinguishes animate from inanimate. Aristotle believed that all living things begin with that in common – life. And in humans he added the ability to know. Life and knowing. At the same time, he noted that animals possess sensation and a purpose of survival."

"So why did you have those kids talking about souls, as if animals died and went to heaven?"

Edward explained, "It's an introductory class. I didn't want to lead them into that maze of Aristotelian complexities. The point was to get them thinking about the survival value, the will to live, of animals and humans, which, by the way, Aristotle presented with some equivalency in *De Anima*."

"A tree bleeds sap to fend off an attack from bark beetles. Isn't that an act of survival?"

"Artistotle's first level of anima," Edward nodded. "Probably every philosopher who has ever contemplated the nature of life has given some thought to those kinds of distinctions. For most of them, it came down to the human intellect, the ability to know. But that distinction doesn't necessarily confer superiority to humans. Schopenhauer, for example, echoed Aristotle but employed starkly different terminology when he wrote that all living things, including plants and animals, have as their basis the *Will* to live. Moreover, Schopenhauer believed that knowledge, the very thing that sets humans apart, diminishes human life because with it comes the awareness of death, the endless agonizing over past regrets and sorrows, a knowledge of evil, and even a susceptibility to boredom. The greater the knowledge, the greater the suffering. If you buy that concept, then plants and animals inhabit a superior place in the natural world. Anyway, many of the past philosophers' conclusions with regard to the human-animal distinctions are pretty much irrelevant today. That includes Aristotle's *De Anima*. He was simply wrong about a lot of things."

"That's heresy, isn't it?" Franklin said with raised eyebrows.

"Not at all. Aristotle would be saying the same thing himself if he were assessing what science has recently revealed about the brains of animals. He would be the first to admit that there's a lot more to animals than just sensation and the instinct of survival. Philosophy, after all, is based on knowledge."

"Sometimes, and sometimes it's based on what we believe."

"I admit I'm surprised, Mister Scott. Not many people bother with philosophy. It ranks right up there with the study of Latin and alchemy."

Franklin smiled his Teddy Roosevelt smile. "I enjoyed the subject. Philosophy was making a come-back on college campuses back in the 60s. We had the post-World War II industrial pragmatism that had shoved it aside for a while and then it faded again in the materialism that followed in the 80s. But there was that brief renaissance of the liberal arts that took hold from Vietnam to Watergate. I was actually surprised to hear that Earl Walters had brought it back."

"I bet he regrets it now," Judith said.

Edward smiled ruefully and said, "Yes, it was a pretty brief comeback for Gennesaret."

"What do you mean?" Judith asked.

Edward was surprised by her look of surprise. He had just assumed that she knew. "Well, Dean Walters canceled my contract for next year. I think he's afraid that we're one news story away from having a mob of parents pulling their kids out of the school. I'll be leaving as soon as I finish grading the final exams next week. I just hope it's before that news story breaks."

"God, I didn't know. That whimp. He's probably running as scared as Jumpin' Jack. I'll talk to him, Edward."

"No, please don't. Foisting me upon him would make it too awkward for everyone involved. He'd be resentful and I'd become a penitent. Besides, I've already accepted another job."

"Well, it really pisses me off," Judith said. "You did nothing wrong."

"Except put radical ideas into those kids' heads," Franklin said. "My granddaughter included."

"Oh, Daddy, Kat has felt that way about animals since she was a little girl. She never made any secret of how she felt about your hunting trips. And I'll bet you that whoever took Jumpin' Jack and then set fire to the lodge harbored strong feelings about animals long before Edward's lecture.

The only thing they took away from it was the symbol, the L, which from a marketing standpoint, is brilliant."

"Yeah, if you're selling souls that don't exist," her father replied. He looked at his watch and said, "Would you mind looking in on your mother? It's time for her pills, and she's always forgetting."

Judith rolled her eyes at something unsaid between them and left the room.

"My daughter has a blind spot when it comes to her daughter," Franklin said to Edward. "You are, I assume, a neutral observer in all of this. Have you any indication that Katrina was involved?"

Edward took a deep breath and answered him as he had everyone else: "I really have no idea. She was not a particularly active participant in our discussion of the value of animal lives. Please don't misconstrue this, as it's possible her passions lie elsewhere, but I sensed that in my class she was generally less intense, less serious than most of the other students."

Franklin responded with another snort and a shake of his head. "Once when she was eleven or twelve she was staying with us at the lodge while Judith was handling some business in New York. I was about to leave for a hunt in Montana, and Kat sprang into action, helping me carry my things to the car. I specifically remember watching her carry my rifle case and thinking it was as big as she was. Then I went inside to say good-bye to my wife. I was gone a few minutes and Kat was waiting for me by the car. I kissed her and told her to take care of Grandma. She giggled mischievously and said in her best biblical voice, 'Deliver to me the head of thine enemy.' I arrive at the camp in Montana and unload the car – no rifle. She had taken it out and hidden it while I was inside. That's my Kat. That's her to this day."

He laughed remembering it, and Edward with him, though he understood the moral of the story: A light demeanor may accompany a seriousness of purpose.

"The happy warrior's 'inward light,' " Edward said.

"'That makes the path before him always bright,' " Franklin added, beaming with pleasure. "That's it exactly! Goddamn that Walters. Kids today could use teachers who can quote Wordsworth."

"I'm by no means a detective," Edward said, "but it seems to me that

Katrina has an alibi. She was camping with some friends the night the fire started. I spoke to one of the students who confirmed it."

"That's what Judith told me. I hope it's true. I love my granddaughter. She has been the light of my life since the day she was born. If she would let me, I would support her in any endeavor she chooses to pursue. But I feel that she has shut me out of the most important parts of her life. There are some things she won't discuss with me anymore, including the hunting that she has always abhorred, and that's why I'm bothered by these circumstances. Putting those trophies in the garage – I felt there was something especially personal about it. Why not burn them if it was intended to be a funeral pyre, as they claimed? What did it mean?"

"I don't know, Mister Scott," Edward said. "Maybe it was just a reverence for those animals that anyone taking that kind of action might feel. Symbolism is important in activism. I was actually surprised that they didn't include pictures of your trophies in the email to the news media."

"And why target me, specifically? Why not that mink farm down in Snowville, raising animals just to skin them for rich European women? Why not Fehrmann's Egg Farm? Four chickens in every cage so small they have to clip their beaks so they don't peck each other to death. And Herriman's cattle ranch. Ranch my ass; it's a meat factory. Jesus, I'd go after Connor's animal control department. Those idiots are still killing strays with their truck exhaust. So why me? I contribute more money to animal conservation than a thousand animal rights activists. The fifty thousand dollars I paid last year to hunt that bighorn sheep in Utah covered the cost of putting ten more of the animals on the mountain. It's hunters like me who are keeping some of the big game reserves in Africa from being wiped out. The sport plows two billion dollars a year into Africa. That makes it worth their while to protect those animals from extinction."

Edward thought it might ease Franklin's mind – take some of the tormenting suspicion off his granddaughter – if he knew that the Herrimans, too, had been targeted, but he couldn't recall if Janet had shared that information in confidence, so he kept it to himself.

"I've only been here for a few months, and I don't know much about you, but I've been told that your big game hunting is widely known. National magazines have featured it, haven't they?"

"It's no secret."

"No, exactly, and Judith said in her statement to the press after the fire that you've hosted community events in your lodge. That means a lot of people have seen your trophies, maybe some of my students. Your granddaughter isn't the only person around here who objects to big game hunting, or hunting of any kind, for that matter. You don't have a social media account, do you? Facebook? Twitter?"

"No, I never have. It doesn't interest me. I leave all that internet business to Judith."

"Believe me, if you did, you'd be buried under an avalanche of abuse and death threats any time an article appeared about your hunting activities."

Franklin sighed and shrugged.

"Have you come right out and asked her?"

"Of course not," he said. "If she had nothing to do with it and then discovers that her grandpa suspected her of such a thing, there'd be no mending our relationship."

Edward nodded.

"Anyway, I suppose this will all play out sooner or later," Franklin said. "They tell me there's a good detective on the case."

"Detective Ellison," Edward said. "She seems very competent."

Edward felt compassion for Franklin Scott. He could only imagine how painful it must be for the old man to even contemplate the possibility that someone he loved so much, his own granddaughter, might hate him enough to have inflicted this wound. A billion dollars couldn't fix that.

"I'm glad we had this talk – Edward is it? Ed? Eddie?"

"I answer to any of them, but it's usually Edward."

Judith just then entered the room with an accusing smile for her father. "Momma said you saw to it that she took her pills before you came down. I wonder if you're becoming more forgetful or just more devious."

"Now, Jude, maybe it's your mother who's getting forgetful," he replied, winking at Edward.

Judith sat down and picked up her drink. She looked from Edward to her father and back.

"Has he persuaded you that my daughter is an arsonist?"

If truth be told, he would have told her that he, for one, was not sure of anything, but that her father had in fact made a strong case for Katrina's involvement. But facts were truth, and he decided to stick to the facts.

"I mentioned to your father that someone told me that Katrina had been camping with friends. It was after I left you at the lodge the day of the fire. I took the trail you suggested, and on the way back to Gennesaret I ran into AnaLise Chen at a campsite. She said Katrina had been there with her and some other friends that night. AnaLise hadn't even heard about the fire."

"Did you hear that, Daddy?"

"Yes, that's what he told me."

"That's what I told you. Now that you've heard it from someone other than me, maybe you'll believe it and just drop it."

"Done!"

Judith raised her glass to Edward and said, "Thank you, Eddie."

"Yes, just say the word," her father said to him, "and I'll have Walters begging you to stay on at Gennesaret."

Edward was tempted, but the idea of facing a scowling and worried Dean Walters each morning deterred him from saying the word. Setting down his empty glass, he thanked Franklin and Judith both and said he thought he'd better be heading back to town. He had exams to prepare, tons of books to pack, an early class.

Judith took his arm on the way out and drew it against her body when they reached the door. She asked him to call before he left so that she could make good on her promise of that primo omelet.

As thin as Judith's fingers were, he still felt a bit light-headed on the winding road down the hill. He opened his window to the cool night air and drove slowly. The rich, he said to himself, are not so different from you and me. Take them out of their Tuscan villa and put them in the Connor Park Apartments, take away their expensive scotch and give them a box of wine, take away their Mercedes-Benz and give them a Subaru, take away their Star Fleet treadmill and give them a pair of sneakers, take away their billions and they are just like you and me.

When he reached the main road back to town, a jackrabbit ran through the light of his high beams and darted into the darkness. But this one didn't trigger the Baader-Mienhof Phenomenon. It was the wrong color and too thin to be Jumpin' Jack. Besides, he was through chasing that rabbit down a hole.

The next morning in class, his last lecture before finals, Edward caught himself stealing glances at Katrina Morrison. And each time, he wondered what exactly was it that he expected to see? The smiling defiance of a happy warrior? Was she looking away from him in guilt? Her usual alert and amused demeanor? He had to once again admit to himself that he was functionally illiterate when it came to reading the human face. The previous night, for example, he had initially assumed from the scowl on Franklin Scott's face that the old man was hostile and itching for a fight. But then Franklin burst into his bully smile and looked as pleased as punch. Had he misread the tycoon's face at first impression, or was he fooled by the second? He couldn't be sure. It was almost as if Franklin Scott had metamorphosed on cue, like an actor. He had either worn the mask of affability from then on that night or he had dropped the hostile facade the moment he entered the room, and there was no telling which one it was. And as they talked about Katrina, did that grizzled old face express a determination to get at the truth or a fear of the truth? It was hard to say.

Katrina didn't look anything like her mother. She was nice looking, but not someone who like Judith would stop men in their tracks. She had long brown hair, large brown eyes, and pale skin. She was shorter and broader at the hips than her mother and not nearly as fit. But, like her mother, she had a confident edge softened by an amused smile, a combination that they both somehow pulled off without seeming smug.

During his first few weeks at Gennesaret, Edward thought that Katrina and JJ were a couple. They usually came into the class together and left together, and he often saw them together outside the class, at lunch, sporting events, and a couple of times having a beer at Lorenzo's Bard & Grill, the college hang-out in town. But just before Thanksgiving, he overheard Katrina and Noah Rosten making plans for a ski trip to Park City, and after Spring break, he overheard them describing their week in Cabo to some of the others in class, including JJ. So it was back to the drawing conclusions board. It seemed that Katrina and JJ had just been friends all along. Coming from the two wealthiest families in Connor, they probably had some shared history growing up in that rarefied environment.

Had been friends, he stressed, because something had come between them. He hadn't seen them walk into class together since the (L) lecture, and, in fact, they seemed to keep their distance from one another.

Looking out at the eleven students in his classroom, he was dismayed by how little he knew about them. What little he did know about them he had only gleaned from their mostly impersonal comments during class discussions and from those snippets of overheard conversations. In other words, he knew practically nothing about them even after all these months of reading and perhaps misreading their otherwise familiar faces.

Take Marty Engerbretsen, who was the one who had brought animals into the discussion that led to the (L) in the first place; he had never seen Marty in the cafeteria, in town, or at any of the school events. He was a short, overweight young man who wore sweaters even on warm days and moved his fingers as if playing the piano whenever he spoke, and he spoke often during class. He seemed very sociable, not shy at all, and yet was nowhere to be found during any of the campus social events.

All he knew about Sofia March-Trevethian was that she believed that riding a bike instead of driving a car was one of the most ethical things a person could do. She had said so in class, and she practiced what she preached. He often saw her zipping through campus on her fat-wheel bike, sitting upright, her golden curls bursting away from her head like solar flares.

Susan Paxton's face, he imagined, reflected the kind of serenity borne by an unquestioning adherence to the Protestant interpretation of Christianity. When she wanted ethical guidance, she'd look to the New Testament and not to the sermons of skeptics, cynics, sophists, agnostics and all of their misguided offspring. She had no use for pre-Christian and postmodern ideologies. She, more than any of the others in the class, was the model Gennesaret Christian College student, Pastor Bartholomew's pet.

Did any of the faces betray the kind of reckless intensity or passion that could have sparked the fire at Franklin Scott's lodge? Not Peter Huelander's, whose eyes peered through thick eyeglasses at some point in the ceiling, as if computing, which was apparently where his passions lay. He was fascinated by and obsessed with the binary brain. Edward only knew that much about Peter because Jerry Moseley had told him. According to Jerry, Peter had even programmed a drone to deliver a Diet Coke on command to the GPA coordinates of his cellphone. Jerry spent time with his students outside of his classroom, talked to them, listened to them, joked around with them, shared Diet Cokes with them, got to know them.

Certainly not Riley Marchant's, whose eyebrows and one corner of his lips often rose with amused skepticism over something being said. If he were to become a cop like his father and his big brother, he'd be the kind who would shake his head and grin while writing out a ticket after listening to the driver's ridiculous excuse for speeding.

Colin McPherson's face was the most irresolute in the class, shifting with the mood of others. He often based his comments on something he had just seen on TV or read online, such as the documentary about elephants that had convinced him of the purity of their souls. Glancing away from Colin, Edward fired his usual starter pistol.

"Today class," he began without having to wait for their attention, "I'd like to talk about that elephant sitting up here behind me."

He almost smiled as the faces of the students turned in unison toward the whiteboard at his back.

"Figuratively speaking,' he added as he drew his (L) on the board.

The dean had warned him to leave it alone, but what did he have to lose?

"As you all know, someone sent an email to the TV station taking credit, or accepting blame – depending on your point of view – for the fire at Franklin Scott's lodge and they tagged the word animal with this," he said pointing to his (L).

"We've all been interviewed by the police, and since none of us has yet been arrested, it's probably safe to assume that none of us has taken credit – or blame – for the email. For all I know, one of us might have shared the concept of the L with someone outside of this class, in which case the police may have many more interviews to conduct.

"There's a lot that I don't know about this matter. I don't know if the fire was an accident or intentional. I don't know if the person who wrote the note was actually responsible for the fire – whether by accident or intent – or simply claiming responsibility for the platform it offered. And I don't know if the fire and the disappearance of Jumpin' Jack are related.

"And while there's a lot I don't know, there are some things I can understand. If someone believes that a class of people, or, in this case, animals, are being abused, mistreated, killed unnecessarily, and that these people or these animals cannot speak for themselves, then I can understand why someone would want to speak out on their behalf. And if someone also believes that the perceived injustice is not being collectively addressed by society, then I can also understand why he or she might act independently. And sometimes, when no one is listening, you have to raise your voice to be heard.

"Was the fire at Franklin Scott's lodge someone shouting on behalf of animals? If it was, I can understand it but I cannot condone it. You've all probably heard that a hundred times before and I share your frustration with the banality of it. It's a cop-out, I know. But the point of it is that there may have been another, less destructive way to make oneself heard. And it's not only about the destruction of a building that in all likelihood will be rebuilt without significant harm to the owner. More importantly, to my mind, it's about the potential long-term damage to the promising future of whoever was responsible. The question becomes, was it worth it? It's a question with a lot of moving parts.

"Which brings me to the topic of today's assignment. I'd like you all to read Chapter 14, *The Ethics of Retribution*. Pay particular attention to the analysis of the following:

"Dialogue," he said as he was writing it on the board.

"Are communication and negotiation moral imperatives? In other words, do we shoot first and ask questions later, or do we talk before we retaliate."

Marty, the student most likely to interrupt, did so, asking, "What's the difference between retribution and retaliation?"

"Good question," Edward said. "And I apologize, because they are not at all interchangeable. Think of retaliation as revenge and retribution as justice. Retribution is the redress of an offense, the seeking of relief from an offense through a variety of means not limited to punishment. It also takes into account mitigating factors, such as remorse, which vengeance tends to discount. To understand retribution, steal my car – you'll probably get probation and a fine. To understand retaliation, steal Don Corleone's car.

"Equivalency," he said, writing it below "Dialogue."

"Equivalency as it relates to retribution. Should the punishment fit the crime or match the crime? An eye for an eye?" He stole a glance at Susan.

"If someone kicks your dog, is the answer to kick their dog just as hard, or would you accept an apology and a fine? An equivalent punishment. In this reading, you'll come across this concept drawn from Herodotus' *Histories*, where instead of a dog suffering for its owner's misdeed, we have the sins of the father being visited on the son.

"Proportionality," he added to the list on the board. "The chapter cites the example of a small-time drug dealer sentenced to life in prison. One of the principles of proportionality is that the redress should not be excessive, out of proportion to the offense. How do we measure proportionality?

"Chapter 14, *The Ethics of Retribution*," he repeated, "There will be a question on this topic in the final exam next week."

With that, he ended the class early, ostensibly to give them more time to study for the exam, but in fact to give himself more time to reach the trailhead for his hike with Detective Ellison.

CHAPTER 7

Edward parked his car behind Detective Ellison's patrol SUV at the trailhead, surprised that she had arrived there ahead of him. The clock on the dash confirmed he was twenty minutes early. He stepped out of his car expecting to find the detective sitting in hers, but her car was empty and locked and she was nowhere to be seen. He called out a "Hello" several times with no response. Assuming she was somewhere nearby, he sat down on the guardrail, where he remained for the next fifteen minutes until she appeared walking down the roadway.

"Hey," she said, "there you are lost in space just like at the gym."

He hadn't realized it, but she was right; he had been turning thoughts around in his head, mostly trying to recall the looks on the faces of his students when he wrote his (L) on the board. Try as he might, he couldn't find any face upon which to pin his suspicions.

"Hi…" He was about to call her Janet, but the uniform, dark glasses and gun belt told him she was on duty. She was carrying a plastic bag that at first glance appeared to contain a beer or soda can.

"I'm sorry I'm late. I walked up to the lodge and then back here to establish some timing," she explained. She set the plastic bag on the hood of her car and pulled out her pocket-size notebook, saying as she wrote, "Forty-eight minutes, minus fifteen or so for the side trips."

"Side trips? Where to?" he asked.

"Looking for this," she said, showing him the plastic bag. "It's the can of spray paint that was used on the garage doors. They tossed it on the way down from the lodge."

"You found it? What are the odds?" he marveled. There were about two miles of dense undergrowth down the road from the lodge.

"I'd say about fifty to one," she replied with a smile. "That's about how many plastic cups, water bottles, soft drink and beer cans and other litter I checked out along the way before I chanced upon it. I figured it would be a good throw, somewhere between thirty and fifty feet from the road, depending on whether it was thrown from a moving car or by someone on foot."

"How do you know it's the one that was used at the lodge?"

"I can't be sure until we run the tests, but I bet it'll prove to be a match. There were maybe a dozen cans of spray paint inside the garage, but no yellow. This one's bright yellow, like the Ls."

He paused, thinking, and then said, "But that means they didn't bring the paint with them. They weren't planning to paint the Ls."

"You could be on the right track, except maybe they knew there was some paint in the garage, or maybe they were planning to use a different marker, a Sharpie or something, and switched to paint when they saw it in the garage."

"Oh," he said, "I wouldn't have made a very good detective."

She placed the evidence inside her car and said, "Okay, professor, lead the way."

As they set off, Edward said he had never hiked this trail before the day of the fire and had only learned of its existence from Judith Scott, who had given him the directions back to the college.

"Have you spoken with her since then?"

"Last night, as a matter of fact. Her and her father, at her house in Connor Heights."

Janet was walking behind him so he didn't her face, but her voice betrayed her surprise.

"Really? Franklin Scott?"

"Yes, I was planning to tell you about that today," he quickly explained, not wanting to get caught withholding information again. He stopped and looked at her. "Honestly."

"It's not that," she said, frowning. "I had an appointment with him last night but then Judith called to say he couldn't see me until later today. I guess his talk with you took precedence."

"I don't know, but it's possible he wanted to hear whatever he thought I could tell him about his granddaughter's involvement before he spoke with you. I'm sure he said some things to me that he wouldn't say to you."

"Like what?"

Edward hated the idea of revealing Franklin Scott's suspicions, but he hadn't been asked to keep their conversation confidential, and he had promised not to keep any pertinent information from Janet.

She seemed to sense his quandary, saying, "I'll treat it as background. He doesn't have to know that we talked. You'd be helping me ask the right questions, that's all."

"Okay," he said, and recounted his conversation with Franklin in as much detail as he could recall. When he had finished, he added his take on it. "It was the party at the camp site, hearing it from me, that seemed to put his mind at ease regarding Katrina."

But now here he was, returning to that camp site with a detective who wouldn't be making this trek if the fact of that party had put her mind at ease regarding any involvement by Katrina, AnaLise and anyone else who had been there that night. What's more, it was he rather than AnaLise who was taking the detective to that camp site. It didn't take a professor to figure out that he might have been too reassuring to Franklin Scott.

"You don't believe AnaLise, do you?" he asked. "About not remembering where the camp site is."

"We'll see," she answered.

He hadn't turned to look at her but guessed her skepticism from the tone in her voice.

"Thanks for putting that plug in for me with Franklin," she said after they had taken a few more steps. "I can only assume he didn't connect my name with my father, Harry Ellison, or he might have replied with a few choice words. He and my father had an acrimonious relationship the whole time my father served as mayor. Mostly involving zoning and building permits for his lodge and the new dorms at Gennesaret Christian College. My father refused to cut corners on the required hearings, environmental studies, and all the other dots and crosses, and it just infuriated Franklin, who seemed to think that we should all be grateful that he was even bothering with his backwater hometown."

"He did come across that way at times, like when he was arguing that the animal rights activists – if that's who's behind the fire – that he couldn't understand why they weren't grateful to him for all the money he shelled out for wildlife conservation. He felt he was targeted unjustly, while the mink farm and Herriman and the others got away with the cruel treatment and exploitation of animals."

"You could make the case," she suggested.

"One man's rationale is another man's rationalization," he replied.

"I'm not surprised he brought Herriman into it," Janet said. "Those two have been feuding as well for as long as I can remember."

"What about?"

"I don't know. I asked Judith about it once, and she said she thought it had something to do with a bank loan that her father had blocked many years ago. He was on the bank's board of directors. Herriman apparently nearly went bankrupt trying to keep his feedlot going, and he never forgave Franklin. More recently, though, it's been about your college. I think if Franklin were living here instead of Chicago, those two would have come to blows by now. Herriman takes his religion very seriously, and Judith said he's been furious at her father for using his endowments as leverage to encourage what he sees as a secularization of the school. Hiring people like the coach and Jerry Moseley – and you," she added, laughing.

"Well, he won't have to worry about me much longer."

"I could talk to Judith about that, if you think it might help."

"Are you friends?" he asked, surprised. They seemed to him like beings from two different planets.

"Her little sister Frankie was my best friend in high school. We did everything together. I think I was closer to Frankie than Judith was. And then when Frankie died, Judith kind of held on to me, I think, for emotional support. I don't see her very often anymore, but to this day, we both cry whenever we talk about Frankie. The hardboiled detective and the tough as nails businesswoman blubbering like schoolgirls."

"I didn't know she had a sister," he said. There was so much he didn't know about the people around him, and there was so much about them that he was learning only now that he was about to move on, now that it didn't matter anymore. "I don't recall anyone mentioning her."

"It was a long time ago. Frankie was only seventeen when she died. A brain tumor. Her father took her to the best doctors and the best hospitals in the country, but it was hopeless."

Edward remained silent for a minute and then returned to her offer. "Last night, Judith and her father both offered to speak to Dean Walters on my behalf. Franklin Scott pretty much guaranteed that I'd keep my job here, but I explained to him that I couldn't stay on under those conditions. I think it would cause a lot of tension between me and the dean and it would end up being unpleasant for both of us."

"It doesn't seem to have bothered Jerry Moseley."

"Jerry doesn't need the dean or Franklin Scott. He's playing along for his own reasons. He could shoot off an email and be working anywhere in the country." He turned to look at her and said, "But it was kind of you to offer."

"Support your local philosopher."

They had reached the foot bridge, and Edward pointed toward the spruces on the other side. "It's just through there."

The camp site was much cleaner than when he first spotted AnaLise picking up the trash from the party, but not nearly as clean as he had left it after helping her. There were several beer cans, a wine bottle, plastic cups, and empty snack packages strewn about, and partially burned paper plates in the fire pit.

"Someone must have been here since that day," he said. "We had picked up pretty much everything around the fire pit."

The detective nodded while writing something in her notepad and then asked him if he could recall the brand names of the beer and soda cans and water bottles, "etcetera," that he had seen there the day of the fire. She repeated as she wrote, "Coke. Bud Light. Evian. KFC. Bacardi."

"And Diet Coke," he remembered.

She added it and remarked, "KFC. I guess they weren't all vegetarians."

"It must have been a large group, judging from all the trash that AnaLise had already picked up. One bag was full and she had started on a second one."

A large group, he repeated to himself, swinging back toward his initial verdict. A lot of witnesses to Katrina's and AnaLise's whereabouts that night, a pretty good alibi, he thought, even if he wasn't a detective.

"You'd think AnaLise could remember who some of them were," Janet observed wryly.

So, swinging back the other way again, he said, "Yeah, I don't understand it. She seems so frank and fearless. She doesn't hold back in class. What about Katrina? Was she also uncooperative?"

"I haven't interviewed her yet. Franklin Scott's lawyers have been stalling it. I hope to break that logjam when I talk to him later today," Janet replied as she leaned over the fire pit.

She scraped through the ashes with a scorched tree limb, pausing to examine each identifiable piece of trash like an archeologist sifting through an ancient midden. She removed only three items from the pit; an unburned package of KFC plastic utensils that must have been buried under the ash of an earlier fire, a crushed Coke can wedged between two of the rocks surrounding the pit, and what looked like the tongue from a leather hiking boot. She placed those items in a plastic bag that she pulled from a pouch in her gun belt, and then she began walking slowly around the pit in an expanding spiral with her eyes focused on the ground in front of her feet.

Edward stepped back twice to avoid blocking her path before he had the sense to move into the area she had already covered,

"Can I help?" he asked.

She stopped and looked up. "Well, you could go out there past the trees and look around for anything that looks interesting."

"Like what?"

"Like the kind of trash you saw the last time you were here. I'll be there in a couple of minutes."

Soon they were both circling trees and zig-zagging through clearings in the undergrowth, where campers apparently pitched their tents or rolled out their sleeping bags for privacy away from gatherings at the pit. At one such spot, Edward came across a stained orange rag and asked the detective if he should pick it up.

She joined him and looked down at the rag. "Yeah, I'd call that interesting. It's a mechanic's rag," she said as she was placing it in a plastic bag, "only those are blood stains, not oil."

After that, they found nothing more to bag. Instead, Detective Ellison took out her cellphone and took pictures of the camp site and the surrounding area, entered a few more notes in her notepad, and declared, "Great, Edward. We're done here. If I weren't on duty I'd buy you a beer, maybe even two."

"I'll take a rain check."

"I'm good for it," she said.

Afterward, Edward decided to return to the college and begin packing up what few personal belongings he had there. Tucked between the cafeteria and the assembly hall, his was one of three adjacent offices the size of closets and the only one currently occupied. The other two had been converted into storage rooms. He didn't mind the isolation or the size of his office, but he wished it had a window, not that it mattered anymore. He usually compensated for the oppressive confinement by leaving the door open and spending as little time there as possible, preferring to do most of his work in his classroom whenever it was available. Besides his desk the only other furniture in the room was the kind of metal utility shelving normally found in a garage or in the adjacent storage rooms and which he had converted into his bookshelf, and an antique oak swivel office chair with a badly split red leather seat. Other than a shelf of books, there was nothing of him in the office; no photographs of family, no mementos, no knick-knacks, not even a coffee mug.

As he was clearing out his desk, the dean walked by more quickly than usual and looking straight ahead. Only now that he was leaving did Edward finally form an opinion about the man. Dean Walters really was a coward, as Judith had said, frightened of everybody's shadow except his own. And he was not particularly intelligent. He couldn't seem to resolve difficulties in his own mind, let alone in practice, so he ran away from them. Or chased them away. Out of sight, out of mind. Don't look at me, Edward thought, and maybe I'm not really here.

Students leaving late classes or heading for a snack and some studying or socializing in the cafeteria walked by alone, in pairs and in small groups, but none from his class. To them, he was also invisible, the adjunct in the closet. Once, early in his non-tenured tenure there, he heard one student say to another as they walked by, "I think he's a philosophy teacher." And the other one replied, "My philosophy is, don't waste your time." He realized that they were unaware of how far their voices carried in that hallway, but he was disheartened just the same.

Philosophy was not dead yet, he knew for a fact, but it had been relegated to irrelevancy by so much of society's emphasis on a magnified and somewhat perverted version of William James' theory of pragmatism. Franklin Scott had that right. There was more interest in the ends than in either the means or the beginnings and little thought given to thought itself. Epicurus, who believed that pleasure was derived not from the senses but from the intellect, would have been horrified by the misappropriation of his philosophy to justify the excesses of the modern appetite. Edward wished that he could have told that student whose philosophy was "don't waste your time" that philosophy was one of the best ways to evaluate what in fact is a waste of time. It could be that philosophy and the other impractical liberal arts were merely going through another dormancy and would re-emerge in in the midst of a new era of introspective appraisal of a chaotic world, as they had in Franklin Scott's college days. But he was not optimistic. It could be that philosophers were an indicator species of sorts and that their ultimate demise in the not too distant future would mark an irreversible turning point in the cultural ecosystem.

Coach Jespperson passed by and curtly nodded to him and then turned back and for the first time ever entered his office.

"I hear you're not coming back next year after all," the coach said, dropping into the leather chair.

"I can confirm that rumor," Edward said with a smile, pleased that someone in the school cared enough to talk about it, even if it was Coach Jespperson.

"I can't say that I'm surprised," the coach said, fingering the whistle dangling from his neck. "Walters sees you as an unexploded grenade, and you know what to do with one of those; you throw it as far as you can and then duck."

"I didn't realize I was that dangerous."

"You're not," Jespperson said. "Don't take this the wrong way, but you're not a live grenade, you're a dud. What I mean by that is that Walters is over-reacting. Hell, it's not your fault if some firebug used that L shit of yours to make a point. Good God, what if one of my players took me literally when I told them to go out there and bring me some heads on their pikes? Would it be my fault? We can motivate these kids, but that's about all. The rest is up to them."

"I know, but for the dean, it's more complicated than that. He thinks that if it gets out that some students are claiming that animals have souls because a Gennesaret teacher said so – even though that's not what I said – there's going to be a stampede toward the exits."

"You don't have to defend him to me. I know what he thinks, and I think it's nonsense. This school has become Christian in name only. Most of the students here go to chapel about as often as I do, which is never."

"It's the parents he's worried about, not the students. I believe most of the parents picked this school for their kids because of its name."

He felt he was trying to explain the dean to himself as well as to the coach, not defend him, but the distinction was not at all clear.

"You're loyal, I'll say that much for you," the coach said, rising. "I'll talk to Walters and put in a word for you, for all the good it will do."

"Thanks coach, but I've already got one foot out the door. I've taken a job at Upland Community College. I start next month."

"The Ogden school? Their basketball team is pathetic, last in the league. And in football, I'm afraid to put in my best players against them for fear of being charged with manslaughter."

Edward laughed and said, "Maybe I'll see you at one of the games."

"Yeah, maybe we'll have our rabbit back by then."

"I thought you could win without Jumpin' Jack."

"We can, but there's a psychological component to sports, just like in war. Psychological warfare. You take it and you weaponize it. You could say that Jumpin' Jack was part of our arsenal. Yeah, we'll win without him, but it's always nice to have something extra to throw at 'em."

"I wish I could have been more helpful, Coach."

"You couldn't have been less helpful," Jespperson said with a snickering laugh. "Good luck."

"Same to you."

"Luck is for losers."

Having filled the only box he had brought with him with the contents from his desk, Edward carried it out to his car and returned to his office with another box for his books. He found Lamija there emptying his trash can into her janitorial cart.

"Oh, I go, come back," she offered.

"No, thank you, Lamija, you go ahead with what you're doing," he said, "I'm just going to leave this box here and I'll finish packing tomorrow."

"Everybody pack for the summer," she noted.

"Yes."

"Mister Edward," she said, hesitating, "I am sorry for telling Dean Walters of the writing you made on the board."

"Oh, don't worry about that," he smiled.

"I saw it on the TV that the writing you made is in trouble and I do not wish to make trouble on you."

"You didn't make any trouble for me. You did the right thing."

"Telling that causes trouble for someone is not the right thing. My brother was shot for telling."

He smiled again and said, "Really, it's okay, Lamija. Put it out of your mind."

"Thank you," she sighed.

Chapter 8

After he had finished handing out the final exams to the class he had one left in his hand and looked around to see whom he had missed. There was one on everyone's desk, so he looked around again and noticed that JJ was absent.

"Has anyone seen JJ this morning?" he asked.

The students glanced at each other and around the room. Most of them just shook their heads, a few said, "No," and Noah Rosten looked at him and shrugged.

"Well, maybe he's just running late," Edward said. "You may all begin and we'll give JJ a few extra minutes at the end."

But after a few minutes had passed, and then ten, and then twenty, he began to think instead in terms of having JJ take a make-up exam later in the day, assuming JJ had a good reason for missing the class. He supposed he'd accept as an excuse something like having to take care of a sick cow or a flat tire on his truck, just so long as it wasn't anything akin to blaming it on an alarm clock or forgetting the date.

At the half-hour mark, satisfied that his ten other students were either scribbling feverishly or gazing up at the ceiling for inspiration, he slipped out and went down the hall to the administrative office. Rosemarie Tidwell, the dean's secretary, was focused on her PC monitor while her two index fingers poked rapidly at her keyboard like a couple of pigeons pecking at birdseed. She acknowledged his presence with a nod and asked him to wait by raising her left finger for an instant without missing a beat.

"Yes, Professor Stathakis?" she said a few seconds later, her fingers hovering over the keyboard.

"Excuse me, Mrs. Tidwell. When you have a minute, would you mind calling Jon Herriman, Jr.'s home? He wasn't here for the final exam and I may have to schedule a make-up with him."

She nodded and her fingers resumed their attack on the keyboard.

Back in his classroom, he waited for the students to complete their exams and then gathered them up one by one, thanking each of the students and wishing them a good summer as he did so. They responded with "Thanks" and a few "I've enjoyed your class," some with smiles that felt to him like genuine appreciation. He doubted they'd miss him any more than he'd miss them, but he, too, had enjoyed the class.

Before dismissing them, he announced that their grades would be posted the following Monday, and then he went to the whiteboard and wrote and underlined, "*Know thyself*," and said, "I wish you all success."

Not long after his students had gone, Mrs. Tidwell entered the room and said she had spoken to JJ's mother. Mrs. Herriman had said that her son had left home at the usual time and that she had no idea why he hadn't shown up for the exam.

"She didn't seem terribly worried," Mrs. Tidwell said, "but then, you know those Herrimans."

Edward didn't know those Herrimans but thought it might have something to do with their Christian righteousness or stoic ranch culture.

"I'm afraid I can't give him a passing grade unless he takes the final exam," he noted unnecessarily to Mrs. Tidwell.

"I told her that, and I told her there isn't much time left. She said he probably just forgot what day it was and that you'll have to give him the test some other time regardless," Mrs. Tidwell replied with a hint of exasperation. "She made a point of reminding me that her husband, '*the chairman of your trustees*,' has a high regard for education and that he has instilled that regard in his sons. So if JJ missed the test, it was not intentional and Dean Walters will certainly understand and make the necessary accommodation. That's what she said."

"I'm sure that's true," Edward said. "We'll just have to wait until we hear from him."

"I'll call you when I hear back from them," Mrs. Tidwell said.

"Thank you, Mrs. Tidwell."

She lingered at the doorway a moment longer and then said, "I'm sorry you won't be returning next year. You have been very polite and professional, and you seem like a kind man. So many of the professors walk around here like heirs to the throne."

He was as touched as he had been by Coach Jespperson's unexpected and slightly backhanded kindness. Perhaps if he had been allowed to stay on for the three-to-five years that the dean had originally proffered, these people he hardly knew might have become his friends. But then he reminded himself that he had had almost nine months to develop those friendships, more than enough time, and that it had taken his imminent departure to finally break the ice. And even now, it wasn't he who had seized the initiative. Still, he wasn't ready to admit to himself that it was he rather than time that was the problem. Given enough time…

"Thank you, Mrs. Tidwell," he repeated. "You've been very kind to me as well."

His arms loaded with the class materials, he walked passed Jerry Moseley's classroom, the largest in the college, where dozens of students were laughing uproariously and stomping their feet. Many of them were waving and sloshing the contents of plastic cups as if at a biergarten during Oktoberfest. Jerry was writing or drawing something on his whiteboard, and while Edward couldn't make it out, it was obviously hilarious. He smiled and hoped he'd remember later to ask Jerry what was so funny. He could use a good laugh, which he was obviously not going to get from the rapidly approaching Pastor Bartholomew.

"Oh, dear, Edward, I'm so glad I caught you before you left," the pastor said. He paused to catch his breath and then continued, "Mister Herriman just called and he is very upset. He wants to know where his son is."

"He didn't show up for the final exam in my class. I asked Mrs. Tidwell to call his home. She spoke to Mrs. Herriman, and I got the impression that she, Mrs. Herriman, was not particularly worried about it."

"Yes, she apparently informed her husband, and he is not taking it quite so calmly. He told Dean Walters to check with all of his classes. The dean sent me to you." The pastor intertwined his fingers at his chest as if praying for a good word to carry back to the dean.

"Well, I can't help you. There's been no sign of him, and none of the other students has seen him this morning."

"I'll walk out to the parking lot with you. Perhaps his truck is there," the pastor said.

If JJ's truck were out there, JJ would have been in class, but Edward could see that the pastor would be better served by action than logic. As they walked together through the parking lot, however, Edward found that he, too, was looking left and right for any sign of JJ's big red Dodge Ram despite the logic, which, of course, ultimately prevailed. When they reached his own car, he set his materials down on the passenger seat and stepped around to the driver's side, where the pastor was continuing his futile scanning of the lot.

"I hate to bring this up, Pastor, but has anyone thought to check with the police and the clinic?" Edward said. There were a lot of curving miles between the Herrimans' ranch and the college, some of them along deep gullies or forested hillsides down which even a big red truck could disappear from view.

"Heaven forbid, but if no one else has, I'll see to it," the pastor said.

The pastor was true to his word, as Edward found out later that night when Janet called while he was in the midst of his initial evaluation of the essays submitted by his class, minus JJ. The elder Herriman had apparently just been haranguing the sheriff by phone, complaining that not enough was being done to locate his son even though every officer in the department had by then already been assigned to the search.

"He wants us to look here and there and everywhere, which we were pretty much doing anyway," Janet said. "What can you tell me?"

"I don't know him that well, but JJ doesn't seem like the sort of person who would just run off, unless that video and the tension between him and the other students just got to him."

"What sort of tension?"

"I've just noticed that the other students in my class aren't interacting with him in the friendly way they once did. Shunned is a bit strong, but something close to it."

There was no response from her, but he could hear police radio chatter in the background and her voice joining the garbled communication. A couple of minutes passed before she returned to the phone.

"Listen. Edward, I've got to run, but I'll get back to you," she said, hanging up before he could reply.

Clearly, her urgency suggested bad news, and Edward was left to speculate as to just how bad. Most likely the crash, the roll-over into a ravine that he had feared all along. If so, maybe JJ had been pinned inside the truck, just hurt, or thrown from the vehicle and lying unconscious in a ditch. Or killed. Or maybe he was reading too much into Janet's haste. She may have just been answering a call from the sheriff, or responding to a personal matter. He shook his head, trying to shake out the pointless speculation. Only the facts mattered, and he had none.

He stepped out onto his balcony and looked out at a lenticular cloud burnished with the faint silver glow that remained of the daylight. A warm and gusty wind was blowing in from the southwest, forecasting a change in the weather. May had been unusually warm and dry, or so he had been told by just about everyone with whom he had shared any small talk. The fields and forests were tinder dry, the fire chief had remarked every time he was interviewed about the fire at Franklin Scott's lodge, giving his crews and, by implication, himself a shout out for their defensive efforts. Edward entertained the possibility that his dislike of Chief Hammond had something to do with Judith Scott, but he attributed it mostly to the man's vacuousness. With the wind howling, he didn't hear the door sliding open at the adjacent balcony.

"Gathering wool for your knitted brow?" Jerry shouted.

Edward stepped over to the railing so that he could be heard above the wind.

"Hey, Jerry. I guess I am a little preoccupied. We seem to be missing one of our students," he said. "Jon Herriman, Jr."

"JJ? What the hell?"

"He didn't show up for finals today and now his father has everybody in the sheriff's office out looking for him."

Jerry shook his head and said, "Can't be good. JJ's the sort of guy who'd ask his father for permission before running away from home. Something must have happened."

"That's what I'm afraid of."

"By the way," Jerry said, "I hear that you are running away from home."

"Not exactly," Edward said.

"Yeah, I know, it's a long story. Well, go ahead, I've got a few minutes."

"Okay," Edward said, and he finally offered Jerry an abbreviated version of the long story about his (L) and its association with the disappearance of Jumpin' Jack, the fire at the lodge, and the video of Herriman's cow. He concluded with Coach Jespperson's analogy of the dean tossing a grenade that was about to blow up in his face.

"Wow, so anima plus L equals animal. Good for you, Edward. Jesus, that's elegant. When I saw it on that note on the news I thought it was just the acronym of some animal cracker offshoot of ALF or PETA. You've been published, man. The dean should be offering you tenure instead of a pink slip. That's exactly what I'm going to tell him."

Another vote in my favor, Edward thought. If it were a democracy, he'd probably keep his job. He thanked Jerry and repeated what he had said to his other supporters. For him, the well at Gennesaret was poisoned and he was moving on.

"That's too bad," Jerry said. "I'm going to miss your imperviousness to humor and sarcasm."

Edward laughed and said, "Speaking of humor, I passed by your class today and it sounded like happy hour at your comedy club hang-out."

"The Bard and Grill? It's not nearly as funny as my class. You must have heard me giving the students the formulas for the absolute minimum pixilation required to blur images of various parts of the human body. So many people use a fig leaf when a shamrock will do."

"Is that what they call higher math?"

"Absolutely. It resolves a distortion in our dimension of absurdity, sort of like your anima plus L. Mathematicians and philosophers love wisdom. Wasn't Pythagoras both? What was his take on souls?"

"He apparently believed in metempsychosis, or what we know as reincarnation. His own soul supposedly passed through four previous lives before his own."

"Really? Well, why not? Why incinerate a perfectly good soul in the fires of hell when you can recycle it instead?"

"The conservation of mass. Isn't that a law of physics?"

"Fucking right!" Jerry said, beaming with admiration. "I really will miss you, man. Listen, my sister is coming in for a visit next week. Why don't the three of us plus Doc go out for a bon voyage drink?"

"Sure, I'd like that," Edward said, especially with Alice Moseley. She was like a female version of Jerry, smart, funny and as thin as Olive Oyl, but prettier.

"Alice thinks you're cute," Jerry said. "If you weren't so long in the tooth I'd give you her hand in marriage."

"I know, you're kidding."

"No, I'm serious."

Jerry promised to set up their night out and then returned to all the "busywork" awaiting him inside his apartment. Edward stayed outside a bit longer and then he, too, went inside to the distraction of the final exams. He toiled through the mostly mediocre essays until his aching neck and blurring vision finally drove him to bed, where he pondered the mysteries of his ceiling for what seemed like half the night before he was overtaken by sleep.

He was awakened by his phone just after 5 a.m., more than an hour before his alarm was set to rouse him for his morning jog. The call was from the sheriff's office main number rather than Janet's cellphone so he was tempted not to answer it but finally did so on the last ring before the shunt to voice mail. His relief upon hearing Janet's voice lasted only through her apology for waking him.

"JJ has committed suicide," she said, the words as incomprehensible to him as the gibberish in the dream from which he had just awakened.

"What? Where?" he asked stupidly, as if the location mattered. "God, I'm so sorry. That poor kid."

"Yeah, it's been a tough night," Janet said. "His little brother Luke spotted his truck behind one of those big hay shelters out in one of their remote pastures. He found JJ hanging from one of the trusses. It looked like he had climbed up on a bale of hay and then kicked it away."

"I'm so sorry," he repeated, finding it as difficult to breathe as to think. He recoiled from the image forming in his mind.

"I know," Janet said. "Could you come in to the office sometime this morning. I'd like to go over a few things with you."

He thought he answered "Yes, of course," but he wasn't so sure when he reflected upon it later. He thought he might have unintentionally hung up without answering her at all. It didn't matter. She would know that he'd be there whether he had said so or not.

He skipped breakfast and his jog all the while telling himself there was no reason to hurry. There was nothing more he could tell Janet, nothing more he could explain, but there was so much more he wanted to understand. As far as he was concerned, he was rushing to her for answers that were not his own.

He got there less than an hour after her call and he was not asked to wait this time before the desk sergeant escorted him down the same hall as before. However, this time, he was led past the conference room to an office next to Sheriff Ortega's. Janet answered the sergeant's knock with a "Come in, Edward," even though as far as he knew no one had informed her of his arrival.

"Security cameras," she explained, pointing to her computer screen.

"I still can't believe it," he said, taking a seat across from her desk. "I wasn't awake when you called and, I don't know, it was as if I had dreamed it."

His distress apparently showed, for she offered him a compassionate smile. Rising with her mug in her hand, she asked him to wait a minute while she fetched more coffee. She returned with her own refilled and a mug for him. It was just what he needed, and she waited until he had had a few sips before explaining the purpose of the meeting.

"Last time we spoke, you mentioned that you had noticed some tension between JJ and the other students, I wanted to better understand that."

"But it was a suicide?" he asked, confused by the suggestion to his mind that others might have been involved.

"We have to wait for the coroner's report, of course, but it's clearly a case of suicide," she said. "You've seen these hay shelters around here, they're like big steel canopies. Well, he drove out to one that's way out on the far east side of the ranch. There are no roads to it, and there were no other tire tracks besides his and his brother's. We think he climbed to the top of the stack, which almost reached the roof and then set one of the bales on its end. He climbed up on top of that, threw a rope over one of the trusses."

Edward nodded. "Did he leave a note?"

"He did, and I think you need to know about it, but I'm going to ask you not to repeat any of it to anyone."

He nodded again. "Of course."

Janet removed a clear plastic folder from a file on her desk and showed it to Edward. It held a sheet of white paper with the handwritten note: "I'm sorry father. There's too much cruelty in it. I can't go on doing this."

Edward stared at the paper until the writing on it began to blur and then handed it back to Janet.

"JJ was a sensitive kid," he said quietly. "I can't help but think that that video of the cow got to him. Have you traced the source?"

The detective bit her lower lip before replying. "Listen. Edward, I'm not at liberty to tell you everything we know. All I can say is that it's an ongoing investigation."

"I'm sorry. I understand," he said. "You were asking about the tension in the class."

"Yes, you mentioned that JJ was being shunned by other students. Could you describe that to me, those involved, anything that was said."

She had seized on his use of the word shunned even though he had qualified it at the time, but he decided to just describe what he had seen in his classroom in the weeks since the fire and leave the definition of it to her.

"It was sad, really," he concluded. "They had seemed like such a cohesive group in the earlier days of the class. In a small class like that, everyone gets to know everyone else. I sometime saw them in groups in the hallway, and there seemed to be a comradery, some genuine friendships developing among them. I heard some talking about getting together for a class party sometime. It was as if they had formed an ethics club."

"Until the fire," Janet said.

"Yes, and then it all changed."

"You said both JJ and AnaLise Chen were on the outs with the others but what about with each other?"

"I didn't see any interaction between them either. I had the impression that they were being snubbed for different reasons."

"What makes you think that?"

"Just that, the fact that they hadn't retreated to the same corner."

"And Audrey?"

"Same thing. But as I said, she's very shy and I may have been misreading her situation. The social dynamics with her were different from the start. It could be that she wasn't being ostracized at all. I don't know."

Janet set her pen down on her notepad and sat back in her chair.

"I know that you're taking this pretty hard, Edward," she observed. "But listen, I've investigated quite a few suicides in my career, and I've never been able to cite a single external event as the cause. Something may come along that determines when it happens, but not why it happens. I think you know that. It's not Jon Senior's fault and it's not your fault and it's not even Jon Junior's fault. It goes much deeper than that."

"I know," Edward said, smiling sadly. "Thank you."

"I'm going to wrap this up soon, and when I do, I'll be able to tell you a few things that might explain the when. Maybe even before you leave town," she said, adding, "And hold on to that rain check for the beer. There's no expiration date."

As he was setting his coffee mug on her desk he noticed another plastic bag containing the half-burned tongue from a leather hiking boot that she had pulled from the fire pit at the camp site.

Pointing to it, he stated the obvious, "That must be an important piece of evidence."

"Yes it is, and we might not have found it without your help."

CHAPTER 9

The Herrimans held a private burial service for their son two days after his body was released by the coroner, whose conclusion, death by self-inflicted hanging, was by then known throughout the Gennesaret community and to a lesser degree throughout Connor County. The school held its own memorial service the following day. Many of the non-resident students had already left for the summer, but most of the remaining students as well as many faculty members, staff, and all of the trustees attended.

Edward arrived early and sat near the rear of the chapel. Mrs. Tidwell sat down beside him and remarked that never in a hundred years could she have imagined such an awful reason for JJ's absence that day. As Dean Walters was walking past them on his way to the reserved pew in front, she told Edward that JJ's father had called the dean three times that morning.

"After each call, Dean Walters looked as if he had been slapped," she said.

As students and faculty streamed into the chapel, Mrs. Tidwell's running commentary on their emotional reactions to the news of JJ's suicide would have been a fitting tribute, thought Edward, if she had shared it with the entire congregation. Devastated. Stunned. Shocked. Wept.

"JJ was so modest and sweet, he probably had no idea how much we thought of him," she remarked.

She and everyone else fell silent when Pastor Bartholomew placed his hand over the microphone on the pulpit and cleared his throat. Edward was not surprised when he opened the service with a reading of Psalms 23:2. During the admittedly few services that he had attended at Gennesaret, Edward had never known the pastor to stray from the well-worn green pastures of his ministry. He spoke of JJ in generic terms as a faithful Christian, a loving son, an excellent student, a fine athlete, and a favorite member of the Gennesaret Christian College family who would be missed by all who knew him.

It was not until the pastor relinquished the mic to student speakers that Edward got a sense of some of the sadness and loss felt by the Gennesaret "family." A few of them, including the football team's quarterback, spoke through tears as they recounted their anecdotes and impressions of their friend. To Edward's surprise, Katrina Morrison also stepped up to the pulpit and between sobs said that JJ had been like a brother to her since they were children. He had taught her how to ride a horse and drive a tractor and she had taught him how to play tennis and golf.

"I'm sorry," she said, sobbing uncontrollably as she returned to her seat beside her mother, who embraced her and stroked her hair.

While Pastor Bartholomew was returning to the pulpit for the closing with the Lord's Prayer, Edward felt the faint buzz of his cellphone in his jacket pocket. He resisted the temptation to peek even when a few minutes later it buzzed a second time.

At the end of the service, he remained behind as everyone else filed out and dispersed and then he, too, walked out. A light rain was falling, almost a mist, so he stepped back under the chapel's portico and checked his phone. Both calls had come from Upland Community College, and the second had gone to voicemail.

The college's human resource manager apologized for leaving a message but said she was about to go into meetings that might last through the day and she didn't know when she'd be able to call again. She regretted to inform him that the college had rescinded its offer of an adjunct position. She was sorry for any inconvenience it might have caused but the decision was unavoidable and she wished him well in his pursuit of a position elsewhere.

He stared at his phone, dumbstruck, the word "inconvenience" flashing through his mind. He had packed. Half of his belonging were already inside his car. He had broken his lease and had to pay the remaining month's rent as a penalty. He had told everyone who cared to know that he had taken a job at Upland. He had been planning to leave the next morning. No job, no apartment, nowhere to go, no explanation, but at least he had a definition for the word "inconvenience." He immediately called back the HR manager's number but there was no answer and he chose not to leave a message. He had no message for them, only a question. Why?

Demoralized, he walked out to his car and sat there considering his options. First, he would have to talk to his apartment manager and try to reinstate the remaining month on his lease. Then he would have to move all of his stuff back inside. And then, he would have to resume his search for a job and hope against hope for a quick breakthrough. Or, he could load his remaining belongings into the car and move on to a big city, where he could knock on college doors for a job. At least there, in the meantime, he could sign up for substitute teaching in the public schools by day and work in a big box at night. Moving on seemed the logical choice but it would require more energy than he could muster at the moment. If he could get his month back at his apartment, he'd have some breathing room, time to think it through.

He was leaning toward the less logical procrastination when he was startled by Judith Scott tapping a ringed finger against his window. He lowered the window, thinking she just wanted to say hello, or good-bye, as the case may be.

"It's wet out here, Edward," she said. "Do you mind if I join you for a minute."

"No, of course not," he said, moving a box from the passenger seat onto the boxes behind him.

"Katrina's gone inside to check the posted grades. I don't know why she bothers; they're all A's," she said smiling proudly. "Aren't they?"

"I can only speak for myself," he said, smiling back at her. Just having her sitting there beside him had cheered him up. "She gave a beautiful tribute."

"Didn't she? I thought so, too, but she's embarrassed for breaking down the way she did. I told her that that's what made her remarks so poignant."

"More than words," Edward agreed.

"Am I keeping you from something? You must have a lot to do before you leave," she said, glancing back at the carload of bags and boxes.

"Well, I did, but now it's all up in the air. I've just been informed that the job offer from Upland Community College has been rescinded. Without an explanation."

She nodded. "I was afraid of that. Jon Herriman called me last night. He said Earl had, in his words, 'come clean' about the source of the L. I don't know if you are aware of it, but there was a gruesome video involving one of the Herrimans' cows that was posted with that same L in parentheses."

"Yes, I've seen it," Edward said.

"It's horrible. I can see how it might have been upsetting to JJ. Herriman said his son was scheduled to drive one of the trucks to the packing plant on the day of his suicide."

The "when" that Janet had talked about, thought Edward.

"Herriman demanded that you be fired, and he was apparently frustrated to find out that Earl had gotten out ahead of him. I guess he wanted the satisfaction. He told me that if it had been up to him, you and a few other faculty members whom he named would have never been hired in the first place. He holds the dean, my father, me and a couple of other trustees, and, in his words, 'the rot in society,' responsible for corrupting the college."

"I'm sure he's too upset about his son to think clearly," Edward offered.

"I can appreciate that, which is why I let him rant. Of course, he's held that view for a long time. The last time he brought it up at a board meeting, I told him he was full of shit. This morning he apparently turned his wrath toward the dean. I was in Earl's office just before the service this morning when Herriman called him. Earl let slip that you had taken a job at Upland, and he told me afterward that Herriman said, 'Not if I have anything to say about it.'"

"He didn't waste any time."

"I'm sorry, Edward. I know quite a few people in higher education around the country. I'll see what I can do for you."

"Thank you. There's not much of a demand for adjunct professors of philosophy, but I'll take what I can get. Right now, though, my first priority is deciding whether to wait here for something to come along or leave tomorrow as planned. My problem is I broke my lease."

"Well, I can help you with that," she said. "You were staying at the Connor Park Apartments weren't you? We own that property. I'll call the manager and take care of it. Stick around for a while and in the meantime I'll check around for a job."

Before the call from Upland, Edward had been thinking about cancelling his night out with Jerry, Doc and Alice to allow for more sleep ahead of his departure the next morning. But now, he was looking forward to it. It was the only thing he was looking forward to. The unpacking, the resumption of his job search, his anxiety over his role in Janet Ellison's investigation and the prosecution to follow – he could set all of that aside for one night. He had arrived at a degree of equanimity following the rejection from Upland that only served as a testament to the aimlessness and disarray that he had come to expect of his life. He had been more distressed at the prospect of losing his apartment, and Judith had seen to that as promised.

The apartment manager had welcomed him into his office with outstretched hand and an obsequious nod. Everything had been taken care of, he informed Edward. He could stay as long as he wanted to, and, please, if he had any concerns, required any maintenance or repairs, he should not hesitate to call day or night. Just a few weeks earlier, the manager had churlishly threatened to withhold his cleaning deposit as well as his last month's rent if the carpets weren't professionally cleaned before his departure despite Edward's assurance that they were spotless.

So, as he was carrying boxes across the freshly cleaned carpets to his kitchen, his steps were not as heavy as they might have been. There was no rush, nothing to rush toward. He was considering not even unpacking. He could leave everything in the boxes and dig out only those things he needed as needed. He'd take a break that night, and then he could devote his time and energy to his next move, whatever that may be.

By the time Jerry banged on his door at the appointed hour later that night, however, he had relented and unpacked his clothing, toiletries and kitchen utensils, leaving only a few scattered stacks of boxes containing mostly his books and teaching supplies.

"Eddie!" Alice cried, giving him a bear hug and a smacking kiss on his ear. "You look great."

"For an old man," Jerry said just far enough under his breath to be heard.

Ignoring Jerry, Edward said to Alice, "You, too."

She did, in fact, look great. He didn't remember her being so tall, three or four inches taller than him, but that was probably due to the illusion of distance. Before, they had only met across the two balconies, not face to chin. Her wavy brown hair had been bleached nearly blonde by the white-hot sun over Egypt, where she had been working at an archaeological site for the past six months. She hadn't tanned, however, which was not surprising considering her views on the care and maintenance of the human body. Sunscreen was a no-brainer, of course. She was a fellow semi-vegetarian with a confessed passion for seafood. A Vinyasa yogi, she was as physically active as her brother, though with some dogmatic strictures. Gyms were cesspools. Swimming pools were cesspools. Hair dyes were toxic. Food additives were poison. She had once penned a scorching criticism of what she referred to as a tattoo culture that defiles the flawless beauty of the body, which, when it appeared as an op-ed in the *New York Times*, provoked a brief but widespread debate and a fair amount of scorn. No smoking, no drugs – street or prescription – and no hard liquor, only the fruit of the vine, red, and only in moderation.

She was wearing a black spaghetti strap tank top that showed off the strong taper of her shoulders, and shorts that revealed that while her legs were extraordinarily long and slender, they were certainly not sticks like her brother's. Admiring her statuesque presence, the "Eddie" with which she had greeted him had barely registered.

"How was the dig?" he asked her.

"Don't get me started," she said with a frown. "We were nothing but cheap labor. Our illustrious lead archeologist sat on his fat ass and reaped all the glory."

"Seniority has its rewards," Jerry said.

"Fuck seniority," Alice replied.

Jerry led the way down the stairs to their awaiting car. Doc, the night's designated driver, was on the phone to his clinic as they climbed inside, Jerry in front and Edward and Alice in back.

"This is what I have to put up with." Jerry said once Doc had hung up. "What makes your profession so special that you have to take calls every half hour? Maybe I should open an emergency mathematics clinic and give you a taste of your own medicine. Edward could start a 24/7 existential crisis hotline, and Alice could be on-call to archeologists with mummy issues."

"Relax, I was just handing it off to the night shift," Doc answered. "And why don't you leave the comedy to the professionals?"

"That's right! I should have been able to call in a professional comedian to deal with this situation instead of trying to handle it myself. Where are the Ubers of comedy?"

"And this is what *I* have to put up with," Doc said to the rearview mirror.

"I've had to put up with it my whole life," Alice said to Edward.

Edward had informed Jerry earlier that day that Upland Community College had been scared off by Herriman, but Jerry insisted that they go ahead with their planned night out since a bon voyage was nevertheless inevitable. Besides, he had reserved a table at the Lamplight Restaurant, where there could be serious repercussions to a last-minute cancellation.

As he pulled out onto the highway, Doc looked into the rearview mirror again and said, "No doubt Herriman is distraught, but why is he targeting you, Edward?"

Having giving an account of his lecture and its ramifications so many times since the disappearance of Jumpin' Jack, Edward had arrived at an abridged version that answered the most common questions before they could be asked. He felt he came across as not so much contrite as baffled by the way events had unfolded.

Doc said, "Suicide is the toughest death to explain and the one that cries out the loudest for an explanation. Herriman appears to have latched onto the only explanation that makes any sense to him. He is not going to accept the possibility that his son had rejected the way of life that he had planned for him in the absence of some subversive outside influence."

"The man's delusional," Jerry said. "To him it's a binary world, good versus evil, and the only thing standing between the two is his army of Christian soldiers."

"So evil must have prevailed when you were hired at Gennesaret," Doc quipped.

Jerry laughed and said, "You could call it that. It was Franklin Scott's filthy lucre. Herriman is losing the fight over the soul of Gennesaret and it's driving him crazy. But he isn't about to surrender. Edward is just the latest casualty but he won't be the last."

"Who decides what's good and what's evil?" Alice asked.

"That's easy," Edward answered. "The winner decides."

"In that case, I guess you must be evil," she laughed.

He was glad that they had gotten everything related to his (L) out of the way during the short drive to the Lamplight rather than having it served up with their dinner. Jerry obviously felt the same way, saying as they stepped out of the car, "Let us now speak only of cabbages and kings."

Instead, the conversation gravitated toward Alice, who among the four of them had by far the most interesting life. Her work took her from one place to another even more often than his. However, her one place might be Caracol or Paestum to his Fresno or Omaha, and her other might be

Xi'an or Giza to his Tucson or Connor. Despite her standing in the field, she insisted that most of her time was devoted to cleaning shards of pottery with a toothbrush or blowing away specs of dust with an atomizer "like some demented housewife."

"You'll appreciate this, Doc," she interjected as she was describing her work in Paestum. "I was on my way down to check out a dig at Ascea and I stopped at this little town called Acciaroli."

"I've heard of it," Doc said. "It's that town full of super agers."

"Yes, exactly, only I didn't know that at the time. So I'm sitting alone in bar with a bunch of old guys at the other tables and one of them comes over to me and says he would like to introduce me to his young son, who is an admirer of American women but also respectful. 'Como no? Con piacere,' I said. And so he brings over another old guy who looks like he could be his brother. 'Scusi, non o capito,' I told him, explaining that I understood him to say young son instead of brother. 'But this is my son. Maybe not so young, but he has only 82 years and he has never been married.' The father was 103, and his brother, whom I had mentioned and who was now also standing there leering at me, was 105. It must be something in their wine."

They all laughed, and Doc explained to Edward, "The DiPietro side of my family comes from Salerno, which is just up the coast from Acciaroli."

"What is it with you Italians?" Alice asked. "I get harassed more in Italy than in any other country, including France and Brooklyn. It's crazy; I get it from adolescents and centenarians and everything in between. They're all mascalzoni."

"Like you said, it must be something in the wine. It fills us with amore as well as longevity."

That was about as funny as Doc ever got, at least in the limited amount of time that Edward had spent in his company. Doc and Jerry were an odd couple, to be sure. Unlike Jerry, Doc had a serious disposition. He didn't kid around very much, and if he held any strong opinions about the people around him, he didn't share them. Though he exhibited signs of compassion, it seemed clinical, a dispassionate compassion, if there were such thing. He often shot hoops with Jerry but he was not nearly as athletic nor was he into any kind of outdoor activity. His interest in sports was chiefly centered around the injuries that he treated. He wasn't judgmental about it, however, once observing to Edward that jocks had their occupational hazards just like everybody else. If Edward had put any stock in that trite nonsense that opposites attract, he'd point to Doc and Jerry as an example.

When they returned to the apartment building, Doc accepted Jerry's invitation to join them upstairs for that drink or two that he had eschewed during dinner. It was almost midnight and Edward begged off, saying he was just too exhausted. Donning the proffered mantle of party pooper, he separated from them at his own doorway and went inside and settled in for the night. He had just changed into sweatpants and a T-shirt when there was a knock at his door. Groaning, he stepped into his slippers and shuffled over to open it. At that hour, he would have been surprised no matter who it was, but he was even more surprised to find Alice standing there barefoot, topless and wearing leopard skin lounging shorts.

"Three's a crowd," she explained. "Mind if I occupy your couch?"

Despite his best efforts, something in his look must have given him away for she quickly added, "I'm sorry, Eddie, I didn't mean to make you uncomfortable. I thought you'd be cool with a little partial nudity."

"No, it's not that, I'm just was surprised to see you, partially nude or otherwise."

He was sincere about that. It wasn't about breasts, it was about her, whom he liked very much and who apparently felt comfortable calling him Eddie and inviting herself into his apartment topless.

"Please, come in, Alice. Of course you're welcome to my couch."

She led the way inside and said, "Anyway, my breasts are so small that most men don't even notice them. I was at a topless beach in Crete a couple of years ago and I felt like one of the boys."

She left him no choice but to look. "You have very nice breasts."

She laughed again, saying, "I wasn't angling for a compliment, Eddie, but you really are a sweet guy. What century did you say you're from?"

"I'm older than I look," he conceded. "At least that's what I've been told."

"No matter what Jerry says ad nauseam, it's not all about numbers."

She walked past the boxes full of books to the couch and looked around.

"It's the same layout as Jerry's," he told her. "I haven't had time to restock the refrigerator, but there are some soft drinks and some oranges and apples in there. Can I get you a blanket?"

"A sheet will do," she said. "You know, Eddie, I probably have more books in my cellphone than you have in all these boxes. Why are you hauling them around?"

"I've had most of these books since I was in college. I think having them around makes every new apartment feel somewhat familiar. I guess it's like a turtle's shell to me; I can't part with it."

"And I thought logic was a hallmark of philosophy."

"Of philosophy, sure, but not necessarily philosophers."

He excused himself to fetch a bed sheet from a box he had yet to unpack and returned with it while she was filling a glass of water at the kitchen faucet.

"Good night," he said. "I'll see you in the morning."

"Okay, good night, Eddie, and thanks again."

He had no idea how long he had been asleep before he was awakened by Alice climbing into the bed beside him but guessed not long despite her declaration that "It's morning." It had been morning, well past midnight, anyway, when she first arrived.

She draped herself over him, and he put his arms around her and kissed her.

"Alice," he whispered into her ear, "I don't have any condoms."

"Why doesn't that surprise me? Anyway, I'm on the pill."

"Okay, and you don't have to worry about any STDs."

She laughed and said, "It didn't even enter my mind. Can we move on now?"

Kissing her again, this time not so tentatively, he rolled over with her and then pulled off his sweatpants. She had already dropped her leopard spots on the floor. He kissed her breasts – he thought them perfect – and then her neck, her mouth and her eyes as she wrapped her long legs around him, squeezing him in a scissor lock.

As she tightened her hold around his waist, she was able to control both the tempo and the pressure exerted. It was disconcerting to him at first, but he soon relinquished his independence of movement and began to feel as if their individual bodies had dissolved and then coalesced.

Chapter 10

It had been so unexpected and happened so quickly that he hadn't had time to think it through, which was probably just as well, he told himself as he reflected upon it while making a pot of coffee. If he had been given time to think, it probably would not have happened. He would have said something suggestive of just enough hesitation to drive her out of his bed, which he almost did with the prattle about condoms and STDs. He would have deprived himself of the softness of her cheek next to his, of the sweetness of her smile, of the sinewy energy of her body, of the serenity of the sleep that fell over him with her body against his, all on account of some well-reasoned uncertainty over its meaning and consequences.

When he first started dating again following his divorce from Sandra two decades ago, he discovered he was incapable of having sex without attributing some deeper meaning to it. He came away from the few encounters he had feeling either guilty or disillusioned. Guilty on those occasions when he was not inclined to take it any further, when, in fact, he never bothered to find out if his date even cared to take it any further, and disillusioned on those occasions when he would have wanted to take it further only to discover that his date was not so inclined. His disastrously short-lived marriage itself had resulted from his inability to set aside his guilt, which he later attributed to his immaturity, only to have it recur time and time again even as he matured. Not so many times, though, and as the time in between the encounters grew from months to years, his ambivalence also grew. He did not want to hurt anyone and he did not want to be hurt, preconditions that had all but excluded the possibility of sex. What he felt was required was a non-verbal, pre-existing synchronization of expectations. In other words, they'd both have to be struck by lightning at the same time.

His college roommate, Charlie, who was the best man at his wedding, had tried to warn him, saying, "You know, Edward, you don't have to marry every girl you sleep with."

No, not every girl, just Sandra, who, he had been too embarrassed to admit to Charlie, had been the only girl he had slept with up to that time.

Of course, none of these ruminations applied to his night with Alice, he told himself. She had initiated the sex, not he. He could take his cue from her. If she were to signal that there was more to it than their one night together, only then would he have to assess his own proclivities. Still, he let slip through his mind a feeling on his part that there was more to it, but he managed to quash it with the more pressing matters at hand. While Alice was in the shower, he'd have a little time to scroll through a few of his bookmarked college job postings.

She joined him in the kitchen a short time later wearing one of his T-shirts, which did nothing to hide her perfect breasts from his memory. Her hair was damp with the "mountain fresh" fragrance of his shampoo. They smiled at each other and kissed as Edward imagined lovers do the morning after, and then true to form, wondered whether they were now lovers or merely the proverbial two ships. She poured herself a mug of coffee and sat on the stool beside him.

"I'm sorry, I can't offer you breakfast," he said. "I had planned to do some grocery shopping after my run this morning."

"Jerry's got anything you could possibly want. We could go over there and whip something up, or I could bring something over here," she offered.

"Thanks, maybe in a while, unless you have plans later. I usually do my run before breakfast. It's not so much a run as a slow jog."

"I know most joggers prefer to go it alone, but if you'd like some company, I'd like to join you. Slow jogs suit me just fine. And don't lie to spare my feelings because I really do get it."

"I'd enjoy your company, Alice."

"Anyway, I'll be gone in a couple of days, so you don't have to sweat a regular intrusion."

"I just hope I can keep up with you. I've developed a healthy respect for your legs. They're as strong as they are beautiful."

She blushed for the first time since he had known her and said, "I thought you were Greek, not Italian."

"Half and half," he laughed. "But the Italian half is recessive and only manifests itself occasionally."

"That explains more than you realize." Finishing her coffee, she said, "I'll go get into my slow jogging outfit. Just knock when you're ready."

Each had offered the other an out but neither had seized it, which Edward took as a positive sign, though dampened somewhat by her caveat that she'd be gone soon. If he chose to, he could have taken that to mean that she could put up with him for a couple of days if he could put up with her, but he chose not to.

His knock on the door a half hour later was answered by Jerry, who stood in the open doorway with his hands on his hips like a fuming father confronting his daughter's deadbeat beau.

"Are you going to ask me if my intentions are honorable?" Edward asked, trying not to laugh.

"Something like that, although the fact that she was smiling when she came in is a mark in your favor. So, what are your intentions, old man?"

"Jogging with Alice and then breakfast."

"Come in, Edward, but leave your sense of humor outside. I'll tell her you're here."

But she had heard him and appeared behind her brother as he was about to turn around.

"Let's go, Eddie, before he says something embarrassing," Alice said.

She flew past her brother and bounded down the stairs with Edward trailing. Once she reached the street, she stopped and waited for him to catch up, and then they started off together, slowly at first.

"Your little brother is very protective of you, isn't he?"

"Yeah, which is kind of funny considering that I'm the one who took care of him from the time he was about twelve up until Doc came along," Alice said.

"What about your parents?"

"Divorced, and Mom had struggles of her own. She was an alcoholic. I stress the word *was*. She's been sober for almost ten years now. She finally stopped drinking toward the end of Jerry's treatments. Thank God they both survived. I love them both so much."

"What was Jerry being treated for?"

"He didn't tell you? Hodgkin's. He was diagnosed when he was sixteen. Then came the chemo and radiation and follow-ups that went on for years. Mom tried her best but she just couldn't manage it, so it fell to me. But she was much better than me at lifting Jerry's spirits. Whenever she visited the hospital – usually after too many drinks – she was the life of the party. Don't get me wrong, Mom is smart, charming and funny even when she's sober, but when she was drinking, she was smart, charming and an absolute riot. As Jerry once said, she would always leave the doctors in stiches. It really rubbed off on him, didn't it? Anyway, a few years ago, Jerry went back into the hospital for a full battery of tests that confirmed he was cured. You can't imagine how relieved we all were. Doc happened to be there doing his residency. They met, and the rest, as they say, is history. My services were no longer required."

"Jerry was the first person to welcome me here. I couldn't have asked for a better neighbor."

"He considers you a friend."

"I would have said friend, but I didn't want to seem presumptuous."

"He also says you're an introvert. He says you're a more socialized version of Hesse's *Steppenwolf*," she regarded him with curiosity. "Are you?"

"Not hard core, I hope. I don't shoot at cars. I think it just takes me longer than normal to get to know someone."

"You got to know me pretty fast."

"Not really, Alice. I don't know you very well at all, but I'd like to."

"A true introvert wouldn't have admitted that, Eddie. Me, I'm an extrovert, and I'll tell you upfront that I'd like to get to know you better as well."

But time wasn't on their side. Two days was hardly enough time to scratch the surface of a new relationship, or even to determine if it actually was a relationship. She'd be gone, they'd drift apart, and if they did ever see each other again, the world would have shifted beneath their feet. Frowning at his thoughts did nothing to drive them away.

"All I know about you is that you're an itinerant, half-Greek philosopher who lures strange women into his bed," she continued as she broke into a quicker jog. "Sorry, Eddie. I should be more careful. Jerry also says you can't always tell when someone's kidding."

Just over a week ago it occurred to him that he was finally getting to know something about the people around him just as he was about to leave them behind. After almost nine months amongst them, watching them, hearing them, occasionally even talking to them, he had discovered for the first time in recent weeks what should have been obvious from the day of his arrival: These were complex individuals with complex lives formed by past experiences, choices and circumstances as varied as his own. Jerry had survived Hodgkin's? Why hadn't he known about it until now? He hadn't asked Jerry about his past, that's why. He hadn't taken an interest. But that wasn't true. He had been interested in his comedic, math-mad neighbor; he had just lacked the self-assurance to pry into his private life.

As he had explained to Alice, he hadn't wanted to presume that Jerry was possibly a friend. Judith had a sister? Detective Ellison and Janet were the same person? There was more to Coach Jespperson than spit and polish? Jon Herriman, Jr., was tormented by the inherent cruelty of his patrimony?

As he jogged alongside Alice, their conversation made increasingly difficult by the exertion, he thought, too, that not only had he become more aware of the "beings" who had inhabited his life the past nine months, he had also become more aware of himself through them. "Know thyself," that overworked Greek aphorism that he had consigned to his students at the final class, required reflection as well as introspection, exterior as well as interior definition. In other words, he reasoned, there were elements of one's self that while not evident through introspection were illuminated by how the self was perceived by others. For example, much as with the smell of one's own breath and the tenor of one's own voice, one's own character faults and virtues are perceived differently and often more objectively by others. So it was that Janet's description of his catatonic musings at the gym, Jerry seeing him as an introverted friend, and even the coach's notion of his loyalty had added some clarity to what he already knew about himself. With that in mind, he believed that given time, Alice, who for reasons known only to herself always called him Eddie, could offer him a wellspring of knowledge about himself.

"Do you have to leave in two days?" he asked her.

She glanced at him before answering. "I'm meeting up with my team in Portland for some advance work. A lot of planning goes into a dig."

"Where are you going this time."

"Back to Belize. We've been granted access to a really promising site at Caracol. Never been touched. What about you?"

"Depends. I'm sending out resumes, submitting applications. Where I land, nobody knows."

They had reached the outskirts of town at a much faster pace than was normal for him, and yet he wasn't nearly as tired as he usually was at that point. The sun was rising behind a gray veil of clouds and the air was cool and smelled of smoke from the fireplaces and wood stoves that many of the resident climate change deniers refused to give up. Traffic was light at this time of day and they were jogging toward it so that they could more quickly shift to the shoulder whenever necessary. Cows and horses and field hands gawked at them as they passed. The driver of one big rig honked and waved, no doubt at Alice. Whenever he dropped back a few steps behind her, Edward was struck by the fluidity of her motion, the graceful rhythm of her cadence and the side-to-side bobbing of her head. It was almost as if she were dancing to a tune only she could hear. He felt that his own gait, jerky and inconsistent and a bit stiff, was awkward in comparison. To the cows, horses, field hands, and big rig drivers, they must have looked like a crazed college professor chasing a gazelle.

As they were approaching the industrial park a mile and a half outside of town, he caught up to her and said, "This is where I usually turn back, but we can keep going if you like."

Checking her watch, she said, "No, let's stick to your routine. We've done good. Let's go get our reward."

He scanned the road ahead and spotted a pick-up truck speeding toward them too fast for a safe crossing, so they waited for it to pass. When it was within about a hundred yards of them, however, the pick-up suddenly slowed down to a sane speed and was practically creeping along by the time it reached them. A lot of drivers were considerate like that. Not all, but most. There were a few sadistic types out there who liked to throw a scare into him with a swerving feint, but they were the exception. Edward waved a thanks to the driver, a young man who, instead of responding with the usual smile or wave, glared at him as he went by. Edward noticed that a female passenger was nodding and had her hand on the driver's shoulder. She looked familiar but he couldn't place her. After the pick-up had gone by, a big RV approached and they waited for it, too, to pass before crossing the highway. They began their return at a walk, which made it easier to have a conversation.

"Have you considered fishing in deeper waters?" Alice asked him.

"What do you mean?"

"Instead of looking for another adjunct gig at another small college, have you ever thought about something more stable, like a public high school, or one of the new online universities. They don't pay very well but they're always hiring."

He bowed his head and frowned, feeling like a boy who's been told to grow up and eat his spinach.

"I substitute at high schools sometimes and I feel like a prison guard.

I just don't think I'm cut out for it long term. Discipline isn't in my skill set. At least at the college level, I have students who choose to be in my class. They're not disruptive or disrespectful, even if they sometimes seem bored. I enjoy my interactions with them, and I wouldn't get even that, at least not in person, at an online school."

"Yeah," she said, and gave it more thought. "What about going back to college for a degree in a different discipline, something more marketable, like psychology or history or sociology? You'd ace it. That would open a few more doors, wouldn't it? Maybe not a tenure track, but it could lead to a regular faculty position."

"I've thought about it, but as Jerry recently pointed out to me, I'm getting a little long in the tooth," he replied.

He could have also added that he lacked the drive, the motivation, the energy, the ambition necessary for such an endeavor, appealing though it was. If nothing else, though, being a student again would move the goalposts.

"You can't take Jerry seriously; you should know that by now. Anyway, Eddie, I've known quite a few people your age – whatever it is – and some a lot older than you who've gone back for a mulligan. It's called the second act. If I ever get tired of archeology, I might give oceanography a try. I love the seas."

"I know," he said. "It's an option."

Satisfied with his concession, she resumed her trot and gradually sped up. She was soon well ahead of him and his slog jog wouldn't cut it anymore. Breaking into a run, he had almost reached her when he noticed what appeared to be that same white pick-up truck once again heading toward them. This time, though, it sped up instead of slowing down, racing toward them, its engine roaring, and in seconds it was upon them. In a flash, Alice vaulted sideways onto the soft shoulder, her momentum carrying her over an irrigation ditch alongside a chain link fence. He tried to do the same thing, a Superman leap for the ditch, but he was an instant too late. As the truck fish-tailed across the gravel, its rear panel caught his right leg and swung him around like a top. With tires spinning, it hurled gravel at him like buckshot and sped away. Lying on his back in the muddy ditch, he looked up at Alice, who seemed to be screaming frantically. He couldn't hear her over the hissing and screeching of air brakes but he felt her hands on his cheeks.

"Eddie! Eddie!" she repeated, gradually getting through to him as a big rig rumbled in the roadway. "My God, Eddie, tell me where are you hurt?"

A few seconds later a big bellied man with a white Santa Claus beard appeared over Alice's shoulder and said, "I called 911. They're sending cops, an ambulance. How bad is it?"

"I don't know," Alice replied.

"Shit," the trucker said, "I saw that son-of-a-bitch hit him. It was no accident, I can tell you that."

Edward began to regain the awareness of his body and felt sharp, stabbing pains in his right leg and left arm. When he tried to raise his arm to look at it he nearly blacked out.

"Don't move, man!" the trucker barked.

Alice leaned over him and said, "Your leg's broken, Eddie, I don't know about your arm."

"Jesus Christ!" Edward groaned.

Long minutes passed before they heard the approaching sirens. One after another of the sirens fell silent as the emergency vehicles nosed in behind the tractor trailer. The first officer on the scene was Sergeant Marchant, who upon assessing the situation, called in a confirmation for an ambulance and directed one of the arriving deputies to handle traffic control.

"Anybody get the plate number?"

"No, it all happened so fast," Alice said. 'It was an old white pick-up."

"It was intentional, man," the trucker said to Marchant. "I saw the whole thing. That truck was gunning for this guy."

"Okay, don't go anywhere until we've taken your statement," the sergeant said. He then radioed a description of the hit-and-run vehicle and identified the victim for dispatch.

"Say again," a voice that Edward recognized as Janet's came back over Marchant's hand-held radio.

"Yeah, Detective Ellison, it's that professor, Edward Stathakis."

"Condition?" she asked.

"Conscious and breathing, possible fractures. Don't know on internals. EMTs just arrived."

Edward drifted in and out of consciousness as a pair of EMTs went to work on him. As they assessed his visible injuries, they also checked his vitals, asked him to describe his pains, put a stethoscope to his chest, inserted an IV needle in his uninjured arm, palpitated his abdomen, and asked him again and again about his pains. As far as he could tell through the fog of the pains, they were just trying to keep him talking.

After what seemed like only a few seconds since he had been jogging with Alice, he was strapped to a gurney inside a speeding, blaring ambulance with one of the EMTs assuring him that he was doing fine, just fine.

"Alice?" he asked.

"She's fine," the EMT said. "Sergeant Marchant will drive her to the hospital. Relax, Edward, you're doing fine."

He was until they rolled him out of the ambulance, when the jolt of the gurney hitting the pavement sent a searing shockwave through his shoulder. His leg he couldn't feel at all. He was wheeled into a large room bristling with stainless steel devices, tubes, electronics, and domes of light descending from the ceiling like flying saucers. He could hear Doc talking to the EMTs but couldn't make out what they were saying. Soon, though, Doc was peering into his eyes behind a concentrated beam of light.

"Hello Edward," he said. "You have a compound fracture of the femur, some damage to your knee cap and a dislocated shoulder, and possibly a concussion. We're going to put the leg in a splint for the time being. After that, I'd like to do a scan of your internal organs to make sure there's nothing more serious that we need to deal with before surgery. Before we get started, we'll give you something to knock down your pain. In just a few minutes, my friend, you won't have a care in the world."

When he awoke, he was in a hospital bed in a small room with a large window overlooking the city park. The clock above the door said it was 7:15, which he knew couldn't be right because he and Alice had started their jog at 6:30. But judging from the light and shadow outside, it was still not long after sunrise.

"No, it's p.m.," a nurse laughed when he expressed his surprise at how much had transpired in just over an hour. "The sun's setting, not rising."

He had no memory of the CT scan that according to the nurse had revealed no internal injuries, nor of the surgery to set his femur inside a scaffolding of titanium rods and screws, nor, thankfully, of the resetting of his dislocated shoulder, and only the haziest memory of the accident that had put him there. And then he remembered that it was no accident. After the nurse had gone, promising to return soon with a dinner tray, he was left alone to confront a fear he had never experienced, a fear for his life. Not from his injuries but from an unknown but very real, very deadly threat. The driver of that truck intended to kill him. What was to stop him from trying again? He put the question to Janet, who arrived a short time later as he was picking at a bowl of red Jell-O.

"I wouldn't worry about that," she said, "This was clearly a crime of opportunity. It wasn't a cold-blooded plot. He obviously had no idea you'd be there, and then when he saw you, his grudge, whatever it is, kicked into gear. It was like road rage except the rage came from somewhere else. So, he had an advantage over you. He was not at risk. This wasn't toe-to-toe. Believe me, Edward, if he ran into you on a sidewalk, he might say something but he wouldn't take a swing at you. Right now, he's probably hiding in his darkened room somewhere thanking his lucky stars that you're still alive and praying to God that no one caught his plate number."

"You're right," he hoped. "I just wish I knew who it was and what it was that set him off."

"We know from the descriptions we got that both the driver and his passenger were young, probably college age, which leads me to believe there's a connection to Gennesaret rather than to anyone in your private life. Unless, of course, you wronged that girl."

"She looked familiar, but really, I don't who she is."

Janet laughed and said, "I was just kidding, Edward. It's not uncommon for witnesses to recognize a face and yet be unable to place it. I had a criminology professor who referred to it as the 'Mona Lisa Context.' If you were to see the Mona Lisa hitchhiking alongside the road or sitting in a bar or thumping a watermelon at the market, you'd say, 'Gosh, she looks familiar.' Put her back in the painting and suddenly it's, 'That was Mona!' Keep your eyes open for her."

"I will, but if she's a student, I won't be seeing her in context anymore."

"No, but you'll recognize her, and him, too. I'm pretty sure their faces are etched in your memory."

"I hate to think they're students," he said.

"We don't know that. Right now, it's all speculation. I don't want to upset you, Edward, but you should know that word has gotten out that you told your class that animals have souls. I know," she interjected as he was about to protest. "I know that's not what you said, but it's what some people have heard. So, it could be that what we have is a blasphemy that to some Christian soldier might have sounded a call to arms. On the other hand, it might have just been somebody who has it in for joggers. We've had more than a few of those, and a couple of them came pretty close to a hit like yours."

If he could choose his assailant, he'd take the latter. And as for people misrepresenting his lecture, it bothered him because he valued truth, but for all practical purposes, what did it matter? That rabbit was out of its hutch and neither he nor Dean Walters could put it back. There was that, anyway. He wouldn't have to face the dean, who at this point would need a back hoe to cover his gimpy professor's tracks. He sighed and thanked the detective for taking charge of the case, which he assumed would have normally been assigned to a traffic cop.

"We appreciate your business, Edward," she said. "With you around, the sheriff may have to hire another detective to keep up with the workload."

"My pleasure."

"Consider yourself lucky. If you had been a centaur we would have had to shoot you," she said with a laugh as she was leaving. "Did I get that right? Centaur, Minotaur, I'm always confusing the two."

"You got it right."

That whole simmering drama over the fire and the missing rabbit that had preoccupied him for the past few weeks seemed so unimportant to him now that he hadn't even bothered to ask her about the status of her investigation. She had hoped to wrap it up before he left town, which would have been two days ago under his now obsolete schedule. Well, he was still here and the investigation was apparently still ongoing, which is probably what she would have said if he had bothered to ask.

Janet's visit had been professional rather than personal – she was in uniform and on duty – but he felt that there had been a personal element to it. When she first arrived, she placed her hand on his chest over his heart while asking him how he was doing, and she had kept up her smile longer than usual. And then while going over the details of what she repeatedly referred to as "the assault," she never once took out her notepad. But what did it say about his yet-to-be-defined relationship with Alice that he was even parsing Janet's visit in such a manner?

Though he vaguely recalled seeing Alice's face close to his, perhaps feeling her face close to his at some point after he woke up in what must have been the surgery recovery room, he knew that he couldn't trust his memory, the same memory that also recalled Santa Claus assisting in the surgery. Not long before Janet's arrival, Doc had dropped by to check on him and told him that Alice had gone back to the apartment to change her clothes and grab a bite to eat.

"She wanted me to tell you that she'll be back shortly," Doc said.

"Is she okay? I don't remember exactly."

"Not a scratch," Doc said. "She was here all day. I told her to go home after you came out of recovery. She left with Jerry."

After Doc left, the nurse who had been there with him said to Edward, "Your girlfriend's a real sweetheart. Let me tell you something, if love could mend a broken leg, you'd be up and dancing right now."

Had Alice identified herself to the nurse as his girlfriend? Edward doubted it, but he thought maybe Doc might have said something to that effect. And love? Who said anything about love? People were so quick to jump to conclusions that they sometimes tripped over their own misperceptions. A different nurse came on duty while he was still toying with his Jell-O. She gave him a handful of pills and reminded him to press the red button any time he wanted a shot of pain relief.

"Don't be stingy with it," she said. "You'll sleep better, and sleep is the best medicine."

He dutifully pressed the red button and fell asleep with a plastic spoon in his hand and the food tray largely untouched over his belly. He woke up to Alice kissing his cheek. She sat down on the bed and waited for him to fully regain his senses.

"I asked Jerry to wait outside for a minute so we could talk," she said when he finally responded with a smile of recognition. "This isn't the way I planned to spend this night."

"Me too," he said. He raised the head of the bed to better see her. "I didn't know how you felt about it, but I thought there was a chance. I meant it when I said I'd like to get know you better."

"I meant it, too, Eddie." She placed her hand on his chest just as Janet had done and said, “I have to leave the day after tomorrow. A dozen people are counting on me to be there. If I don’t show up, it will set us back in what’s already an extremely tight schedule.”

“I understand, Alice. Anyway, I may still be here the next time you visit your brother. Maybe we can pick up where we left off.”

“If you’re still here, it’s you I’ll be visiting, not Jerry.” She leaned over him and kissed him on the lips. “Jerry has your cellphone. Call me if you need anything.”

“And you’ll hop on a plane and rush to my bedside?”

“Yes, as a matter of fact, if it comes to that.”

“I was just kidding,” he said. “See, I’m getting the hang of it.”

Chapter 11

The day after Alice left, Edward had no visitors at all, except Doc, whose professional duty, like Janet's, was tempered with what Edward allowed himself to take, or mistake, as personal interest. The prognosis was good, Doc told him after he was wheeled back from an X-ray of his leg. In just six to eight weeks, he'd probably be able to put some weight on it. And once his arm was out of the sling in a week or two, he could begin a regimen of occupational therapy to learn how to manage his life on crutches along with physical therapy to build up his strength for the slog ahead. In the meantime, he'd be in a motorized wheelchair, which meant moving to a ground floor unit at his apartment building, which Jerry had already arranged.

What a mess, he said to himself after Doc had gone. Hobbled, no job, no telling how much the medical bills would cost him, no Alice. If only Janet could identify the road warrior who was the cause of all of this he'd at least have someone to sue for his injuries plus mental anguish and pain and suffering. He figured he'd settle for a million dollars, all the while dismissing it as fantasy. A hot-headed pick-up driver who believes running over a jogger is a good career move probably hasn't had the kind of career that would generate that kind of money. The most he'd get out of a lawsuit was the old white pick-up truck, and there was probably an outstanding loan and mechanic's lien on that. Can't squeeze blood out of a deadbeat. At least he still had his health and an appreciation of his own absurdity.

The day before he was to be discharged, an occupational therapist named Josh rolled into his room in the promised motorized wheelchair, crashed into his bed and pumped his fist like a kid in a bumper car.

"These are some sweet wheels," Josh said. "The brakes take some getting used to, but you'll have your right leg sticking out there to cushion your stops."

As ridiculous as that sounded, it actually turned out to be true. His right leg, rigid in a brace, was like the bumper on a rail car. The trick was to come to a rolling stop before hitting anything too hard. He spent practically the entire morning playing with his new toy, taking hard turns in and out of his room, zipping down the hallways and making a merry-go-round of the nursing station. When it was time for lunch, he parked at the foot of the bed and pulled the tray over his knees. The TV was on mute, which suited him until he looked up at it and saw the reporter Mindy

Dumont standing outside of the administration building at Gennesaret Christian College.

"Dean Earl Walters declined comment," she was saying as he ramped up the volume, "but many others I've spoken to on campus expressed shock that anything like this could happen here. Bob?"

The anchorman appeared on the screen, nodding solemnly, and asked, "Mindy, do we know whether the students have been arrested?"

"Bob, we're told by Sheriff Ortega that four resident students including Franklin Scott's granddaughter and two of the non-resident students have been arrested. Warrants have been issued for the other four non-residents. If those four fight extradition it could be weeks before they're taken into custody."

"Thank you, Mindy, it truly is a shocking development."

Edward coughed out a mouthful of scrambled eggs and almost choked in the ensuing fit as he focused on the Chyron at the bottom of the screen that was scrolling the headline: "10 Gennesaret Christian College students charged in the arson of billionaire's lodge." He read it over and over again as Bob moved on to other news, weather and sports.

As much as he hated to echo Bob's commentary even if only in his own mind, it truly was shocking. All of them? He had accepted the possibility that more than one of his students was involved only because of the sheriff's eminently logical conclusion that it would have taken more than one person to take Scott's trophies off the walls and move them into the garage. So, two, maybe three, he had presumed. But all of them? And what about JJ? Would he have been charged as well?

He was finding it difficult to just sit there fingering the joystick of his go cart while this whirlwind was whirling around him. It was only a matter of time before he was caught up in it, before Mindy Dumont was thrusting her microphone in his face and demanding to know if he felt any responsibility for what had happened. He had to talk to Janet whether it was appropriate or not, even at the risk of annoying her.

On his first call to the sheriff's office, he was told that Detective Ellison was out. On his second call a half hour later, he was told she was still out but that he could leave a voice mail message, which he declined. On his third call a half hour after the second one he left a message asking her to call him if she could.

He grew increasingly anxious, occasionally agitated as the hours wore on with no news to add to the dumfounding confounding astounding news at noon. If he could walk, he would have been pacing to the mantra "All of them?" which had after a while evolved into an ear worm. Every once in a while, he'd take it in segments: Katrina? AnaLise? Riley? Susan? Marty? Sofia? Peter? Colin? Noah? Audrey, for God's sake? And JJ? What about JJ?

He had looked them all in the eyes in his classroom and hadn't seen it. AnaLise had more or less lied to his face, toyed with him, or at the very least withheld the truth from him. He couldn't help but take it personally. They had all sat there with poker faces while he congratulated himself on his ability to understand what they – whoever "they" might be – had done out of compassion for animals; to understand it without condoning it. Thanks, professor. Now could you teach us the perp walk? Was it any wonder that none of them had confided in him?

And there was Janet, playing her cards close to the vest as well, all the while methodically building her case. She must have been harboring suspicions about the students, all of them, for weeks. What finally broke it? He was planning to ask her that whether she was at liberty to answer it or not.

She had still not called by the time the evening news came on with Bob announcing. "We begin with team coverage of the bombshell story that has rocked Connor County."

Almost the entire newscast was devoted to the story, leading with the charges and arrests, followed by the release on bail of the six students who were arrested locally, a background piece on the fire, the predictable reactions from other students and local officials, a shrewdly crafted non-statement from the college, and a brief interview with Judith Scott.

"I can only say that as the mother of one of those arrested and as a trustee of the college, I'm personally devastated by these developments. There is still much we don't know. Until we have more information, I really cannot comment further."

She seemed to him as cool and self-assured as always, though he detected an undertone of anger in her voice, a note he had never heard before. To a casual viewer, however, it had probably come across as a parent simply trying to control her emotions. She did that well, he thought.

She was polite without smiling, and managed to cut the interview short without appearing defensive. If anyone could manage this crisis, he said to himself, it was Judith Scott.

Though to think of it as a crisis was a bit of a stretch, he thought. Crisis was too strong a word. But he changed his mind a short time later when the story popped up on one of the cable news networks. Then, as the evening wore on, he switched from channel to channel and watched as the story kept growing and spreading, being talked about everywhere he turned. Ten Christian college students charged with torching real estate mogul's lodge. Tycoon's own granddaughter among those charged. The community of Connor in shock. Motive said to be animal rights. It was metastasizing into big fucking news!

Edward himself was largely spared until a Fox News reporter scored an interview with Jon Herriman, Sr., who was identified as "the chairman of the Gennesaret Christian College Board of Trustees as well as the grieving father of a student who shared a class with the ten suspects and just last week committed suicide."

Wearing a black Stetson and a dark suit and tie, Herriman glared at the camera as if he were speaking directly to the "liberal crackpots" and "subverters of Christianity" who had infiltrated the college and brainwashed these students. Maybe it was just the Stetson, but there was also something unforgiving about his eyes that reminded Edward of his old schoolbook depictions of Calvinist witch hunters.

"My own son," he said, "was made to feel guilty for our way of life, which has been the way of life for our family for five generations."

"In what way was he made to feel guilty?"

"This professor at the college, some kook named Stathakis, told him, somehow convinced that whole damn class that animals have God-given souls and that they deserve the same rights as human beings. That's the kind of BS I'd expect from a professor at some elite secular cesspool but not from Gennesaret Christian."

Hearing his own name mentioned swept over Edward like an out-of-body experience. Yes, Stathakis, that was him, but not really, it was just his name, a label like "kook" with no basis in reality, or least none that he recognized. He was detached, incorporeal, hovering over his name, while Herriman cut the truth out of it like a coroner removing the heart from his body. He was numb to the pain. At that moment, and for only that moment, he was merely a dispassionate observer.

"But you're the chairman of the trustees," the reporter noted. "Why was it allowed?"

"I'll tell you why. Money. Enrollment. People with inferiority complexes who were hell bent on joining the fashionable wing of academia. People like Franklin Scott. And look what it got him. If I had wanted my son to get that kind of education I would have sent him to UC Berkeley or CUNY. What I've come to realize is that the devil's own were smuggled into Gennesaret Christian like invaders in a Trojan horse."

But it was about to end, Herriman vowed. He said he now had the votes on the board to "clean house from the top down" and restore Christianity to its place at his once virtuous institution.

And then Edward's phone began to ring with calls from the local media, the AP, a couple of the national networks, and several major newspapers interspersed with anonymous callers. He was tempted to answer the unidentified calls on the chance it was someone he knew, and more than once his finger nearly tapped "accept" but ultimately he restrained himself. Why take the chance of having to utter a "no comment" and then try to hang up while some journalist nevertheless persisted? He couldn't. Not yet. He didn't have Judith Scott's self-assurance or Herriman's wrath to see him through an interview. He couldn't answer questions on the fly. He needed to think, to hone his story and then stick to it.

Each time his phone rang anew, his heart stopped until he checked who was calling, and then raced ahead when the screen identified another news organization instead of Janet. When the night nurse arrived and checked his vitals, his pulse was forty beats per minute faster than that morning's resting rate.

"You've been very active, I hear," she noted as she removed the cuff. "You need to get a good night's sleep if you want to go home tomorrow."

"Okay," he said, but he knew that sleep wouldn't come easily. What he wouldn't have given just then to once again have access to that little red door bell at the gateway to opiate addiction. He was still wide awake an hour later having checked another five calls, none from Janet, when his phone rang again, this time with a text message from oddreD. He mouthed the tag, "odd red," and "o ddred," and then was about to reject it unread when with a brain stutter accompanying the double dd came the name, "Audrey D!"

He opened the message and read, "JTLYK It was NOT an accident!"

He wanted to ask the meaning of JTLYK, but thought first things first and replied, "Audrey?"

"Attys have lie to but we dont. Truth matters or it was all for nothing!!"

"I don't understand. Where are you?"

"more L8R & thnx"

The first acronym that came to his mind after she had signed off was WTF? He had no idea what she was talking about, or rather, texting about. But at least that part of it made some sense. Talking was so excruciatingly difficult for her, it was only natural that she'd prefer to communicate with him through text messaging. But what was she communicating? Could she have meant the hit-and-run? No one was calling that an accident, and so far as he knew, there were no attorneys involved. So she had to be talking about the fire. Even if the fire was set intentionally, it wouldn't surprise him at all if the students' attorneys were already mounting an accident defense. To do otherwise would constitute legal malpractice. Audrey, however, apparently wanted no part of it. What did she want? He started to raise his left hand to scratch his head but was saved by the sling.

Sleep finally did come to him, but it was neither deep enough nor long enough for him to feel rested by the time he was awakened by the morning nurse. She and a CNA wheeled him into a sitting shower and afterward helped him into a pair of sweatpants and a zippered hoodie that Jerry had brought to him for the discharge. With time to spare before the clinic's van was scheduled to take him home, he had breakfast and surfed the news channels, which had nothing new to offer. His phone rang twice as he ate, both of the calls from news hounds who had called repeatedly the night before. The second call was still ringing when Jerry walked in.

"That might be fame calling," Jerry said.

"As a matter of fact, it is, but it's not the kind of fame I want."

"Get with the program, man. People these days take fame any way they can get it."

"Even infamy?"

"Sure, it's all coin of the realm."

Edward was glad to see Jerry, while at the same time embarrassed that he had had to rely on him, a neighbor, for so much these past few days. Of course, if it was true that Jerry considered him to be a friend, as Alice had said, that would put a different spin on it. Relying on a friend in a time of need would not seem quite as desperate as relying on a friendly neighbor.

"A reporter with a cameraman showed up at your old apartment last night. He was pounding on your door. I stepped out and told them to stop wasting their time and my sleep. I said you were gone, and I even opened the door for them and showed them it was empty to prove it. I told them that I had heard you were leaving town. I spoke God's truth."

"Jerry, I don't know how I can ever thank you for all you've done for me."

"With fame come riches. I'm sure you'll remember your friends when that time comes."

When he first regained consciousness in the hospital, his first impulse was to call his parents. But he was alert enough to recognize that instinct as infantile and irresponsible, The injured child running to mommy and daddy. Only in this instance, it would have been the middle-age son running to old and ailing parents who, but for another more caring son, would have been left to fend for themselves in their declining years. And how could he ask his brother for help when he had been of no help to him?

"If I had had a child when I was first married, he or she would have been about your age by now," he said to Jerry. "I wouldn't have had to rely on the kindness of strangers."

"Who are you calling strange? Besides, children are greatly overrated. Sure, if you're lucky they might be around to visit you in your hour of need and then at the end to send you off across the River Styx, but that comes with a price, a lifetime of freedom, that I, for one, would not be willing to pay."

"We're the only species that has a choice when it comes to reproduction," Edward said.

"Exactly! The only animal on earth with the brains to know when to stop this insanity. What's to be gained with all these random genetic permutations? Every one of them carries the genetic death sequence. The sum is always zero."

Edward laughed and spun his wheelchair around to gather up his toiletries, phone and wallet from the countertop outside the bathroom. A nurse appeared at the doorway a few minutes later and said the van was waiting.

His new apartment was a convenient disappointment. It was easy to access with his wheelchair and would certainly be preferable to his old apartment when he graduated to crutches, but instead of a balcony with a view of every sunset, it had a small concrete pad for a patio with a view across a strip of grass to the back sides of the carports. But also on the positive side, it was cheaper. After Jerry left, he set about organizing his new environment to accommodate his limited vertical mobility while periodically checking his phone calls, one of which was finally from Janet.

"Where the hell are you?" she said. "I went to the clinic and you were gone, and now I'm standing outside your empty apartment."

He explained his move to the ground floor, and a few minutes later she was at his door,

"The local station had video of your unit upstairs and they said that you had apparently skipped town. The sheriff asked me to check it out. I didn't believe that you'd leave without letting us know."

"Of course not," he replied, swinging his leg around like a turnstile so that she could step inside. "I called you yesterday and left a message asking you to call me back."

"May I see your license and registration, please," she said with a laugh.

"But officer, I thought U-turns were allowed here."

"Yeah, anyway, my mailbox is full and I just haven't gotten around to it."

"That's okay. I just wanted to talk to you. After everything that's happened, I'm just trying to understand it. It was so totally unexpected," he said, and then held out his left hand like someone begging for alms. "All of them?"

"It's not as surprising as it seems," she said, sitting on the arm of the easy chair. A bag with his personal belongings and toiletries from the hospital occupied the seat. "They all got together for a going-away party and then it just spiraled out of control."

It must have been a send-off for those who were leaving at the end of the semester. That would explain the party at the camp site, not that a party among college students required an explanation.

"But my class didn't seem like the kind of cohesive unit that would party together. I'm surprised that they were the only ones there."

"It was a going away party for Jumpin' Jack," she said, relishing the big reveal. "They got together to release the rabbit in the woods. It was all about your L from start to finish, although the finish may not have turned out the way they expected."

"They were all involved in taking the rabbit as well?"

"Not at the beginning. Listen, Edward," she said, turning serious, "The D.A. has taken over and he doesn't want the details of our evidence to leak out. There are a lot of high-powered lawyers on the other side, as you might have guessed. The six who we arrested were released right after they were booked. Not a minute in a jail cell. That should tell you something."

"I understand."

"I feel I owe you some explanation before it all comes out because without your help, it would have taken a lot longer to tie it all together."

"You mean my encounter with AnaLise at the campsite."

"Right, and taking me to it. After I found that ear in the fire pit, I had something besides the Ls on the doors that placed them at the lodge. Anyone could have painted the Ls, but they had the ear."

"That was an ear?"

"A moose ear from one of Scott's trophies. What did you think it was?"

"A piece of a leather boot. You know, like the tongue."

"Really? Well, it was accidently ripped off a moose head while they were moving it to the garage. Someone put it in his pocket and carried it back to the camp site. When he realized his mistake, he threw it into the fire pit. We also had some DNA from the blood on that rag you found. We think someone cut themselves while hauling the trophies into the garage. So I was able to hold all that over their heads, which scared a few of them, the ones who didn't yet have lawyers. They broke ranks and to some extent decided to come clean. I have a feeling they're still hiding something, but it won't matter much."

"So they confessed? The fire? Jumpin' Jack?"

"I can tell you that AnaLise has admitted to taking Jumpin' Jack. She was returning to her dorm room after your lecture and as she was walking past the pen, she just acted on impulse. She put the Post-It Note with the L on the cage and carried the rabbit up to her room. A little later, she revealed what she had done to Sofia, Susan and Audrey, who also had rooms in the dorm. Once the search for the rabbit began in earnest, Sofia put the rabbit in her bike bag and took it to Noah, who's renting a room in town. They hatched the plan to release it in the woods, and then they decided to turn it into a party. They invited everyone else in your class. They all showed up for it. Depending upon who you ask, it was either a harmless stunt or a noble act."

Edward was shaking his head. "If they had only stopped there, I think even Dean Walters might have let it pass."

"Yeah, but once they were at the camp site, they watched the rabbit hop away into the forest – they said it looked back at them before it was gone – and it was apparently a turning point for some of the hold outs. I know, it sounds like something out of a Disney movie, but there were even some tears. And then they picked up where they had left off in your class. Cruelty to animals, animal rights, the same issues you had raised. It apparently got pretty heated and passionate. That's when Katrina described her arguments with her grandfather over all the animals he kills for sport. Or as she puts it, 'for fun.' She talked about how much she hated seeing those animal heads on his walls. Well, after a few more beers and maybe a joint or two, they all decided to march up there and liberate those heads as well. None of them wanted to talk about JJ, but as far as we can tell from what little they said, he may have refused to go along with them.

"Katrina knew there was a house key hidden under a pot beside the door. There were tools and ladders in the garage. One by one they moved the trophies into the garage. The plan was to load them into and on top of the cars that were there and then drive them down to the cemetery. They intended to take pictures of them propped up against tombstones and then post the pictures across the web to shame Franklin Scott. You see, up to that point, it didn't matter to Katrina if her grandfather knew she was involved. She actually wanted him to know.

"But as they got into it, it became apparent to them that there were just too many heads. Someone got the bright idea of burning some of them in that huge fire place. There were arguments about that, and one of the heads was pulled out of the fireplace, thrown back in. You can guess where it went from there."

"But if it really was an accident, why send that email to the TV station?"

"Yeah, pretty dumb, right? A signed confession. It was AnaLise's doing. She admits it was mistake. She intended it as a manifesto against big game hunting, but she had had a few too many and apparently wasn't thinking clearly. If she hadn't included that L in parenthesis, it might have been difficult to prove it came from them instead of some outside activist who wanted to get in on the action."

"But they also painted the Ls on the garage doors"

"That was before the fire. And it actually helps their case. They might as well have painted their names on the doors. You can be sure that their lawyers will argue that if they had intended to burn the place down, they wouldn't have done anything so stupid, even drunk. The email, though, is a higher hurdle."

"That's why they were angry with AnaLise," he surmised.

Janet shrugged, saying, "If it was, it was misplaced. The D.A. would have charged it as arson even without the email. Intentional or not, they caused the fire while in the commission of a felony and they did nothing to stop it. Any one of them could have called 911. No one did. That's arson, compounded by breaking and entering, burglary, and the willful destruction of several trophies worth thousands of dollars. On top of that, they made no effort to ensure that there was no one in the burning dwelling. That's aggravated arson, a first degree felony. If you accidently shoot and kill someone while robbing a bank, you're going to be charged with murder. Accidents don't happen in a vacuum."

"Okay, but if everybody including AnaLise thought the email was a stupid mistake, why put the L on the video of the slaughterhouse? That doesn't make sense."

"No, and we were trying to make sense of it, especially after JJ committed suicide. JJ had his cellphone with him that day, and when the coroner examined it, he came across edited versions of the video. Our IT people confirmed our suspicion: JJ posted that video himself. Which does make sense, since he was the only one of them who had access to the slaughterhouse. He was the only one who could have stood there filming it without arousing the suspicion of the workers."

"He wanted to explain himself."

"I don't know. Edward."

As he processed the information that she had shared with him, he continued to struggle with the tragedy of JJ's suicide, which was beyond his comprehension, and the folly of the others' missteps.

Shaking his head in bafflement, he said "I don't understand why they wouldn't have just come forward and explained what happened 'It was an accident. We're sorry.' Why keep quiet until they're caught? And they must have known that they'd be caught, Janet. These kids aren't stupid."

"No, Edward, but they're also not the Mafia or a street gang with a criminal skill set and a code of silence. They were a bunch of college kids out on a lark. It got crazy, they got scared. When you're scared, you step back, not forward. Sooner or later, probably after things settled down a bit, one or more of them probably would have done exactly what you expected them to do. Unfortunately, they waited a little too long."

"So you believe they've told the truth?

"Well, so far, what they've told me squares with the evidence. But if I come across something that says otherwise, you can be sure I'll set it on the other side of the scales."

Edward thought a long and hard minute about whether to tell the detective about his text message from Audrey. He wished he knew why Audrey wanted him to believe the fire was not an accident, and also whether she had conveyed the message to him in confidence. For all he knew, she might have sent the same text far and wide. He needed more information.

"Who were the six who were arrested?" he asked.

"That's been on the news," Janet said. "Katrina, Noah, Marty, AnaLise, Sofia, and Riley Marchant. It broke my heart watching Don as his little brother was being booked."

"Do you know where Audrey is?"

"As a matter of fact, she's the only one we haven't tracked down. She hasn't returned to her home in Wisconsin." She paused, eyeing him with suspicion. "Why, do you know something?"

So Audrey apparently didn't want to be found, which made him hesitant to reveal her message to him until he knew what, if anything, she did want. He convinced himself that he wasn't withholding information from Janet, which he had promised not to do, just giving it time to ripen before sharing it.

"I'm worried about her ability to handle all of this. You know, she's not like the others."

Janet looked away and bit her lower lip, signaling that she recognized a non-answer when she heard one, but to his relief she didn't press the point.

"Her parents are worried as well," she said. "She's probably just been scared off for a while. She'll surface before long. The D.A. has assured her parents through their lawyer that we're not going to make things any more difficult for her when she does turn up. We'll cut her some slack, Edward, but it goes only so far."

Chapter 12

He was prepared to convey Janet's warning to Audrey the next time he heard from her. But days passed and there were no new texts from her, and his attempt to reach out to her through the reply number from the first one went unanswered.

Confined as he was to his motorized wheelchair, he found himself devoting most of his time to watching and reading news reports, ignoring the diminishing number of calls from reporters and sampling the bottles of imported wines with which Jerry had displaced the five liter box under the sink. He had decided to put off his job search at least until he was up on crutches and his name was no longer in the news. The news media were already tiring of the story, though it had just flared up with the arraignment of seven of the ten students. Susan Paxton had surrendered voluntarily and joined her six classmates in court, while Colin McPherson and Peter Huelander were challenging extradition from their respective home states of Maryland and Ohio, and Audrey was still nowhere to be found. The seven entered pleas of not guilty, and as there was not much more to say on that subject, most of the news programs reprised some of their previously aired background reports and interviews.

One segment that Edward had not seen before showed Franklin Scott, with rifle at ease, delighted as Teddy Roosevelt beside the huge body of the giraffe he had just dispatched with a single shot behind the shoulder blade. It was an image that was sure to inflame the growing number of animal rights activists who had been flooding social media and news comment forums with full-throated support for the "Connor 10" and increasingly hostile attacks on Scott and his businesses. Dozens of the activists from all over the country had even showed up for the arraignment, cheering as the seven defendants, shielded by their legal teams, were hustled into the courthouse and again on the way out. AnaLise, Sofia and Noah acknowledged their supporters with smiles, but the other four looked straight ahead coming and going. The lead defense attorney, a silver haired man who responded to the cameras rather than to the reporters asking the questions, declared that neither he nor the defendants would comment on the unfortunate circumstances of this case until it was resolved, at which time the truth would absolve these innocent young people.

Edward shut his laptop and aimed his leg toward the avocado sandwich he had left in the kitchen. Before he could take a bite, his phone rang, Alice calling.

"God, Eddie," she said, "were you watching that interview with Jon Herriman just now?"

"No, but I saw it a few days ago," he said. He had changed channels when it came on. Hearing his name once again spoken in a moment of grieving wrath would have just upset him, as it apparently had done to Alice. "It's okay, Alice, I haven't let it get to me."

"No, not that. Didn't you notice that truck behind him? The white one between the horse trailer and the Escalade? It was the one that hit you, Eddie, I'm sure of it!"

"I didn't notice it."

"Call it up on their website, you'll see it. It's the one."

"Alice, how can you be so sure? The truck that hit me looked like half the trucks I see around here every day. I don't think I'd recognize it even if were to hit me again."

"It has a spotlight on the driver's side. You know, the kind you see on police cars? I noticed it when I jumped out of the way."

"I didn't see it."

"Doesn't it make sense? Someone connected to Herriman? He practically choked on your name. It could have been one of his sons, someone who works for him, maybe even someone he hired to run you down and make it look like an accident."

That latter theory was nuts, but Edward had to admit the first two were very real possibilities. First though, he'd have to be convinced that the truck that Alice saw on the news was the same truck that hit him.

"I don't know, Alice, it's possible," he said. "But I've seen those spotlights on other trucks around here. They apparently use them for hunting at night. I can't accuse Herriman based solely on that."

"It's too much of a coincidence," Alice insisted. "I think you should at least mention the similarity to the police."

Edward said he would, and then he would have wanted to continue talking to Alice about other things, just talk, but her lunch break was over and it was back to work for her. He on the other hand had nothing to look forward to except a visit from a home health care CNA who would help him get past his embarrassment and into the shower.

It was that daily humiliation along with the occasional drop-in by Jerry that kept him from going stir crazy while waiting for Doc to clear him for crutches, which he did a week later. Out of the sling, his left arm was still vulnerable, but he found that if he was careful to distribute the pendulum of motion between his left leg and right arm he could teeter totter along without too much difficulty. There was a part of him that hated to part with his much faster chair, but now he was free to shower on his own and even drive with his right leg slung awkwardly over the center console of his Subaru. That much he could manage, he found upon venturing out to the grocery store, but pushing the shopping cart through the aisles and afterward carrying the bags out to his car were beyond his capabilities, forcing him to accept the assistance of an old man who was stocking shelves, who, it turned out, had once taught chemistry at Gennesaret Christian.

"I retired twelve years ago," he said to Edward as he hoisted the bags into the back of the car. "I hear the enrollment has more than doubled since then. If we had had that many students when I was there, they might have paid me what I was worth."

Which reminded Edward that before Herriman sabotaged his job at Upland Community College, he had asked Mrs. Tidwell to hold his final pay check and mail it to him once he was settled in Ogden. With that prospect gone, he supposed he could now just call and ask her to mail it to his new apartment number, but after being cooped up for a week, he felt like extending his excursion.

The campus was almost deserted, though he noticed a cluster of expensive cars in the VIP lot near the administration building, He thought he could get away with parking in a handicapped stall near the door even without a tag, but he had heard the stories of cars being towed within minutes of violating the rules. He could just imagine Dean Walters watching him from his window while frantically scrolling through his phone list for parking enforcement's number. Anyway, his physical therapist had recommended long walks and threatened him with blood clots, pulmonary embolism, and death if he sat on his ass too much. It was a cool, cloudy day, and it felt good to be outdoors again.

As he clumsily banged his way into the administrative office, Mrs.

Tidwell leapt out of her chair and rushed toward him with outstretched arms as if toward an erratic toddler tilting toward a fall.

"Professor Stathakis, my goodness, I imagine you're here for your pay check. I've been meaning to call you about it. I didn't know where to send it."

"That's okay, Mrs. Tidwell, I'm back up on my feet now, as you can see."

"I heard about your terrible accident. They said it was a hit-and-run. It's just outrageous. Those kinds are usually drunk or talking on their cellphones or driving without insurance. Well, I hope they are caught and made to pay for what they did to you."

"Thank you, Mrs. Tidwell. Justice will be done, I hope."

She returned to her desk and rummaged through a stack of papers until she found an envelope with a note clipped to it.

"Here it is," she declared, discarding the attached note and handing him the envelope.

He leaned his left crutch against the counter and folded all of his earnings for the foreseeable future into his back pocket.

"I was surprised to see all those cars in the VIP lot," he said. "I thought Dean Walters would have turned out the lights and hung his 'Gone Fishin'' sign on the door by now."

"Oh, professor, you have no idea! It's been pure pandemonium around here. Dean Walters is gone, fired. He cleared out yesterday. The trustees have been meeting here almost every day ever since the arrests. They've been poring over all the personnel files and calling faculty members into their meetings one by one. Coach Jespperson said it was just like the Star Chamber."

He could never tell whose side Mrs. Tidwell was on. She sometimes expressed some exasperation or annoyance with this person or that person but with forbearance or, failing that, resignation. Amidst conflicts or quarrels, she was the Switzerland of Gennesaret Christian College. Edward had always found refuge in her neutrality. Even now, surrounded by the pure pandemonium of his making, she had nevertheless welcomed him into her office with open arms.

"I've been taking quite a few calls regarding your class," she said.

"Reporters," he said, shaking his head. "I'm sorry, Mrs. Tidwell, they've been hounding me at home as well. But I guess you don't have the luxury of just ignoring their calls as I do."

"Them, too, but I meant calls from students. Both current and prospective students. They have wanted to know if you would be teaching the same class next year. They were interested in taking you class. Goodness, if you were coming back, you'd have to offer the class two or three times each semester to accommodate them all."

"Really?" he said, more than a little surprised. Maybe some of that fame that Jerry was talking about was catching up with him. "I expected just the opposite. Complaints from parents, students dropping out."

"Oh, we've had a few of those as well. It's mostly been the others, however. They seem very disappointed when I tell them you won't be returning next year. I always tell them that if they are really that interested in your class, they could enroll at Upland Community College instead."

"I appreciate that very much, Mrs. Tidwell, but I won't be teaching at Upland either. Mr. Herriman saw to that."

"I didn't know. I'm sorry, professor. I'm sorry, too, for Mr. Herriman's tragic loss of his son, but he can be unnecessarily antagonistic. The trustees have relinquished control of the college to him, you know, at least until a new dean is hired."

"What about Judith Scott?"

"She resisted, of course, but he had the votes."

He sighed, thanked Mrs. Tidwell again, and exited as clumsily as he had entered, the door hitting him on the way out. To his dismay, a number of trustees and faculty members had gathered in clusters outside the board room down the hall that he'd have to traverse to exit the building. Moving like a clown on stilts, he had little hope of passing by them without being noticed. He tried, however, sticking as close to the opposite wall as he could and averting his gaze with the logic of an ostrich: If I can't see them, they can't see me. Whether because the tactic actually succeeded or, more likely, his old colleagues knew better than to fraternize with him in full view of the distinguished councilors of the Star Chamber, he managed to escape unscathed by either curiosity or castigation.

Once outside and on his way to his car, however, he heard Judith Scott calling his name. With all that had transpired since they last spoke, he turned and waited with some trepidation as she approached. What if she, too, had come around to the theory that he was responsible for ruining the lives of students, primarily her daughter, and also precipitating the retrenchment underway at her family's treasured college? He braced himself for her typically diplomatic style of disapprobation if not outright animus.

"You can hobble but you can't hide," she said.

It was the sort of snarky remark he had some to expect from her, but she had delivered it with a weak and quickly waning smile rather than her usual aplomb.

"You caught me," he replied.

After she had ascertained that he was alive and well enough considering the severity of his accident, she said, "I'm glad I did catch you, Edward, I wanted to talk to you."

"I've been meaning to call you, Judith. I wanted to tell you how sorry I am about the mess Katrina is in, and also about what's happening here. I'm at a loss…"

"Edward, stop! I've told you before that you are not responsible for the actions of others, whether it's Katrina or that idiot Herriman. Katrina is fine. She's staying with her father in San Diego. This will all be over soon and she will come out of it without a scratch. All of them will. Years from now they'll all look back on it as a fond memory of their rebellious youth."

"I hope so, Judith, but I can't help but worry about them. They are facing some serious charges."

Judith shook her head and said, "You can stop worrying about that. Our lawyers have it all under control. You can stop worrying, period. Since it's not going to come out in a trial, you might as well know now that what happened at the lodge had nothing to do with your lecture. Katrina regrets that they dragged you into it with those Ls. What happened was a foolish accident. They never intended to burn down the lodge. Their plan, Katrina's plan, was to shame her grandfather by exhibiting what she refers to as his cruelty to the world. What she did was driven entirely by her antipathy to her grandfather's hunting, an antipathy she has harbored since she was child."

"Your father told me about it," he said. "But what do you mean it won't come out the trial?"

"All I can tell you right now is that it won't. We have no intention of airing our personal affairs in public."

"Your father seemed very protective of her."

"Yes, despite their disagreements. But it was bound to come to a head sooner or later with one or the other of them compromising for the sake of their relationship or the two of them becoming permanently estranged. Daddy, to his credit, has finally waved the white flag. No more hunting. He was not willing to lose his granddaughter over another trophy. The sad part of it is that Katrina was willing to lose him rather than abandon her own principles."

"It must be very difficult for all of you, Judith."

"We'll survive. What about you?" she asked, taking him in head to foot. "You look so thin, almost frail."

"I lost some weight, and I haven't been able to exercise. It's amazing how fast the muscles atrophy."

"Isn't it? I broke my leg skiing once and the same thing happened to me. You need to exercise, eat and exercise. Hydro therapy is the best thing for you, Edward. Believe me, a broken leg won't hold you back in a pool. As a matter of fact, why don't you come up and use our pool? I'll tell the staff to expect you."

"Thank you, but I wouldn't think of intruding on you like that."

"Nonsense. You've seen my house. It's like a hotel. I wouldn't even know you were there. But if I did, I might challenge you to a race."

"I read your bio in the school catalogue. I wouldn't stand a chance against you."

"That was a long time ago," she laughed. "Anyway, remember, the pool is at your disposal any time."

"I'll consider it, Judith, thank you."

She glanced at her watch and said, "I've got to get back."

"How's it going in there?"

"The battle for the soul of Gennesaret? Herriman is winning, but it's certain to be a pyrrhic victory. Once the enrollment and budget numbers start to come in this fall, there will be some serious soul searching for sure."

"Good luck," he said.

"Oh, Edward," she called out as she, too, was about to leave. "Jumpin' Jack's disappearance had everything to do with your lecture."

He nodded and laughed, saying, "I'll take the credit for that one."

Could he really? he wondered as he lurched away. Could he take credit for the one positive event associated with his words, whether misconstrued or not, while at the same time disavowing all the others? There it was again, his obsession with guilt. It was an itch he had to scratch. Even if the fire at the lodge was an accident, it had spread from that camp fire that he had stoked. He was the reason the students were there that night. And by conjuring up his words, whether slurring them or not, they conjured him up as well. He was there in spirit, doing jumpin' jacks right along with them as Jumpin' Jack disappeared into the woods to live free and die as a rabbit, as an animal rather than a toy. Sure, he'd take that. But what about JJ's suicide, the video of the slaughterhouse, Audrey's erratic behavior, the firing of Dean Walters, and the decline and fall of the college? And the attempt on his life, for God's sake? But then it was he, after all, who had sown the wind.

As he crossed the parking lot, he felt that his walking was becoming easier. He was getting the hang of it. Getting into the car, though, was a different story. It had seemed simple enough the first time he did it that morning, but now for some reason he had to twist and tilt his body into a half dozen configurations, like a child's Transformer toy, before he found the winning combination. Exhausted, he drove straight back to his apartment, turning his thoughts along the way to Judith's invitation, and then to Alice, and then back to Judith.

He had much less trouble extricating himself from the car and then he balanced on one foot while lifting the tailgate to unload his groceries. He grabbed one bag in each hand and swung them alongside his crutches until he reached his door, at which time he faced a dilemma. Pondering the two bags and the door knob, he was reminded of the puzzle of the fox, the chicken, and the sack of grain. He would have to drop one bag in order to open the door. But then he wouldn't be able to bend over to pick it up again. He had no choice but to return one of the bags to the car and content himself with twice as many round trips. Well, he told himself, it was exercise, and the bags held some of the foods he had been craving the past week. Exercise, eat and exercise.

Just as he had finished placing the last bag on the kitchen countertop, Jerry walked in through the still open front door and noted that he had been gone a long time. He explained his errand at the college and described the scene outside the boardroom.

"Mrs. Tidwell made it sound like an inquisition. She told me Dean Walters is gone. Have you been through it yet?"

"I was in the room for less than a minute," Jerry replied. "I sat down, Herriman thanked me for appearing before the board, complimented me on my credentials, and then he asked me if I adhered to the principles of Christianity in the performance of my duties. I stood up, thanked him for inviting me to appear before the board, informed him that mathematics had not yet confirmed the existence of God, and then I walked out."

"Wow, Jerry, good for you. But what about your job?"

"Apparently, they were warned by their legal counsel that firing me would cost them not only the endowment that paid my salary but my full salary out of their own pockets for the four years remaining in my contract. Franklin Scott's lawyers drew it up when I was hired, and those guys belong to the iron workers of America. I was told that Herriman was still willing to throw me out on Christian principle but a majority of the board decided that depriving me of four years of well-paid vacation was punishment enough. I may appeal their decision."

Edward laughed, but his mind was drifting elsewhere. Even though he knew it might be hard to pin him down, he wanted to ask Jerry about Alice, all kidding aside.

"Alice called me yesterday," he began. "She saw Herriman being interviewed on TV and noticed a truck parked at his house that she thought looked like the one that hit me."

"No shit?" Jerry said. "Well, you can take it to the bank. Alice has an eye for detail. She doesn't guess."

"I told her I'd mention it to the police, but given the circumstances, I don't think they'll drop it on Herriman without something more to go on. He would probably just accuse me of retaliating against him for what he said in the interview."

"Of course he would, but if Alice says it was his truck that hit you, then someone needs to investigate, arrest and prosecute whoever was driving it that day."

Edward nodded, "He could have hit Alice instead of me. Whenever I think about that, it makes my head spin. It was just insane. Alice means a lot to me."

"You hardly know her, Edward."

"I know, but I think we hit it off. I wish she was still here."

Jerry's smile gave away his sympathy. "She'll be back in about six months, and I wouldn't be surprised if she wishes you were here as well."

He wanted to believe she felt that way, but hearing it from Jerry hadn't convinced him of it after all. Jerry may have just said it to be kind, satisfied that his sister had escaped the clutches of an unsuitable suitor.

"I may still be here," Edward said obstinately.

"I'll be sure to check the classifieds every day for 'philosopher wanted' ads. But if nothing turns up, you two can send each other postcards from wherever you happen to be: 'Having a great time, wish you were here.'"

Edward picked up and rattled his 30-count bottle of oxycodone and said, "Doc's prescription is good for two refills. That should be enough to get me started in the retail drug trade."

"I've talked to Doc about that," Jerry said as sternly as Edward had ever seen him. "I've told him he's overprescribing that shit, but he won't listen to me. Listen to me, Edward, take two aspirin and throw those fish hooks down the toilet. Believe me, I've been hooked by well-intentioned doctors, and if I had known better I would have filed a malpractice lawsuit against them."

"Jerry, as a philosopher unwanted, I submit that there is no such thing as happiness. There is only pain and the absence of pain."

CHAPTER 13

After a couple of weeks of physical therapy, Edward's left arm was almost back to normal, allowing him to work on his upper body with only the normal exchange of pain for gain. He was also able to transfer a fraction of his weight onto his healing leg, though that part of it remained a delicate process. The hydro therapy that Judith had recommended was in fact part of his routine at the clinic. It did not involve swimming, however, only paddling and swinging his legs against a current of water in a pool no bigger than a king size bed. He broached the subject with his therapist, who enthusiastically endorsed a vigorous swim as the superior alternative, which was all the encouragement he needed to take Judith up on her offer.

Not entirely sure that she had meant it, or really expected him to show up unannounced, or bothered to mention it to her staff in case he did, he thought it best to call first. He was put through to Sonia, the house manager, who told him that Judith was away on business, but yes indeed, she had been informed of the invitation.

"Would today be alright?" Edward asked, sounding to himself like a guest from the boondocks speaking to the front desk at a swank hotel.

"Anytime. Would you like directions?"

"No thank you, I know the way."

He arrived at Judith's estate wearing his baggy knee length bathing trunks, flip flops and a striped T-shirt. Sonia, a sturdy woman with aging Nordic features and golden braids coiled above her ears, seemed surprised by his crutches and leg brace.

"There is no lifeguard," she said. "No one to help you."

"I'll be okay," he assured her.

She led him past the sitting room where he had met with Franklin Scott, down one of the two hallways that flanked the stairway to the second floor, and through the kitchen to a long and narrow conservatory that looked out at a large shimmering blue pool and tennis courts in the distance surrounded by a manicured privacy hedge of blue-green yews.

As he stepped out onto the quarry tiles, his right crutch hit a wet spot and slipped out from under him. Fortunately for him, Sonia was there to catch him in arms as strong as his therapist's. Her grip caught his bicep like a steel trap.

"I wasn't told of your handicap," she complained.

"I'll be fine, Sonia. I'll be careful," he promised.

"If you need anything, there's an intercom in the conservatory," she said, with a sideways glance at the pool that suggested just how worthless that lifeline might be.

Left alone, he tried to concoct some way to sit down at the edge of the pool either with or without his crutches, but no functional method came to mind. He knew then what he had to do. He moved to the deep end of the pool, set the crutches down on a lounge chair, and, since jumping was out of the question, he toppled into the water face first. After the initial sting wore off, he dog paddled to the shallow end and commenced walking as the therapist had taught him to do. It felt good to be using his right hip and to flex his knee, even if only through a third of its normal arc. The resistance from the water forced him to lean forward, swivel his torso and pump his arms as if walking against a gale. Tiring quickly, he switched back to the dog paddle and took a lap around the pool. He could see why Judith recommended hydro therapy, especially in a swimming pool instead of the big, stainless steel bath tub at the clinic. He had taken her at her word that his use of the pool would not be intruding upon her, but he was nevertheless a little disappointed that she wasn't even home to intrude upon, let alone to kick his ass in a race.

He alternated between swimming laps and the underwater power walk for what he guessed was about a half hour and then he hoisted himself up onto the lip of the pool at the spot where he had entered it. He warned himself that if he slid over to the lounge chair, he'd either have to end the therapy session or face the prospect of another face flop back into the pool. Undecided, he sat where he was with his right leg stretched out on the tiles like a beached piece of flotsam and his left leg dangling in the water. Shortly, the thirst that had been creeping up on him took over and decided it for him. He pushed himself over and up onto the lounge chair. Then with the crutches under his arms, he squatted with his right leg extended like a Cossack doing the Hopak dance and with the requisite yelp "hop!" he was upright. There was no water hose or fountain in sight so he headed for the conservatory to call for a bottle of water or a soda, something to keep him going for another round in the pool.

Stepping inside, he was surprised to find Franklin Scott sitting in a cushioned wicker recliner, a tall glass of sparkling water and a smartphone on the glass top of the wicker side table next to him, and Judith's melodious voice rising up out of the speaker.

Interrupting her, Franklin said, "Your professor just walked in, or should I say toddled in?"

"Hi Edward," Judith said. "I'm glad you're trying out the pool. How is it?"

"Great, Judith, thank you," he said loudly. "You were right about the benefits."

"Good, make it part of your routine, oaky? And Dad, I'll get back to you after the meeting in Vancouver. Bye now," she said, ending the call from her end before her father could reply.

Franklin reached over and tapped the screen of his phone, telling Edward, "She works much too hard. I think it gives her the sense of control she finds missing outside of her work. Either that, or it's simply a distraction, a form of entertainment. What's your guess?"

"I really don't know her well enough to say. She has seemed very competent in every situation that I've seen her in. Very much in control."

"That's right, in control of herself and everyone else." He motioned to Edward to take the seat on the other side of the table. "When she's working, she's in her element, in command. She knows what needs to be done and she does it, quickly, efficiently and without the huffing and puffing you typically get from the musclemen in the business. But when she's not working, she seems to flounder. Drinks too much. She doesn't really have any interests outside of work, except maybe the college. She thought it had the potential to become a small jewel in academe. I thought so, too. But now it appears to be headed back into the Dark Ages."

"I know, and I'm sorry for the role I played in that."

"Judith said you like to blame yourself for everything. Why is that?"

Edward smiled and shrugged. "I don't enjoy it, but I'm willing to take whatever blame I have coming to me. With regard to what's happening at the college, the rabbit, the fire at your lodge, everyone has been telling me the same thing; that I'm not responsible. Well, with the exception of Mister Herriman and whoever tried to kill me, that is. And I was starting to believe it myself for as long as I thought that only a couple of students were involved. It was a simple rationalization, really. What I said in class I said to eleven students, but if only a couple of them took something away from it that was unintended, then I could conclude that the mistake was theirs, not mine. Otherwise, they all would have misinterpreted the lecture. Do you see what I mean?"

"Yes, but you're assuming that it was your words, your lecture that drove them to do what they did at my lodge, and that's where you are wrong."

"All of them!" Edward interrupted, leaning forward. "My entire class, not just one or two of them. All the students in Pastor Bartholomew's religious studies class didn't get together and kidnap Jumpin' Jack and then burn down your lodge. Nor did Coach Jespperson's entire football team, or Jerry Moseley's math class, or any of the other classes, clubs or teams at the school. It was only my class, and it was all of them. I somehow brought them all together in common cause."

"So what?" Franklin demanded. "They got together because you inspired them to free a caged animal. After that, my friend, it was all Katrina. Forgive me, but it had nothing to do with all that crap about souls or the equivalency of man and animal. Katrina loves animals. She can't stand to see them abused or humiliated or killed *unnecessarily*. I'm cruel because I end an animal's life for no good reason, or no reason acceptable to her. She has said so many times before, and this tableau with the trophies that she had planned was just her way of putting one more exclamation point on it. Everyone else went along with it because, well, because it was a party."

"I don't know, maybe, but the fact remains that Katrina's escalation of her feud with you happened to coincide with her participation in my class and it involved everyone else in my class."

"Coincidence. There you are! Listen, Edward, psychology is not my strong suit, but I think there may be some part of you that wants to take the credit for what happened. You molded minds! Your words were powerful! You inspired action! Rebellion! Isn't that what all good teachers aspire to? A discernible impact on the lives of their students?"

The thought, albeit fleeting, had occurred to him as recently as his encounter with Judith in the Gennesaret parking lot. She had laid out the same facts as her father to absolve him of responsibility, and he had embraced only that morsel of credit, the freeing of Jumpin' Jack, that she had tossed to him as an afterthought. Could it be that he was blinded to the facts by the glare of the limelight shining upon *his* class, *his* (L), and *his* starring role in all of the accompanying drama? After all, here he was sitting in a luxurious mansion chatting with one of the richest men in the country who before any of this had transpired would not have even deigned to acknowledge his apology if he had bumped into him on the street.

Deflated, Edward said, "I was wondering if I could have a glass of water. My throat is parched from the chlorine."

"Water, lemonade, soda, whiskey, beer, name it," Franklin said, reaching for his cellphone.

While waiting for his choice of lemonade to arrive, Edward said, "Judith told me Katrina's motives aren't likely to come out at a trial, which I took to mean there will be plea bargains instead."

Nodding, Franklin said, "A couple of years ago, a young animal rights activist from Minnesota released twelve hundred minks from their open air pens. He was caught and charged with a felony under the federal Animal Enterprise Terrorism Act. He was convicted and sentenced to up to fifteen years in a federal penitentiary. Three young people raided a pig farm in Iowa and stole I think it was about fifty piglets. They are serving five years in prison. Another young man, twenty-two years old, bombed a feed lot in Wisconsin ten years ago. He may still be in prison when he's fifty. Do you get my drift?"

"Yes, of course, I would not want to see that happen in this case."

"It won't. My lawyers have arranged for the ten defendants here to plead guilty to criminal mischief. It's a misdemeanor punishable by up to six months in jail. But the prosecutor will accept pleas in abeyance, which means if these kids stay out of trouble for a year, the charges will be dismissed. No criminal records. I have waived any claim to restitution and I will also reimburse the town of Connor for the costs incurred fighting the fire at the lodge. Naturally, the students and their parents are all on board with this. I'm hoping that very soon we can put this all behind us."

"What about Audrey Davenport?" He had a nagging feeling that she would not be on board with it.

"Ah, the fugitive. Well, her parents have promised to reason with her when she surfaces. If for some reason she refuses to cooperate, the D.A. will go ahead and prosecute her on the criminal mischief charge. Though I expect if it comes down to it, he'll simply dismiss the charge rather than go to the expense of a trial. So, if she's looking for some kind of a bullhorn, she won't get it here."

"So her obstinacy could actually pay off," Edward said, taking comfort in the thought. "She would be the only one who gets off scot-free."

"Spelled with two ts," Franklin said with one of his hearty laughs.

"That was unintended," Edward confessed. "But you know, Mister Scott, Audrey is probably the last person I'd suspect of angling for a soapbox or, as you say, a bullhorn. She is one of the least assertive people I've ever met. She's painfully shy. She never speaks unless spoken to, and when she does, she's not looking at you, her face reddens and her voice is a hesitant whisper. She's not going to stand up in front of a camera or issue a manifesto from the witness box."

While he was speaking, Sonia carried in a tray with a pitcher of lemonade, a bowl of ice, and two frosted glasses. As she was setting it down on the table, Edward felt as if she were giving him the once over, focusing mostly on his leg, for any sign of the injury she had feared. She accepted his thanks for the lemonade and then asked him if he'd be returning to the pool.

"No, I think I'd better stop for now."

"Yes, come back when you are a little more steady on your feet," she advised.

After she had gone, Franklin said, "Don't mind Sonia. She feels personally responsible for everything that happens in this house. Judith was sued once by a guest who slipped and fell on a floor that had just been mopped, and Sonia, of course, blamed herself. Judith is right about the hydro therapy. Come back whenever you like, fall and break your other leg if you want to, just don't sue Judith."

Edward was reaching for the pitcher of lemonade when the cellphone beside the tray beeped. Franklin tapped the screen and said, "Yes?"

"Chief Hammond is here," Sonia said over the speakerphone.

"I'll see him in the sitting room," Franklin said. Rising, he said to Edward, "My wife and I will be returning to Chicago tomorrow, so I may not see you again for some time. You've taken some hits over this mess, your job, your leg there, but I suspect you'll glean some sort of meaning out of it all. Isn't that what philosophers do?"

"I'm working on it," Edward said.

"Fine, good luck!" Franklin said with an immensely satisfied grin as he strode out of the room.

Edward finished his lemonade and then he, too, headed out. He had only gone as far as the hallway outside the kitchen before he was intercepted by Sonia, who insisted upon escorting him the rest of the way. The doors to the sitting room were closed as they walked past it, but Franklin and the fire chief could be heard talking over each with raised voices. Franklin's voice just then silenced Hammond's mid-sentence with, "I said it doesn't matter, goddamn it!" Setting aside her fear of a fall, Sonia hurried Edward along and out the entrance doors and shut them quickly behind him.

Franklin's revelations regarding the plea bargains lifted Edward's spirits, mostly for the sake of his students but also because it meant he would not have to testify at a trial. Franklin's psychological diagnosis notwithstanding, he had no desire to be the center of attention in a courtroom with those students' futures hanging in the balance. He might not have minded it quite so much if he were examined and cross-examined solely about his lecture and the derivation of the (L). In spite of everything that had happened, he was still proud of that lecture.

In fact, as far as that went, he was actually looking forward to setting the record straight, publicly, on the record, once and for all. "No," he would have testified under oath, "I did not say that animals have souls." Never mind that as an agnostic he would have already perjured himself by invoking the help of a god whose existence or nonexistence was beyond his knowledge, his *gnosis*. "Yes, I encouraged the class to explore the comparative value of human and animal life, by which I meant the value of life to the human or to the animal living that life." Let them call a rebuttal witness who would dare testify that animals would choose, were they capable of choice, to sacrifice their own meaningless lives to feed and entertain the more worthy human species.

However, he also would have undoubtedly been asked to put the lie to AnaLise's account of the campsite party, recount JJ's emotional struggle with the incriminating evidence he possessed, describe the students' damning conspiracy of silence, and reveal the text message from Audrey, all the while facing them as he had in the classroom. He would give them a lesson in trust and betrayal. He would fail them all.

Maybe now with no trial hanging over him, his association with Gennesaret severed, and his departure from Connor no more than a few weeks away, he could set this year of his life aside for some future, dispassionate reassessment. Just setting it aside for a while, he reiterated to himself, not putting it behind him. There were some occurrences, episodes in life that if shelved in receding memory without first being preserved could over time deteriorate, lose their meaning. He intended to keep working on the meaning of it, as he had said to Franklin, because, yes, that is what philosophers do, but there was no urgency. His more immediate mission was to find a new job. To recover his mobility. To take a load of clothes to the laundromat. And to make a run to the bank that he had been putting off. His last pay check would not carry him much further, and the only option left open to him was to pay the damn early withdrawal penalty and dip into his IRA, his only bulwark against old age in a homeless shelter. Every spare dollar he could muster since his divorce from Sandra, to whom he had naively entrusted his end of life aspirations, had gone into his retirement fund, which he had declared inviolable, even if it meant stocking shelves at a grocery store like the retired chemistry professor. But with a bum leg, he couldn't even do that.

At the bank, he eased himself into a chair across from an assistant bank manager named Lorraine and explained his predicament, saying he'd have to take the hit from an early withdrawal.

"Not necessarily," Lorraine said with a nod to his crutches. "You obviously qualify for the disability exemption to the early withdrawal penalty. That will save you the ten percent."

"Great," he said, feeling like he had just pulled off a heist. His bum leg was saving him a bundle.

He was sitting across from her at an angle to accommodate his rigid limb, which required him to twist his body while filling out the forms. After he finished, Lorraine summoned her secretary to scan the documents and fetch the check from one of the tellers. Edward had his back to the secretary and he didn't see her face until she was standing at the teller's window. She turned her head slightly, just far enough to steal a glance at him, and then she quickly looked away when he noticed her. There was nowhere to hide, however, when she returned to the assistant manager's desk, and Edward came face to face with Mona Lisa in context.

He didn't know her name, had never spoken to her, but while depositing his paychecks he had noticed her many times in the company of the bank officers, or feeding papers into the copy machine, or scurrying between desks and teller windows with office supplies, slips, fresh stacks of currency. She had short, dark brown hair parted high on one side with bangs sweeping across half her forehead and over the top of one ear. Her complexion was the same Mediterranean hue as some of his full blooded Italian cousins, not tanned, and she was not stingy with her eye shadow and lipstick. She seemed a little younger than his students and also younger than most of her co-workers, with whom she often exchanged whispered remarks that led to smothered laughter. There was no mistaking her. She was the passenger in the truck that hit him, and judging from the frightened look she gave him, she suspected he knew it. Handing the forms and the check to Lorraine, she hurried away and found something to occupy her behind the tellers' counter.

Edward signed over the check to be deposited into his account and hesitated, weighing pros and cons, when Lorraine asked if there was anything else she could do for him.

"No, thank you," he said, deciding not to ask for the secretary's name.

Doing so might have required some sort of explanation that he was not ready to provide. There was also a chance that he had misread the girl's expression and that she was not at all sure whether he recognized her. She might have figured that if he had, wouldn't he have leapt out of his seat and confronted her, demanded to know the name of the driver, called the police? If there was any doubt in her mind, asking for her name, which was likely to get back to her, would only serve to remove it.

He paused again outside the bank, trying to imagine the scene if he were to go back inside and do exactly what he had just imagined that the girl would expect from someone identifying her as an accomplice in the attempt on his life. Accusations, denials, tears, police, handcuffs. Was he ready for all that? There was no telling where it might all lead, how it might all end. He could pursue justice, demand his retribution, the ensuing legal and personal strife be damned! Or he could walk away, leave it behind – and not simply set it aside – so that he could move on from

Connor without this new unpleasant entanglement holding him back. He elected to give it some thought, a lot of thought, and not give in to an impulse he might later regret. Gripping his crutches, he headed for his car and took his usual safe route home.

Chapter 14

The sun rose on the following day, a Saturday, through a fiery vanguard of crimson and yellow clouds propelled by stuttering gusts of wind. By mid-morning, a towering bank of storm clouds brought up the rear, unleashing a fierce thunderstorm and heavy rain. A perfect day, Edward thought, to concentrate on his job search. He resolved to complete the applications to traditional colleges that he had already started and then after lunch to swallow his pride and take a dip in the murkier deeper waters that Alice had recommended. He had to admit that she was right; the private for-profit and online schools didn't pay as well but, indifferent to conventional academic calendars, they were always hiring. However, he was not willing to even consider public middle or high schools despite Alice's encouragement, even if it meant exhausting his retirement fund.

While the morning went as planned, he procrastinated through most of the afternoon, convincing himself that it was more important to finish unpacking and tidying up what he could rather than extend his search to the job postings of last resort. By evening, the gray dome of clouds had shattered and the sunset cast a light orange light over the carports that dominated the view from the sliding glass doors that led to his patio. The sunsets were what he missed most about his old apartment upstairs. If he had been able to manage the climb up the two flights of stairs, he might have barged in on Jerry and had a beer on his balcony. Instead, he poured himself a glass of wine and satisfied himself with the orange glow of the carports while waiting for the delivery of his "Garden Deluxe" pizza.

"Come in, it's open," he yelled when the doorbell rang. He stood up and reached for his wallet.

"It will cost you more than that to get out of this jam." Janet said as he turned toward her with a twenty dollar bill in his hand.

"Janet, I thought you were the pizza delivery guy. Come in."

"I can't stay too long," she said, taking the recliner where he had been sitting.

"Would you like glass of wine?" As it was a Saturday night and she wasn't in uniform, he thought it safe to offer.

"No, sit down, Edward, I have to ask you a few questions and also give you another little lecture about cooperating with your friendly neighborhood detective."

"What do you mean?" He had an idea but thought it best to play dumb at first in case he was wrong.

"I think you know what I mean," she said with a disappointed smile. "We had a visit at the station last night from a bank employee named Angela Nieto. She assumed you had done what any law-abiding citizen would have done and reported her to the authorities. Imagine her surprise! She thought if she came to us first, we wouldn't arrest her in front of her friends at the bank or at home with her parents looking on."

It had occurred to him that she might turn herself in if she were sure he had recognized her, but he didn't think he had been that obvious.

"Janet, I'm sorry. I did recognize her at the bank yesterday, but I couldn't decide what to do about it. There were so many repercussions to consider and I wasn't ready to deal with them."

"Well, you're going to have to deal with them now. She told us the driver was her boyfriend, Luke Herriman. She had gone with him to his brother's gravesite at the cemetery. On the way back, Angela saw you jogging and told Luke who you were. She said he just flipped out. He turned around and came after you. She insists he was just trying to scare you but the truck skidded on the gravel and he lost control of it."

"Have you talked to Luke?"

The doorbell rang again before she could answer. Edward asked the pizza deliveryman to set the box on the kitchen counter and paid him with the twenty dollar bill that was still in his hand. After the deliveryman had gone, Edward shuffled back to the couch and looked over at Janet.

She looked back at him with knitted eyebrows, as if trying to solve a puzzle.

"You know what?" she said after a long silence. "That pizza smells great, and it looks like an extra large. Are you going to eat it all yourself?"

"Leftovers for breakfast unless you help me out," he said, brightening.

She fetched the pizza, a couple of plates, napkins, and poured herself a half glass of wine from the spigot on the box.

"Luke is only sixteen," she said between bites. "If you want to push it, I'm sure the D.A. would be more than happy to move to have him tried as an adult. Based on all the witness testimony and the skid evidence at the scene, we're not buying Angela's story. There was no evidence of a hard brake. He wanted to hit you. He's looking at attempted second-degree murder. Attempted manslaughter, if he's lucky. A lot depends on you."

"Has he been arrested?"

"This morning, and then he was released to the custody of his father."

He gave it some thought and said, "Remember when you told me that it wasn't a premediated act, that it was probably someone who was just momentarily crazy with rage?"

"Yeah, and I still believe that's true. But it doesn't change the fact that he wanted to hit you."

"No, but it changes who he is. He's not a murderer," he said, indulging an image of the boy standing there with his girlfriend at his big brother's grave. "He's a kid who let his emotions take over. Like Angela said, he flipped out. Can't we just accept her version of it? Reckless driving, hit and run?"

A full smile this time brought out her dimples. "A littering ticket for trashing a body on the side of the road! You Greek philosophers would make lousy cops. But you're the victim, not me. I'll run it by the D.A."

"Good," he said, catching sight of a quicker end game with no sore losers. "I mean if the truck was insured, I should be able to at least get my medical bills paid for."

"Absolutely. But I'd advise you to find a good personal injury attorney. The insurance company will try to settle with you for as little as possible. Threaten them with a lawsuit and they'll spring for a bundle."

"Right now I'd be satisfied with having the bills paid," he said truthfully. "You know, Janet, it's just a big relief knowing that there isn't some maniac out there waiting for a second shot at me."

"Not for a while, anyway. No matter which way it goes, the kid's license has already been suspended. You won't be seeing him on the road any time soon." Checking her watch, she set down her wine glass and said, "I've got to run. I've got a date."

"What, on a Saturday night?" Edward replied, vaguely disappointed and a little surprised considering the pizza and wine she had just had.

"I know what you're thinking," she laughed. "Must be a cheap date if she has to eat a big slice of pizza first. Well, it is, kind of. I'm having dinner with my uncle at the assisted living center. Mushy peas and carrots and Salisbury steak somewhere under the gravy."

He followed her to the door and pleaded again for her forgiveness for once again withholding information.

"I'm getting used to it. In fact, I'm actually seeing a pattern developing," she said, then stopping just outside the door. "So, have you heard from Audrey?"

Hating himself for it, he replied, "No, I haven't."

"Okay," she said, and walked away.

He went back inside and, naturally, he called Alice, actually mouthing the word "naturally" as he was dialing her number. The call went into voicemail, and he left a message telling her of the arrest of Luke Herriman and asking her to call back for details and the opportunity to say, "I told you so." That left him time to consider what he meant by "naturally." Thinking back, it wasn't the first time his thoughts turned to Alice after seeing Janet. The same thing had happened when Janet visited him in the hospital. But then, too, Judith had come to mind following his date with Alice as well as after talking with Janet, who had never been far from his thoughts since the day he met her. Janet's easy-going nature, optimism, empathy, and understated competence had held him up better than his crutches. She seemed like someone who had come as close to knowing herself as anyone he had ever known.

He really had to concentrate on finding a job, he told himself. He had to put his mind back to work to keep it from drifting off in all these aimless ruminations. Adrift is what he was, reaching for one delusion after another. What was the point of imagining Janet, Alice or Judith by some defect in the path of reason falling into the emptiness of his life? He had through idleness succumbed to an easy, satisfying lull in the pursuit of his illusive self, and in the process, he had been losing ground. Moving to a stool at the kitchen counter to be closer to the pizza, he opened his laptop and picked up where he had left off at noon.

In the morning, he got up early and drove to the gym for a few extra sets of the upper body workouts he had been doing two days a week at the therapist's clinic. The gym was always nearly deserted early Sunday mornings, but by mid-morning it would be jammed with weekenders working up an appetite for the all-you-can-eat brunch at the Lamplight Restaurant. He was greeted with an encouraging thumbs up from Laurie, a fitness zealot whose management style mixed inspiration with perspiration.

Arriving on crutches was just the sort of thing that would make a good impression on her.

He had his choice of weight machines and decided to start with the lat pulldown, which felt a lot like the prolonged, vigorous stretch with which he had started the day, except for the repetition. From there, he moved on to the butterfly press, where he found himself sitting across from the fire chief.

"Hey, it's the professor. Stathakis, right?"

"Yes, it's Edward," he replied, postponing the first set. "How are you, Chief Hammond?"

"Fine, and it's Nate," the chief said, also pausing his workout. "My EMTs told me about your incident. I'm telling you, Edward, the roads are war zones. You're a lot safer over there on those treadmills."

"I know, but they can get pretty boring."

"I hear they picked up one of Herriman's boys, Luke," the chief said, shaking his head. "It doesn't surprise me. You know those Herrimans."

Mrs. Tidwell had said the same thing to him, and even with everything he had learned about the Herrimans since then, he still didn't know what they meant by it.

"Except for JJ, I've never met any of the Herrimans. And JJ was really a nice kid."

"The best," Hammond nodded solemnly. "But the rest of that family seems to be holding some sort of grudge against the world. Lola, that's Mrs. Herriman, she calls me and complains any time our trucks run past their ranch with the sirens on after she's gone to bed. She insists there's no need for sirens on the highway. We try to accommodate her, but sometimes we have to nudge the slow traffic out of the way. And Jon's impossible, but I guess you've found that out for yourself. I saw him tear into you on TV."

"He's understandably upset about JJ. Luke, too."

"Luke's just as hot headed as his old man but without that old time religion to channel it toward some purpose, whether you agree with it or not. Did you know that just a couple of weeks before he ran you down, we had to cut him out of a new Mustang his father had given him for his high school graduation?"

"No, I hadn't heard about that."

"Yeah, he and another kid were drag racing down the frontage road

inside their ranch and Luke spun out coming up out of a dip and rolled the car. Totaled it. If it hadn't been on private property, his license would have been suspended right then and he wouldn't have been driving the truck that day. I bet he caught hell from Jon."

"What about the other brother?"

"Matthew? Matt's a year older than JJ. He enlisted in the Army when he was eighteen. He was just discharged but he told me at JJ's funeral that he was considering re-enlisting. He says his dad is worse than a drill sergeant. There will be a fight over it. With JJ gone, Jon's going to expect Matt to step up and take on more responsibility at the ranch."

Listening to the chief, Edward began to have a more favorable impression of him. Nate didn't seem particularly thoughtful or sympathetic, but he was straightforward with his thoughts and not shy about sharing them, traits he had originally attributed to a shallow mind. Maybe that explained his appeal to women; Nate made no secret of his admiration for them. They simultaneously resumed their workouts, with Edward surreptitiously trying to keep up with the younger and more muscular man.

At the end of their first sets, Edward said, "Nate, I was up at Judith Scott's house the other day and I heard you talking to Franklin. It sounded like it got pretty heated."

Nate let go of the arm press and said, "What were you doing up there?"

"Judith invited me to use the pool for some hydro therapy."

"Oh, well, Judith is like that."

Like what? Edward wondered. Considerate? Careless? Imprudent? Thoughtful? He settled on that one, saying, "Yes, she's very thoughtful. She wasn't home, but I spoke briefly with Franklin. He said the arson case is likely to be settled with plea bargains."

"Yeah, I get where he's coming from on that, you know, with the involvement of his granddaughter. But I told him that if it were to go to trial, we could make a strong case for felony arson. That's why I was there. I brought him the fire marshal's report. It showed multiple ignition points with evidence of an accelerant. He insisted that those were due to some of the kerosene lamps in the lodge getting caught up in the fire as it spread. He argued that every time one of those lamps fell over, it accelerated the fire and made it appear as if it were another point of origin."

That sounded like a reasonable explanation to Edward. "Isn't that possible?"

"Sure, a burning beam falls from the roof, hits one of the kerosene lamps and you have a new flash point with an accelerant. But there were about a half dozen of them, and I told Franklin that the computer modeling done by the fire marshal wouldn't support that theory. Of course, I also told him that I'd be willing to admit under oath that it was possible. A jury might buy it, but it would be a hard sell with the insurance investigators. That didn't matter to him since he wasn't planning to file an insurance claim anyway."

The fire chief finished his workout ahead of Edward and then hung around at the counter with Laurie discussing the efficacy of certain exercises on specific muscle groups, which necessitated some comparison flexing and squeezing to confirm the firmness. They took no notice of Edward as he passed by them on his way out.

Dreading the scrolling lists of job openings awaiting him at his apartment, he crossed the street for a breakfast of scrambled eggs, hash browns, and toast with a coffee and two refills at the café. On his way out, he reached over a dog lying against the newspaper box and bought the Sunday paper. The dog, some kind of terrier with a scraggly-haired snout, perked up and, lured along by the crutches, followed him down the street to the city park. Edward sat down on the steel slats of a bench facing away from the rising sun.

"Hey, buddy," he said to the dog, who looked up at him with what he interpreted as anticipation.

He subscribed to the prevailing belief that a dog understands when it's spoken to. It may not know it in the true sense of *gnosis*, but it is aware that something has taken notice of its existence. Cats, too. Say "kitty" and they sense that they've become the focus of your attention.

So, he imagined from the questioning look the dog gave him that it was asking him, "What?"

It clearly expected some kind of progression from the "Hey, buddy" that it had just heard. A scratch behind the ears, a tousling of its hairy snout, a ball thrown for it to retrieve, a treat, a "good boy" compliment, a "go home" command, an interaction pertinent to itself.

Edward was reminded of something Wittgenstein once said: "If a lion could talk, we could not understand him." By which he apparently meant that an animal's reality is so different from our own that there could be no shared understanding upon which to base a dialogue. It would be like trying to communicate with an alien from another galaxy. That "What?" that he had attributed to the dog was only ventriloquism, his own understanding projected through the dog. For all he knew, the dog was conveying contempt for the weird creature that barked so unintelligibly.

Nevertheless, he persisted. "What do you want, buddy?"

Finding him not only incomprehensible but also about as stimulating at the now stationary crutches, the dog sniffed at the crutches one last time and then ambled back the way he came.

Edward turned his attention to the newspaper. There wasn't much there of any interest to him. Most of it he had already seen online, including a brief item about the arrest of an unnamed juvenile in the "hit-and-run accident three weeks ago that injured Edward Stethakis, a Gennesaret Christian College professor who was jogging with his girlfriend along State Highway 12 a mile outside of Connor." Stathakis, not Stethakis. Former professor. Girlfriend? He just wasn't sure about that one. A mile-and-a-half outside of town. If he had had a pen, he would have circled the errors and graded it a C. That detachment to himself, the out-of-body-like experience, that he felt in the hospital while listening to Jon Herriman berate him on TV crept over him again as he re-read the article. What does all of this have to do with me? he wondered.

He set the newspaper down beside him and then impulsively pulled out his cellphone and drafted a text message to oddreD, starting it as she had with "JTLYK," which he had had to look up to decipher.

"JTLYK fire marshal says fire was no accident but it will be plea bargained as one. All have agreed to it. Audrey U should come back and get it over with. 4 the best. Stathakis."

He set the phone down on the newspaper and leaned back, chuckling at the silliness of the acronyms. Was it really that hard to just spell out the words? A few extra taps? He had just done a dozen sets in the gym, three reps each, totaling close to a half ton of weight, for God's sake. That took effort. It was as if text messaging had just picked up where telegrams left off – stop – prune it – stop – words cost money.

A couple of joggers ran past him at a faster clip than he had ever attempted. In the distance, he spotted Sofia peddling her bike into town, as usual without a helmet. Wearing a long full skirt, white ankle socks and black sneakers, she resembled a bobbysoxer from a 1940s Mickey Rooney film. Her arrest for arson and the attendant notoriety didn't have her holed up in her dorm room with the curtains drawn. She was the only one of his students he had seen in public since their arrests. Maybe all of the others had like Katrina been spirited away by their parents until things blew over or, more likely, he just hadn't been out in public much himself.

Startled by a "ding" from his phone, he picked it up and was startled a second time to see a text in conversation mode from oddreD.

"Y cant we tell the truth? Y does a good thing become bad just cause its done with passion? Silence is better than a lie."

She was at that moment sitting somewhere waiting for an answer.

"I agree but lives can be ruined by this. They are scared. Prison is not an abstraction."

"I know thats Y. But we own it. It means something. People R listening. Weve got their attn for a few secs – we must say something important! Lawyers can lie all they want & doesnt matter."

Where was this subversive intensity coming from? He wondered. This was Audrey speaking, the devourer of YA romance novels.

While he was still composing a reply, she continued, "JJ understood cared suffered. He was 4 anima(l)s truly. We all were."

He wrote, "Plea in abeyance is not admission of guilt. No one can silence you but jail can. Come back."

"Ull hear from me. Details. Give me YR email address?"

He typed out his address and asked again, "Where are you?" If she didn't answer, he would take it to mean she wished to remain in hiding and that their communication was confidential.

"I know you care. B4N" she wrote.

"Audrey be careful," he replied, not knowing whether she had already ended the session.

He thought about Janet and took a deep breath. She said she was getting used to his concealments, but he could tell that her patience with him was wearing thin. He hoped there would be something in Audrey's email that would clarify to whom he owed the greater duty.

Once he was back at his apartment, he checked his inbox for Audrey's email. Nothing but the usual spam, offerings, newsletters, notices, etc., the usual items that would normally fill or kill some time if only to delete them all. However, less than an hour had passed since their texting conversation, so he wasn't particularly surprised or disappointed. He checked again an hour later, then after lunch, then whenever he took a break from filling out job applications, then after dinner, and a couple more times before giving up and going to bed. What was the urgency, anyway? he asked himself lying awake. She had already told him the fire was not an accident. Nate Hammond had said as much. What did the details matter, assuming that that was what she intended to offer? What did it matter, period? The case would soon be resolved to everyone's satisfaction, no details required.

When he got up in the morning, he brewed a pot of coffee and set out a bowl of Cheerios before he even thought about Audrey. Opening his laptop, he found her email there waiting for him with the subject line of "Pyre." She had sent it at 1:48 a.m. The body of the email was blank but there was an attachment, a file in the format he required in his class term papers, including a title and subtitle:

<u>Ethics 101</u>
Audrey Davenport

Liberating Jack
A Defense of Illegal Acts in Defense of Anima(l)s

When AnaLise Chen walked into my room with Jumpin' Jack in her arms, my first thought was that the cheerleader squad would be furious. The "goon squad," as some of us in the dorm called them, were the only ones allowed to touch "our mascot" in or out of his cage. "Fuck them!" AnaLise said. She planned to return the jackrabbit to its natural habitat and she was recruiting members of the Ethics 101 class in the endeavor. Why us? Because we had all participated in a philosophical exercise requiring us to place a value, worth, on the lives of animals with which we share our existence. When Professor Stathakis described the horrible bludgeoning death of a rabbit that he witnessed as a child, it struck many of us in his class as a testament to the cruelty we inflict upon ourselves when we are cruel to animals.

The professor's methods of stimulating thought included a clever dialectic hinting at a soul, anima, within anima(l)s. As the soul is unknowable except as a concept of faith, we might as well have been asked to consider how many angels can dance with the devil on the head of a pin. However, it can serve as a tool for comparison. Apply it to animals, and any cruelty directed toward them would be morally insupportable. Apply it solely to humans, and the question becomes, what does such cruelty say about our own souls? If we can cage, humiliate, torture and slaughter a rabbit, one of the gentlest creatures on earth, how can that not leave a stain on our souls, and if not on our souls, on our conscience? The (L) is not about the souls of animals, it is about us.

So, of course, I agreed to join AnaLise's conspiracy without hesitation. It was not at all a complex ethical decision. The only defense an animal like a rabbit has against inhumanity is humanity. We enlisted the enthusiastic assistance of Sofia March-Trevethian, who concealed the compliant creature in her bicycle bag and delivered him to the apartment of Noah Rosen, who had agreed over the phone to participate. Riley Marchant and Marty Engerbretsen joined us at Noah's and all together we decided to release Jumpin' Jack in the forest and to celebrate his liberation with a party to which everyone in the class would be invited. We all gathered at a campsite near the river below the college and there we set the rabbit free. We shared a moment of indescribable joy as the creature returned to the life from which it had been snatched. And yes, we recognized the dangers it faced, but those were the natural dangers of a natural life. In fact, Katrina Morrison mentioned the case of several activists who were publicly berated by authorities for releasing hundreds of minks knowing that many of them would be killed by predators, starvation or vehicles running over them. One of the activists had responded that *all* of the mink would have been killed and skinned in captivity. He said if even one of them survived, it had been worth it. And even those that hadn't survived had at least died running free rather than thrashing against each other in cages so small that they couldn't even turn around except by climbing over one another.

Yes we celebrated with alcohol and marijuana, but the more potent intoxicant that night was pride in that small accomplishment and a growing sense that we could and should do more. Katrina inspired us with her impassioned denunciation of her grandfather's horrendous "sport." She told us that she had always hated his lodge, which she called a "museum of death." She was powerless to stop him. She had tried talking to him, but he wouldn't listen. AnaLise said we could make ourselves heard to him and all the other big game hunters. Vandalize the trophies, or steal them. Katrina said that would make him more intractable. He would never allow himself to be bullied by anonymous animal rights activists, whom he considered misguided and misinformed. Katrina said if it were up to her, she would burn the place down. Why not, then? AnaLise said. Burn it down, get everyone's attention, make the case. Riley said we would all end up in prison. Noah said it could be made to look like an accident. Ideas then flew in from every direction. Yes, we could burn it down for the attention that it would attract and then issue a manifesto against the so-called sport. Afterward, we could claim that we didn't intend it to happen. We wanted only to exhibit Franklin Scott's stuffed animals to the world, to heap shame upon his infantile indifference to life. But if we were identified, we would still face arrest, or at the very least civil liability.

Jon Herriman, Jr., JJ, who had spent a great deal of time with the Scott family, disagreed. He told Kat that her grandfather would never allow her to be jailed if he had anything to say about it. At that moment, Kat looked as if she had just seen a unicorn. She gave JJ a big kiss on the cheek and said he was absolutely correct. If she were involved, she would face the same consequences as the rest of us. And if her grandfather had a say in the matter, she, and therefore all of us, would be protected from those consequences. But we believed that the only way her grandfather could have a say was if the fire were an accident rather than a criminal act. She thought it a brilliant plan. The hated museum of death would be destroyed and our abhorrence of big game hunting would be heard far and wide.

As you read this, *Lord of the Flies* may come to mind, but this was no descent into a mob mentality setting out to conquer an imaginary beast. Perhaps we were in high spirits, but we had a higher purpose. Even JJ, who struggled so much with his conscience, believed so much in the cause, perhaps even more than the rest of us. But he felt that he could not justify to himself any action against Kat's grandfather while remaining silent about his own father's ranch. It must have been so very difficult for him to post the video of that gentle cow being bludgeoned to death like Professor Stathakis' rabbit.

It was a simple plan. Move the trophies to the garage, "accidently" set fire to one of the heads in the great room, and then spread out into the lodge and ignite other fires to make sure the whole place burned to the ground. There was some debate about painting the (L)s on the garage doors, but if the accident narrative were to be believed, it would be necessary to demonstrate an expectation of being identified. A simple plan, brilliant, indeed, in the abstract. But once we began putting it into action in the main room, there were some defections. By then, however, it was too late to stop it. Once our merry little band gathered outside and caught sight of the raging inferno engulfing that huge structure, we all fled (some with cold feet) back to the campfire below and scattered into hiding from there. As we had anticipated, the investigation closed in around us. Every one of us either remained silent or stuck to our story, including those who now regret their participation. Only a few of us remain steadfast in our contention that this was a counterattack against the cowardly snipers like Franklin Scott who are engaged in an overt war against animals.

(Note: I have remained silent and watchful from afar, and increasingly fearful that most of my classmates may have been persuaded by their lawyers to openly confess their actions as a "prank," and to denounce our defense of animals as expressed in the email to the TV station as a "hoax." If they engage in this lie, if they discredit our actions, it is my intention to publicly disclose what really happened. However, recognizing that it is fear rather than disaffection that motivates my friends, I will remain silent for now. JTLYK)

Chapter 15

The legal process unfolded exactly as foretold by Franklin Scott with the only unanticipated aspect for Edward being the skillfulness with which Judith directed the public perception in its aftermath. His nine students had filed into the courthouse wearing their Sunday best and poker faces flanked by solemn attorneys and legal aides. Afterward, the lead attorney stood before cameras with the defendants gathered like a chorus line behind him and announced that justice had been done. These were not criminals, the lawyer declared with a firm nod to his left and then to his right. These were good students from good families who had engaged in an unfortunate night of school year's end hijinks motivated by their compassionate feelings for animals. All parties in the matter, including the fair-minded District Attorney, had recognized that while the students' well-intentioned but nevertheless imprudent actions had led to the accidental destruction of Franklin Scott's lodge, there was no criminal intent, only mischief gone awry. Therefore, he explained, the charges had been reduced to criminal mischief with the students taking a plea of guilty in abeyance. In a year, even that charge would be dismissed and these fine young people could move on with their lives without the stain of a criminal conviction. He thanked the Scott family as the victims in the matter for joining with the prosecution and defense in acquiescing to this fair resolution. He concluded by saying there would be no comments from the students.

But it was the later interviews with Judith Scott that most impressed Edward. She managed to frame the case as a constructive rather than destructive event in the lives of the young people as well as the victim, her father.

"My father's lodge can and will be rebuilt. My father's only regret – and mine as well – is that his granddaughter, my daughter Katrina, and her friends felt that a public censure of his hunting activities through an unflattering display of his trophies was the only way to be heard."

Judith's remorseful pause here appeared genuine, but Edward wasn't convinced. In his limited experience, the only emotions she had ever allowed herself in public were impatience, irritability, amusement and anger. If remorse, regret and sorrow were in her repertoire, she had managed to conceal them up until now.

She repeated her foundational explanation at every turn of the channel but tailored the details that constructed her overarching positive narrative to the questions posed by the individual reporters.

"Assuming the lodge is insured, is it fair that an insurance company and its other policy holders are left holding the bag for millions of dollars in damage caused by their carelessness?" one cable news reporter put to her, which Edward thought a good question.

Judith shook her head indulgently, not defensively, and replied, "Absolutely not, and that's why my father has chosen not to file an insurance claim."

A reporter from a competing network must have heard that exchange, for she followed it up with, "What about the costs incurred by the community? The cost of fighting the fire, the law enforcement costs, the costs to the criminal justice system?"

"Yes, that issue was raised during the course of the plea arrangements, and our family along with contributions from the families of the other students will fully reimburse the community. We do not take the risks taken by the fire fighters lightly, nor would we expect taxpayers to bear any of the burden. In fact, in gratitude for their bravery, my father has decided to pay for the new fire station that the community has long planned for the forest district."

When one reporter noted that the students' ill-fated activism had failed miserably, hadn't it? Judith played her ace in the hole.

"Not entirely. These are smart, passionate young people," she smiled warmly. "Their dedication to the welfare of animals as well as many persuasive arguments from my own daughter over the years have caused my father to re-evaluate his future participation in the sport of big game hunting. Moreover, he intends to contribute what he had intended to expend on a safari later this year to the local Humane Society."

"But doesn't that in a way legitimize their illegal actions?"

"Of course not. We certainly don't condone what they did. What I'm saying is that they could have achieved the same results through their passionate powers of persuasion. I truly believe that my father would have loved discussing this with them and he would have kept an open mind. I hope that this is the lesson these young people will take away from this: Reasonable people will listen to reason."

Neither the lead attorney nor Judith mentioned Audrey or any way suggested that one member of the "Connor 10" was missing from the proceedings. They spoke only of "these young people," while the news reporters blindly referred to "ten students," "ten defendants," and, of course, "the Connor 10." That only nine students were standing there behind the lawyer during his remarks had apparently gone unnoticed by every member of the press with ten fingers to count on until Mindy Dumont from the local TV station noted it during the late broadcast.

"That's right, Bob," she said to the anchorman, "I went back and checked our footage from the courthouse and I counted only nine students. I have asked for a clarification from the D.A.'s office but I have not heard back from them, so we have no explanation at this point for what may turn out to be a wild card in all of this."

As he watched and read the many iterations of the news coverage of the "Connor 10" plea deal, Edward wondered how Audrey was taking it. Her friends had kept their mouths shut through it all, probably at the direction of their lawyers, so they hadn't directly renounced their actions. But he thought she would have bristled upon hearing the word "hijinks" as well as the perception that they had bungled their ludicrous attempt at activism.

On the other hand, they had apparently achieved some success in their efforts to draw attention to the abhorrent killing of wild animals for sport. Hadn't they caused Franklin Scott himself to cede to their view? On balance, it was a win, wasn't it? He thought so, and maybe Audrey would as well. He hoped that she'd now be willing to return to Connor and take the plea deal before she found herself standing alone in the media spotlight. If she were to balk and release her account of the events at the lodge, she would be the only one who'd pay a price for the truth.

He had to hand it to his students. Their plan had indeed been brilliant. They had carefully sowed the seeds of doubt that misled the investigators, even Janet, and they had played Franklin Scott. They had essentially laid the groundwork for their own defense without the help of all their high-powered attorneys. He suspected that their behavior in his class, the apparent shunning of AnaLise and JJ and their defiant silence disguised as fear and guilt, was also a performance. They had accomplished what they set out to do and had outsmarted everyone, including him, in the process. If he were grading them, he'd give them all As.

Judith as well. She had succeeded in casting the students' misdeeds in the most positive light possible. She had portrayed them as principled and persuasive kids who though they had stumbled in the process had nevertheless achieved their goal. Instead of an ogre, a killer of animals and a vindictive victim prepared to toss ten young people to the wolves, her father emerged as a thoughtful, forgiving and magnanimous man who was willing to shoulder the cost of the lessons they had all learned from their respective missteps. Edward admired Judith more than ever. Beautiful, of course, and poised, she had presented her polemic without a hint of equivocation. She had brought her best marketing skills to the game. She spoke as if reading from a script off of a teleprompter, and more smoothly than Bob the anchorman.

The only dissonance was sounded by a local self-proclaimed "animal right-to-life guy" who identified himself to a reporter as "Cap, just Cap." The "Connor 10" case had been added to the court calendar only the day before, leaving no time for the out-of-town activists to muster a presence at the courthouse. High-priced lawyers know the drill. Cap, though, showed up on the steps wearing a black T-shirt with a white (L) blazoned across the chest.

"Where's the lawyer for the animals?" he shouted while the silver-haired and tongued lead lawyer for the defense was addressing the press.

A police officer approached Cap with a few magic words that silenced him until everyone began to disperse, and then a few of the reporters sought him out.

A short, thin man with a gray beard shaped like a shovel, and round, wire rimmed glasses, Cap had an affable though serious manner about him. Unlike the lawyer, he peered into the eyes of whichever reporter was asking him a question and ignored the cameras.

"Sure, I think the animals that Scott killed should have been represented in that courtroom. Why not? Isn't that what it was all about? Who speaks for them?"

One of the reporters played along, asking, "Well, if you could speak for them, what would you say?"

"I'd call what's happening to animals a crime against humanity," Cap replied, momentarily crossing his arms over the (L) before dropping them and clasping his hands behind his back. "The animals are innocent. They live and die in innocence, in a state of grace. We can't hurt them, we can only hurt ourselves, and that's what I'd say. I'd say people like Franklin Scott are committing crimes against who we are as humans."

When a reporter pointed to his T-shirt and asked him if he subscribed to "that college professor's claim that animals have souls?" Cap answered, "Sure they do, and if you don't believe me, just look into their eyes. I mean really look into their eyes, through their windows, and then you tell me they don't."

Edward had as usual cringed at the reference to him and the misrepresentation of his (L), but there were no reiterations from other sources in the immediate aftermath or in the days that followed. After those few days, he began to breathe easier, convinced that the worst was over. His role in the whole affair would soon be forgotten, and he, like his nine students, could move on with his life without a "stain" on his reputation. He considered it a stain only because that maddeningly pervasive misrepresentation had made him look like some kind of crackpot, like Cap.

He put off another visit to Judith Scott's swimming pool until he could demonstrate to Sonia that he was steadier on his feet. The physical therapy and visits to the gym had strengthened his upper body and improved his balance. At the same time, he found he was able shift some of his weight to his healing leg. According to Doc, he was progressing faster than expected. A couple more weeks and he'd be walking with a cane instead of crutches, Doc predicted.

Despite Judith's open invitation that Franklin Scott had reaffirmed the last time he was there, Edward once again called first and was told by the wary Sonia that he was welcome to use the swimming pool that afternoon. Upon his arrival, she escorted him through the house and kept an eye on him until he was safely sitting on the lip of the pool and then reminded him to use the intercom in the conservatory if he needed anything. He dropped into the deep end of the pool and then swam as he had before to the shallow side, where he went through his underwater walking routine followed by a couple of laps, and repeat.

The sun was high in a cloudless sky and hot, but he was kept cool even between reps by a breeze and the water washing over him as he bobbed in and out of the pool. Knowing that Judith had been in town as recently as a week ago for the settlement of her daughter's case, he gazed up at the second-story windows of the house and wondered if she was home. He hadn't inquired, and Sonia hadn't offered to say. Telling himself to get on with the business at hand, he sank under the water and launched into another lap around the pool. When he got back to his starting point, he found Judith standing above him in a swimsuit the pale blue color of her eyes with a darker blue mesh wrap around her hips. It was as if he had willed her to materialize right there before his eyes. She was carrying a tray of tall glasses filled with ice and a pair of crystal decanters.

"You look like you could use a break," she said, setting the tray down on a table.

"Hi Judith, I didn't know you were home." He stood up and swept his hair back. "I hope I'm not intruding."

"God, I could use a few intrusions," she said. "With Daddy and Kat gone, this place is like a mausoleum."

She leaned over him and held out her hands. He grasped them, and with a push from his good leg and a surprisingly strong twisting pull from her, he plopped down on the edge of the pool.

"Perfect. That's how we did it with my old swim teams," she said.

He slid backwards and raised himself onto a chaise lounge. She remained standing and asked him if he'd join her in a cold Aperol spritz.

"Just the soda, please," he said. "I had an oxycodone a little while ago."

"Oh, c'mon, Eddie. Two fingers, remember?" she said, displaying her long, thin fingers in a Scout's honor. "After all, we're celebrating. We finally got to the bottom of the missing rabbit. We took quite a detour along the way, didn't we? But we got there."

"Well, okay," he said and watched her as she poured the alcohol into his glass. But with the crushed ice, there was no way to tell if she limited herself to the promised two fingers.

From her breezy demeanor, he surmised it wasn't her first of the day, or perhaps she was simply breathing easier having successfully tamped down the tumultuous events of the past few weeks. She certainly deserved a celebratory lap.

Having only seen her in casual street clothes or her power businesswoman garb, he had had some sense of her contours, her beauty and bearing, but he had not imagined a body so perfectly proportioned, toned and taut. She was about the same age as him, for God's sake, and yet she would have turned a pool full of twenty-something bathing beauties green with envy while turning the heads of all of their boyfriends. She reminded him of the pin-ups from the glamourous golden age of Hollywood, right down to the one-piece swimsuit which highlighted rather than hid what in that golden age they might have called her charms. Maybe the rich really were different than you and me, he mused, though he found it hard to believe that even money could buy that kind of beauty.

"I saw you on the news last week," he said as she was handing him his spritz. "I was really impressed with the way you handled it. I mean your presentation, your coolness under pressure. You stole the show."

"I should have been in pictures," she laughed.

And she could read his mind, he marveled. "You must be relieved that it's all over."

"God, yes," she said, pulling another chaise next to his and stretching out into it. "It could have turned into such a circus. It would have, too, if Kat hadn't been involved. Daddy would have hung them all out to dry and then sued their parents for every dime it will cost him to rebuild the lodge. She cost him a small fortune, but I told him to just withhold it from her trust fund, for it's worth. At a certain point, even that kind of money doesn't mean much. Believe me, Kat won't miss it."

"How are you people able to breathe in the stratosphere?" he asked, trying to keep it light.

"Good question," she said. "Seriously, there are times when I feel like I'm suffocating."

"Has Katrina gone back to her father's?"

"Yes, she's gone back to San Diego. She wanted a little more time away from here to consider her next move. However, I doubt she'll be returning to Gennesaret. I don't blame her, with Herriman in control. In fact, I even advised against it. She had been accepted into my alma mater, you know, but chose to stay here. She thought my school was too elitist. Now, I think she's taking a second look at it."

"Please don't misconstrue this, but I was wondering about something," he began, determined to ask. "That day when you first offered to help me track down the person who took Jumpin' Jack, did you suspect that Katrina was involved?"

"Of course. That's why I wanted to talk to you about it. If she had taken it, I didn't want you marching her into Earl's office to be punished, or rather embarrassed for something so trivial. It would not have ended well for you."

"I had no idea she was your daughter."

"She told me that! She thought it was pretty funny that even after all those months in your class you never brought it up, even after I dropped in on you a few times. Never once a 'Your mother is a very considerate person' did she hear. You were apparently the only person in the school who didn't know it. That's why I was afraid you might humiliate her and then find yourself in even more hot water. Don't you ever talk to the people around you?"

Each time Judith had dropped in on his class, he had taken it as a personal compliment, a kindness directed toward him, the newcomer. His social antennae were so askew as to be totally unreliable, he concluded, and not for the first time in his life. His had been the only humiliation in the whole jackrabbit affair.

"I've been trying to do more of it lately," he pleaded.

"Good for you," she said, raising her glass. "Ask a question and ye shall receive an answer. You think I'm overprotective of her, don't you?"

"Not being a parent myself, I have no frame of reference. But I hope she doesn't take it for granted," he answered, knowing full well that Katrina had relied upon it all along. "Were your parents just as protective of you?"

"I don't remember needing it as much as Kat. She can be quite combative as well as rebellious, and that sometimes puts her up against a much tougher foe, as just happened. If I or my father didn't step in to referee those conflicts, she would get pummeled.

"My mother was always there for me and my sister as we were growing up, but after Frankie, after my little sister died, she had no fight left in her. That's when my father took over, reluctantly at first, but he saw to it that I had every opportunity to achieve my goals. Unfortunately, my goals included marrying one asshole after another, and there was nothing Daddy could do about it except try to warn me without actually coming out and saying the humiliating words he had in mind: 'cash cow.' By the time Kat came along, I could take care of myself. I jettisoned her cow-milking father before she was a year old. I was managing motherhood and kicking corporate ass by then, and Daddy began to transfer his papa bear instincts over to Katrina."

"Janet Ellison mentioned that she and your sister were close friends in high school."

"Do you know Janet?"

"She questioned me several times about the fire, you know, and then the hit-and-run case," he explained, puzzled by her surprise.

"Oh, of course, but why would Frankie have come up?"

"We were discussing Katrina and your father – it was the day after I met with him here, as a matter of fact – and she mentioned her friendship with your sister, and you, as well."

"Janet's a gem. I think we could have been much closer friends after Frankie died if her father and my father hadn't been at each other's throats. Her father Harry was the mayor back then and he just wouldn't budge on the red tape. It drove my father crazy."

"She told me about that as well."

"I'm surprised she told you even that much about her personal life. Janet doesn't usually share much about herself until she really gets to know someone. Nate Hammond went out on a date with her a few months ago and he told me afterward that she seemed very reluctant to talk about herself. I told him he had to give her more time, but apparently she had already shut that door. I asked her once why she didn't go out on more dates. She said the only men she meets in Connor are either intimated by her gun or attracted to it, and she doesn't care for either type. I gathered that Nate Hammond fell into that later category."

"I've really appreciated the way she has handled everything. She's been thorough and persistent and yet also patient and respectful," he offered, her patience with him uppermost in his mind.

"That doesn't surprise me. She's one of the most unflappable women I've ever met."

"Nothing seems to faze her," he agreed. "You know, though, Judith, after seeing how you handled yourself in the public spotlight with all of those reporters throwing difficult questions at you, I have to say you're pretty unflappable yourself."

"Fooled you, too, have I," she laughed. "I'm able to perform on cue, like a good politician, or that lawyer of ours, or a cute dancing dog. Put me in front of a camera, or at the podium at a real estate investment conference, or in a boardroom – whether corporate or Gennesaret – and I will put on a good show for you. Away from all of that, I'm anxious, restless, irritable, or just lethargic. Ask my parents or Katrina or Sonia. It doesn't take much to make me want to scream. You had your oxycodone this morning, well, I had my Xanax. How's that for unflappable?"

"I think most people have a public persona that's different from their private persona."

"Do you?"

He gave it some serious thought and replied, "Definitely. When I'm alone, I'm not particularly restless or anxious except when I can't totally shut out some unresolved external difficulty. And when that happens, I just try to talk myself through it, you know, an inner dialogue."

"Please don't tell me you hear voices!"

"No, nothing like that. It's just a thought process I have, that's all, a way to soothe my nerves. It works fine when I'm alone, but when I'm with other people it's not an option because I come across as spacey, or so I've been told. No, it's among people that my anxiety kicks in. I always have a bout of stage fright whenever I get in front of a class, for example, or even when I'm sitting around a lunchroom table with colleagues. Some of the news reporters have been trying to reach me, but I've avoided them all. If I were put in front of a camera the way you were, I wouldn't have anywhere near your command of the situation. I get flustered just having a one-on-one conversation."

"You don't seem flustered now."

"Fooled you, too, have I," he said.

Her laughter never struck him as forced, as a performance. It always came across as a genuine appreciation of an ironic revelation or the exposure of some kind of nonsense or absurdity. He couldn't imagine her laughing at, say, Pastor Bartholomew slipping on a banana peel, but she'd probably guffaw if you were to tell her that the pastor had purloined a banana from the dean's fruit bowl and slipped it into his pants pocket. She'd get it.

"How about that race we talked about?" she demanded, rising and reaching out to help him up out of his chair.

"Not a chance, but I'll do a few more laps in the slow lane."

In the pool, they swam at their own speeds, Judith gliding past him as smoothly and effortlessly as a dolphin while he towed his bum leg like a barge dragging an anchor. Worn out by the effort and the effects of the alcohol, he gave up after only his second lap and stopped to rest with his back against the wall at the shallow end of the pool. Swimming under water, Judith was nearly invisible until she rose up out of the water alongside him. She was breathing deeply but not gasping for air and beaming with self-satisfaction. Her gleaming blonde hair clung to her cheeks and the nape of her neck.

"You're doing fine," she assured him. "I could see your knee flexing. That's really a good sign. I told you this would be good for you."

"Doctor DiPietro says my recovery is progressing faster than he expected. He thinks I could lose the crutches in a couple of weeks."

"Great. You've managed to stay in shape despite the limitation."

"Physical therapy at the clinic and regular visits to the gym. That's been my life the past few weeks."

She turned sideways and placed her hand on his chest and seemed to be counting. "Sixty-four," she said after about a half minute. "I'll bet your resting heart rate is something closer to fifty. That's not bad."

Her hand was still on his chest, but he couldn't tell from her expression if she meant anything by it. He had long ago given up trying to read something into what may or may not be a signal. Alice had obviously been literally flashing a come-on from the moment he opened the door, and yet he had been blind to it until she climbed into his bed. That Judith Scott might be physically attracted to him seemed unlikely but not altogether impossible. Of course, socially she was out of his league, as his colleagues at Gennesaret were quick to point out to him, but sex could be played on an entirely different field. When she finally pulled her hand away, the only way for him to find out if the signal had been real or imagined was to risk a response. He reached over and brushed a strand of her hair away from her eye. They were now facing each other, and their arms slipped around each other. She was weightless as he rotated her against the wall of the pool, with his arms cushioning her back.

Chapter 16

"What happened to your arm?"

Jerry was referring to the scratches on the back of his right forearm, which he had sustained while shielding Judith's upper back from the abrasive concrete below the water line. His left forearm, which had encircled the arch in the small of her back, had only grazed the side of the pool.

"It looks like road rash," Jerry said. "Did you take a fall."

"No, I scraped up against some concrete," he said truthfully, while deceptively swinging his arm back and forth and slightly away from his body in a gesture suggestive of someone who might have been walking too close to a wall.

If he had wanted to be completely truthful, he would have told Jerry that he had injured his arm while cheating on his sister. But that wouldn't have been completely truthful, either, he said to himself. There could be no cheating absent commitments in a relationship. And as far as that went, he didn't actually have a relationship with Alice. All the same, he didn't feel right about it, it being both what had happened with Judith as well as revealing it to Jerry or anyone else. For one thing, whereas with Alice he had contemplated the possibility of a relationship, with Judith it fell within the realm of fantasy, as if he had brushed that golden wave of hair away from Veronica Lake's sultry eye. He may have entertained the idea for a moment or two in the pool, but then Judith said, "God, Eddie, thank you; I needed that." Having initiated the sex and gotten as much or more of it than she he had, he certainly hadn't felt used, but her words were sincere and real and not open to interpretation, no matter how much he tried.

"I was in a charity bike ride last Sunday when one of your students riding up in front of me got clipped from the side and tumbled. She didn't get nearly as scraped up as you. What are you, a power walker?"

"Who was it?" he asked, side stepping Jerry's question.

"Sofia something something. I stopped to help her and we walked our bikes for a bit until she shook it off. We got to talking about Gennesaret and she said you were her favorite teacher. I mentioned that we were friends."

"Sofia March-Trevethian. She was one of the Connor 10, you know?"

"Yeah, she told me. She drove the getaway bike with Jumpin' Jack. I like outlaws. She said you inspired her and her friends. I said, 'Wow, Sofia, if you were all doing Edward Stathakis' bidding, he must be one hell of a criminal master mind.' She said it wasn't like that. She said they did it without your knowledge, but they knew you would approve of it. She asked me if you had said anything about them. I had to say no, at least not to me. I had the impression, Edward, that she wanted your approval of her misbehavior and that you've disappointed her."

They were standing outside their apartment building, Jerry with his bike, a couple of baguettes poking out of a pannier, and Edward on his crutches. Standing was the worst. He tended to rest his full weight on his armpits instead of distributing some it to his hands and up through his forearms to his triceps and shoulders as he did while walking. Bowing his head seemed to make it even worse.

"I don't blame her, Jerry," he said, watching his foot wagging a few inches above the ground. He had suspected as much but it was nevertheless a difficult thing to hear. He looked up at his tall friend, who clearly expected an explanation. "The best I could offer them was to say that I understood why they did what they did but that I couldn't condone it. I wish I had done a better job of explaining the limitations under which I was operating at the time."

"Edward, I can't believe you pulled that 'I understand but don't condone shit.' You couldn't just tell them and everybody else what you really think?"

"What do I think?"

"That their cause was just. That they demonstrated the courage of their convictions, which you, by the way, helped to shape."

"I was starting to like it here, Jerry. I was walking a tightrope trying to keep my job."

"Believe me, I get it. I understand what you did but I don't condone it."

"Thanks," Edward said, shaking his head. "Another thing. At the time, I didn't know who did what or why. Neither Sofia nor anyone else was particularly forthcoming."

"Okay, you're off my hook. But listen, if any of those reporters comes calling, maybe you'll put in a good word for your junior partners in crime."

"Maybe. It depends on how some of the outstanding issues get resolved."

"What issues?"

"It's a long story," they said in unison.

But after the resolution of the "Connor 10" case and the lull that seemed by mid-summer to strike everyone like a sun stroke, there were no more calls from reporters. Not even after Mindy Dumont had discovered that the missing defendant was Audrey Davenport, whose whereabouts were unknown. Since she hadn't been served with a warrant and there was no evidence that she was eluding authorities, she would be offered the same plea bargain as the others when she turned up. And given the reduced severity of the charge that awaited her, there was no active attempt to locate her. End of story.

He half expected Mindy or one of the other local reporters to contact him when Luke Herriman appeared in court on the hit-and-run charge, but that went unnoticed, perhaps through the intervention of Jon Herriman, who apparently exerted considerable influence in election years. That was Janet's theory, anyway. Normally, the D.A. would have notified the local media of any high-profile case, but he passed on this one, she explained over the phone. She had called to tell him that Luke's license had been suspended for one year and that he was ordered to pay restitution in the amount to be determined after the insurance company settled the claim for medical costs and expenses.

"The judge had read my report and he was pretty disgusted with the measly charge he was left with, especially with the smirk on Luke's face the whole time he stood there. I think he would have sent him off to detention for the full two years of his minority if the prosecutor hadn't stated that you were on board with the recommended penalty."

"I'm just glad to have my bills paid and get it over with. Besides, taking away a 16-year-old kid's driver's license for a year is like sentencing him to a year in prison."

"True enough," Janet laughed.

He wished they had been talking in person so that he could have watched her as she laughed. It always cheered him up, left him feeling as if there truly was no deeper meaning to anything. Just the facts, ma'am. He hadn't seen her since the night they split a pizza. As his leg improved and he transitioned to a cane, he had taken to going to the gym more often, ostensibly for therapy but always on the lookout for her.

"How's the job search going?" she asked him.

“I have a couple of prospects. Nothing definite yet.”

He was too embarrassed to tell her that he had actually received only one offer, and that one had come from a community college in Los Angeles that was looking for a writing coach for an ESL class, hourly pay.

“Call me before you leave town and we’ll have that beer,” she said.

In the days that turned into weeks that followed, he began to think about leaving town without a job waiting for him wherever he decided to go. He thought he might have better luck applying for work in person in a big city, where the schools had a lot of turnover with replacements needed on short notice. The “Can you start tomorrow?” jobs. There was nothing but inertia holding him in Connor. His aquatic fling with Judith had, as expected, led nowhere. She hadn’t even asked him to stay for dinner. He had returned to the pool a week later and was informed by Sonia that Judith was away on business for the next two weeks, possibly three. Funny, Judith hadn’t mentioned it, he noted to himself, and then he asked himself, why would she? Some days, that inner dialogue that he had described to Judith was the only conversation he had. On those days, he would have even welcomed a conversation in text.

He hadn’t totally given up on hearing from Audrey but he was still surprised when in mid-August he received another email from her containing no message, just a link. Risking a virus, he clicked on it and was taken to an article in *The Plain Dealer* with the headline, “Activists Thwart Annual Charity Hunt at Buckeye Trophy Preserve.”

According to the article, someone had used a drone with strobe lights and an ear-piercing, hawk-like shriek to scare away the targeted animals and fluster the hunters, some of whom had paid as much as $10,000 to shoot trophy elk and whitetail deer. The article pointed out that the preserve guaranteed kills, even if it meant giving the so-called hunters a shot at an animal corralled just a few yards away. Animal rights activists had protested the “kill fest” many times in the past, derisively comparing it to shooting fish in a barrel, but they had never before succeeded in stopping a hunt.

“The hunt this year had to be cancelled because of the risk posed by the low-flying drone, which at times flew directly toward the hunters as they were about to fire their rifles,” the article said. “Witnesses said the drone was flying a black pennant with a white (L) insignia.”

There was so much there to digest that Edward didn't know where to begin. Obviously, Audrey was somehow involved, but she had never given any indication of the skill necessary to operate a drone with that kind of precision. Peter Huelander came to mind. Not only did he have the expertise with drones but he also happened to live in Ohio. However, Edward found it difficult to believe a mild-mannered techy like Peter would risk the almost certain jail time for violating the terms of his plea deal. Besides, there were a lot of skilled drone operators out there, and Audrey or whoever else might have been behind it could have easily found someone willing to fly under that damning flag, which is what brought Janet to his door a short time later.

She had received a call from a detective in Ohio who described what had happened at the preserve and recalled the (L) on the drone's pennant from the news reports about the "Connor 10" case. He was curious about the missing member of the group and had asked for any leads that might connect Audrey to their case in Ohio.

In for an inch, in or a mile, Edward decided, claiming, "I don't know of any. I think she's from Wisconsin. Peter Huelander is the only one from Ohio."

"Yeah, I know, I told him about Peter and he said he'd check him out. There could be a connection, of course, but I also told him that that L of yours has spread far beyond your class."

"I saw a local guy named Cap on TV wearing a black t-shirt with a white L, just like the flag you described," he offered.

"If Cap were involved, he'd be the first to say so. Besides, he's not the only one wearing that t-shirt. I've seen a few of them around town. Did you know they're for sale online? You should have taken out a trademark, Edward. With some creative marketing it could have been the next mark of Zorro."

"I had no idea."

"You Greek philosophers need to get out of your caves more often."

Her visit was brief. She had only come by as a courtesy to the detective in Ohio and hadn't expected to turn up anything new but thought she'd check just the same. As usual, he felt bad about deceiving her and yet he was not free to do otherwise. As soon as Janet left, he planned to respond to Audrey with a request that she clear up the question of secrecy once and for all.

"Hey, Janet, I may be leaving Connor at the end of the month, and I was wondering if you'd let me buy you dinner, with that beer, of course," he said. "I've really appreciated everything you've done for me and I'd like to thank you."

She regarded him for a moment, smiling, and said, "Sure, but I'll expect more than a slice of pizza this time."

"Absolutely, and wine from a bottle, unless you really have your heart set on a beer."

"I'll make an exception."

Lacking the sensational elements of Christian college students burning down the multi-million dollar lodge of a big game hunting mogul, the drone attack at the Ohio game preserve drew far less national media attention, and not much was made of the (L) that connected the two. Searching with the applicable keywords, Edward called up one broadcast where an Ohio law enforcement official said the flag appeared to be a copycat's attempt to take advantage of the publicity lavished on the Connor case. Since no one was hurt and no damage done other than the cancellation of the charitable killing of the specially selected animals, some of the news coverage even treated it with humor: "Angry Bird Dive Bombs Buckeye Event" "Under Attack From Snipers, Animals Call In Air Strike" "Deer Slayers No Match for Bird of Prey"

From Edward's perspective, while the staged "hunting" at the preserve would likely recover from the humiliating drone strike, the disrupters had achieved their purpose. They had been effective in focusing an unflattering light on a "sport" that if anything was even less defensible than trophy hunting in the wild. But would it change any minds that hadn't already been made up? On the other hand, was conversion the only measure of success, or was proselytizing itself the reward? As he pondered those questions, he wondered again how it was possible that his purely conceptual analysis of the relative worth of living beings could have motivated *every* student in his class to engage in anomalous and risky behavior. It was as if they had all been infected by the same virus, a case of collective obsessive behavior, like the unexplained twitching outbreak involving nine girls at a Virginia high school that had made news a few years back. The image of his grandfather killing a rabbit had been seared into his brain; so perhaps he had inadvertently passed that very real affliction on to his students.

It wasn't until after protesters struck at the venerable San Diego Zoo a few days later that reporters came calling again. The zoo had been hosting an outdoor, black-tie fundraiser with live music, international cuisine, champagne, and "star-studded performances," by which they meant animal acts, when hundreds of black balloons bearing the white (L) insignia drifted overhead and began to pop. Droplets of red dye fell like rain over the banquet, ruining tuxedos and gowns and rendering the plates of sous-vide rack of lamb, pheasant coq au vin, and butternut squash ravioli inedible, though the latter dish was presumed collateral damage. A few of the balloons also dropped recipe cards with messages mocking the event for frightening the zoo's animals with the loud music, serving meals containing the flesh of animals it purportedly cherished, and humiliating animals for laughs. Investigators discovered that the "pranksters," as they called them, had placed vegetarian capsules filled with limonene in each balloon along with a small amount of dye. The dye had been warmed to just the right temperature to dissolve the capsules as the balloons flew over the gathering. It must have required extensive planning and preparation along with exhaustive trial-and-error to get the necessarily staggered timing just right, along with the flawless coordination among the possibly dozens of individuals involved, one of the investigators explained with a tone of grudging admiration.

Just as he had associated Audrey and Peter with the drone attack, if only circumstantially, Edward thought of Katrina Morrison the minute he heard about the balloon drop in San Diego. It was not just her proximity to the incident, however, she also had motive and means. She had the resources necessary to put together such an elaborate scheme, and her recently acquired celebrity status might have attracted the small army of loyalists it would have taken to pull it off.

Mindy Dumont was not the first reporter to call him after the zoo story broke, but as she was local, she was the first to interview him in person. He arranged to meet with her in the city park. He sat waiting for her on the same bench where he had communed with the curious terrier following his talk with the fire chief at the gym. She arrived with her cameraman in tow and asked Edward if he'd mind doing the interview standing and facing the morning sun.

She began by asking him to explain the (L). He realized only after seeing the edited version of the interview later that night that he had answered with a much more detailed and nuanced explanation than she cared to hear. He gave her his by now stock answer that he had tacked the (L) onto Artistole's *De Anima* – "anima being the Latin word for soul" – to elicit debate and discussion. *De Anima* was an exploration of the nature of human, animal and plant life, Edward said, and he wanted his students to contemplate those distinctions, particularly in terms of what life, of what *being* means to both humans and animals. It had come up, he further explained, during a standard ethical exercise where an individual imagining himself as the driver of a car must choose whether to run over a jaywalker or swerve and hit an innocent person standing on the sidewalk. Throw in some variables, such as numbers of victims, ages and relative culpability, and then add a seeing eye dog to the mix, and "we were off to the races," he said, which was also cut in the edit.

"So you were suggesting that animals have souls?"

Recalling Cap's approach, which he thought had come across as more natural than that of the slick lawyer's, Edward looked at Mindy rather than into the camera as he answered.

"No, this was a class in philosophy not theology. I was suggesting that animals have an existence as meaningful to them as ours is to us and that their existence matters to them. And it matters to us as well, especially when we exercise control over their existence. When you recognize that fact, and I believe that most people do, whether or not it alters their behavior, the mistreatment of animals becomes indefensible."

"Your students were apparently motivated by your class to take certain actions that led to the fire at Franklin Scott's lodge. And now we've seen that L showing up in a drone attack on a hunting preserve in Ohio and last night at the San Diego Zoo. Do you feel any responsibility for what's happened?"

He had prepared for this one, and replied, "It's my responsibility as a teacher to share with my students as best I can some of the tools that were passed on to me by my teachers. What I hope they took away from my class was a willingness to ask the hard questions and to keep their minds open to the inconvenient answers."

It hadn't sounded quite so scripted when he had practiced saying it to himself. Mindy glanced at her cameraman and looked as if she were about to roll her eyes, offering Edward some hope that this comment, too, would be cut.

She quickly turned back toward Edward and asked the question another way: "Do you condone the actions of your students and anyone else who might be using the animal soul idea to justify these recent criminal acts?"

"Well, first of all, I doubt these activists were waiting around for a reason to care about the welfare of animals. They didn't need a lecture from me or a flash of light from heaven to break through apathy or indifference. Their own observations and consciences had already done that long before I wrote an L in parenthesis on a white board.

"As for condoning it, I believe they acted in accordance with their principles and I'm not about to condemn them. I'm sorry that Mister Scott lost his lodge and that some easy-chair hunters didn't bag their trophies and that some nice clothes were ruined, but I'm even more sorry that animals continue to suffer unnecessarily and be abused at the hands of humans. And I'm also sorry that my students and so many others find it necessary to make so much noise and even create some havoc over and over again to get the point across that animals' lives have meaning. I admire them for their courage and their tenacity, and I hope they never give up."

Jerry approved. He called to say so later that day and invited Edward upstairs for a drink with him and Doc, who, by the way, was curious to see how well his patient could manage the stairs. The climb was actually more difficult than Edward had expected, forcing him to rely more heavily upon the handrail than the cane. Stepping inside Jerry's apartment, he was surprised to find Sofia there.

"Hi Professor Stathakis," she said cheerfully. She set down the beer she had in her hand and stood up from the couch. "I saw you on TV and I called Jerry to tell him because we had just been talking about your class. He invited me over and said you might join us."

He awkwardly held a hand out to her and said, "It's nice to see you, Sofia. It's been an eventful a couple of months, hasn't it?"

"I guess so," she said, blushing. "I'm sorry I lied to you about Jumpin'

Jack. We were planning to tell you all about it eventually, but then things got crazy after the fire at the lodge."

"No need to apologize, Sofia. I understand. And I'm happy for Jumpin' Jack."

Sofia laughed and said, "I know, right? I wish you had been there to watch him hopping away."

"Me, too."

At Jerry's suggestion, they all moved out to the balcony, where a strong breeze and the setting sun gave Sofia's hair the same sunburst treatment that it got while she was riding her bike. Presented with the opportunity, Edward asked her if she had been in touch with any of the others from the class.

"AnaLise and Riley are the only ones left in town. I see them around, and I Facebook with Susan and Marty. No one's heard from Audrey."

"Judith Morrison told me that Katrina is staying in San Diego with her father," Edward said.

"I know," she replied. "Wouldn't it be wild if she had something to do with what happened there at the zoo? I thought it was beautiful, breathtaking!"

"It was hilarious," Jerry remarked. "I would have paid the price of admission and I might have even worn a tux if I could have been there to see it."

"I hope they get away with it," Sofia said. "I'd hate for them to go through what we what went through here."

Doc, who as usual hadn't said much after the greetings, leaned forward.

"When I was in medical school, some students broke into the research lab and escaped with an irreplaceable rhesus monkey that was being used in a critical stage of a cancer study. They also took away a few rabbits and cats, and they released all the mice and rats somewhere outside the city. I knew one of the students involved. He told me, not boasting or defensively, just as a matter of fact. And apparently the identities of the half dozen others who participated in the raid were also common knowledge on campus. But you know what? Not one of them was ever turned in, not by me, not by anyone."

"Oh," Sofia said, smiling uneasily. "Well, I think everyone in our class feels that way. We all have strong feelings about animals, and it was so exhilarating to discuss it at a philosophical level. It meant a lot to me, Professor Stathakis."

"That's very kind of you to say so, Sofia. If I hadn't already given you an A, which you deserved, you would be getting one now."

She had finished her beer and declined a second from Jerry, saying she had plans for the rest of the evening.

After she had gone, Doc said, "I noticed that she calls you Professor Stathakis and Jerry is just Jerry. Why is that?"

"R.E.S.P.E.C.T," Jerry said. "I don't get any."

"It's just the opposite, Doc," Edward asserted. "Jerry connects with the students. They respect him enough to say things to him they'd never say to me. It might be our difference in age, but I think it goes deeper than that. It's a formality that I've never been able to shake."

"Alice calls him Eddie," Jerry wryly noted, "but I think that's reserved for his girlfriends."

"That's an entirely different situation," Edward protested.

"I was just kidding," Jerry replied, rolling his eyes at Doc. "I bet you introduce yourself to your classes the way my elementary teachers used to write their names on their blackboards the first day of class: 'Miss Anderson' 'Mrs. Bowerbank' 'Mr. Fitzpatrick.' Even if they had first names, I would have never known what they were."

It was true. He always wrote "Professor Stathakis" on the board the first day of classes before the students entered the room. What Jerry was saying made perfect sense. If he were to write Edward or Eddie, that's who he'd be from then on.

"Would you like us to call you Eddie?" Doc asked as seriously as always.

"Thanks, Doc, but I've grown into Edward. That's who I am."

CHAPTER 17

He had just assumed that speaking out as he had in his broadcast and print interviews would sink what little chance he still had to land a job at a traditional college. After all, what reputable institution would hire someone who appeared to not only defend but actually promote criminal acts? So, he further assumed that the email he received a few days later from Joshua Forge College, a "historic bastion of liberal arts" in upstate New York, was some sort of internet scam or phishing expedition. The college, which he had never heard of, was inviting him to submit an attached application for a spot in its special "Sesquicentennial Issues Curriculum."

Having no Facebook, Twitter or other social network presence on the Web, he had been spared the pro-hunting, pro-gun, anti-lib, Bible thumping, meat and potatoes venom he was sure would have come his way online after all the exposure. But it was possible that his email address had somehow been compromised, possibly from all the applications he had submitted to dodgy for-profit schools which were known to sell their lists of gullible students to other racketeers. Originated by shady charities and magazine subscription services, the trade in these "sucker lists" supplemented the schools' harder-earned ill-gotten gains. He wouldn't have put it past some of those schools that he had contacted to pad their lists with any email address that happened to fall into their laps whether it was from a sucker or not. He dared not risk opening the attachment, and he deleted the email and thought no more about it until he began to receive similar invitations from other schools, some of which he had heard of, including Upland Community College. The same HR manager who had called to rescind the school's earlier offer wrote to say that they had received a significant number of inquiries from students who had been misinformed by Mrs. Tidwell at Gennesaret that he'd be teaching at Upland. Was he still interested? He also received an offer from Yale, of all places, to participate in a seminar that fall on "The Great Human-Animal Divide; Is the Gap Narrowing?" Not a job, just travel expenses and a modest honorarium.

Retrieving the email from Joshua Forge College from the trash bin, he researched the school and discovered it was a legitimate institution and that it was celebrating its sesquicentennial. Not only that, photographs of the school revealed a picturesque campus even more idyllic than

Gennesaret. The only drawback was the limited one-year term, which was always the drawback. Scrolling down through his inbox, he hadn't felt this overwhelmed with all the possibilities that life had to offer since the day he was awarded his PhD, never mind that nothing much had come of those possibilities in the many years that followed. He decided to give all the offers some serious consideration rather than act precipitously and pick one based on flights of fancy that had him wearing tweed and smoking a pipe into his twilight years. And whatever his choice, he'd soon have his destination.

He would have liked to have shared the news with Alice, to tell her he wouldn't have to lower his sights after all, but she had arrived at her dig in Caracol and would be inaccessible by phone except when she ventured into the nearby town of Belmopan. He couldn't think of anyone else he knew who would care. Jerry, with his own fat portfolio of job offers from the most prestigious universities in the country, would probably respond to his pathetic list with an indulgent verbal pat on the head, "just kidding." Then there was Janet, the only other person besides Alice who had cared enough to inquire about his job prospects, but he was not comfortable calling her on a personal matter while she was on duty, and he never knew when she was on duty or off.

Restive in his isolation, he grabbed his cane and headed into town for lunch. As he was passing Babe's Bakery, an emaciated cat with matted clumps of orange fur crouched defensively against the wall and then scurried away. A few steps later, another cat darted out from an alley and ran across the road and was nearly hit by a car. Then a small retriever without a collar ambled by, brushing against his leg but otherwise taking no notice of him. Another dog in the distance, possibly an unkempt poodle, ran out from under a parked car and disappeared into the city park. While it was not unusual to see an occasional stray animal around town, by the time he reached the café, he had counted five unattended dogs and at least a dozen cats, including a cluster of kittens that resembled a turtle wearing a fur coat racing in fits and starts across a parking lot.

"Say, Maggie, have you noticed more stray animals than usual roaming around town?" he asked the waitress after she had taken his order for the café's signature buckwheat Jumpin' FlapJacks and coffee.

"Yeah, no kidding," she replied, pulling a folded sheet of paper out of her apron pocket and handing it to him. "These flyers were all over town this morning."

The top half of the flyer consisted of a photograph of a man lifting a shaggy white dog by its rump and the scruff of its neck into a large metal container that was connected with a hose to the exhaust pipe of the Connor County Animal Control truck.

The large text that filled the bottom half read, "YOU PAID FOR THIS WITH YOUR TAX DOLLARS! THAT'S YOU KILLING THIS INNOCENT ANIMA(L)! DEMAND A NO-KILL SHELTER!"

"They broke into animal control and released all the animals," the waitress told him as she was pouring his coffee. "To tell you the truth, I don't blame them. It's just cruel killing animals like that, don't you think?"

Edward rubbed his forehead and handed the flyer back to her. "Yes, it's hard to believe."

"The mayor was in here for breakfast this morning and I told him it's outrageous. He claimed they were planning to do away with it anyway. The truth is, this kind of thing could cost him a lot of votes and he knows it. I told him he'd better do away with it or he won't get my vote."

As he was waiting for his FlapJacks and staring out the window lost in thought, someone tapped his shoulder.

"Hello Professor Stathakis," Audrey said, shyly pressing her chin into her shoulder.

"My God, Audrey!" he said, nearly toppling the table and splashing coffee out of his mug as he jumped to his feet. He didn't know where to begin. "What are you doing here? What's going on?"

"I was walking by and saw you in the window."

He must have looked right past her or, more likely, his mind had been elsewhere altogether. She was, however, someone who could walk into a room without being noticed or vanish in a crowd. If the police were to put out an ATL on her, which they very well may have, it would say: "Female Caucasian, age twenty-one, medium height, medium weight, medium length brown hair, eyeglasses, last seen wearing faded blue jeans and a loose fitting gray sweatshirt and carrying a green backpack." That's how he remembered her from his class, entering alone and then silently taking a seat in the back. She looked exactly the same standing there before him.

"Is it all right if I sit down?"

"Of course, please," he said. "Would you like some lunch?"

"No, thank you, I won't be long."

Her face had already reddened and she averted her eyes as usual, but except for her pronunciation of his name, she wasn't stammering at all. She dropped her backpack on one of the two chairs across from him and sat in the other.

"I just came back to pick up some things I had left at the dorm," she said. "I'm sorry I didn't answer your last email. Riley told me that you had been talking to a detective and so I thought I'd better not."

"Audrey, I wanted us to be clear about it that's all. I wouldn't share anything you tell me in confidence without your permission."

"I didn't think you would. I was just trying to be careful just in case. I guess it doesn't matter too much anymore. Riley said they're not looking for me and there's no warrant or anything. I got together with him and AnaLise last night," she said, reaching into her backpack and handing him a copy of the flyer he had just seen.

He looked at it once more and then at her. The change in her was astonishing. It was not only her unfaltering speech but also a directness in engagement and an air of confidence that he had never seen in her before. No longer the shrinking violet of his class, she was sitting up straight and smiling proudly, almost defiantly. Being a fugitive rebel with a cause had apparently done wonders for her self-esteem.

"Audrey, I admire what you're doing, really, but I'm worried about where it might lead. The three of you could end up in jail. Riley and AnaLise for all practical purposes are on probation. They could be sentenced right away."

"Riley took that picture," she said, lifting her chin as if to take a hit. "He saw that poor dog being killed, you know. Like you and the rabbit. He had to do something. We all did. Oh, I know, people will say, 'They'll just catch most of those animals all over again anyway and some of them will die out there.' Well, maybe some of them will get away and find a new home or just live free a little longer. And the ones that don't, they will have had a few more days of life, won't they? If you were going to die tomorrow, Professor, would you want to spend today in a cage or living out there taking the same chances that every other living thing takes every day of their lives?"

"I can't argue with that, Audrey, but you and others are taking too many chances with your own lives."

"Did you see what Peter and I did in Ohio?"

He nodded, his assumption confirmed. "Yes, that was amazing, Audrey. I have to admit, it was a very inventive way of drawing attention to those kinds of animal preserves. They should be outlawed."

"I know! They harass and kill animals and it's all legal, but when we harass the hunters, we're breaking the law. And did you see what Katrina and Noah were able to organize in San Diego? I couldn't believe it! It was even more awesome than our drone attack. I am so proud of everybody."

"Audrey, I appreciate your trust in me, but I hope you'll be more discrete. And I wish you would all step back for a while and maybe use a soap box instead of open warfare."

"We've been talking about that since the San Diego thing caused such a stir. It's made more of a splash than anything else we've done, including the lodge. I think maybe we'll cool it for a while, but this isn't a hobby, Professor Stathakis. After JJ set fire to the lodge, we all knew that we were involved in something bigger than ourselves."

She had lowered her voice and tilted her face away, as if someone nearby might be listening, and he wasn't sure he had heard right.

"JJ set the fire? What do you mean?"

"I didn't tell you the whole story in that last message because I didn't know what would happen in court. I didn't know what the others would say."

"They didn't say anything, Audrey, but their lawyers claimed that it was an accident even though the evidence suggested otherwise."

Maggie interrupted with his lunch and asked Audrey if she cared to order. This time, glancing at his FlapJacks, Audrey hesitated, and Edward persuaded her to have half of his stack while another order was being prepared. Maggie fetched another plate for Audrey and the glass of orange juice that she had requested.

"You said there was evidence?" Audrey asked when they were alone again.

"The fire chief told me there were signs that multiple fires were started with kerosene lamps on the second floor. He said it was persuasive evidence of arson but that Franklin Scott chose not to pursue it. Isn't that what you were counting on?"

"Yes, but it didn't happen the way we planned. It all changed after we started to burn some of the trophies in the big fireplace to make it look like an accident, you know, as if the fire spilled out of there and just got out of control. All at once, Katrina decided she couldn't go through with it. I think she had begun to sober up and realized that it was really happening. She started crying and screaming to stop it and put it out. She said she couldn't do it, she couldn't burn down her grandfather's lodge. So then Noah rushed to pull one of the heads out of the fireplace and tried to smother the fire with a blanket he pulled off a couch.

"And then JJ ran into the room and shouted, 'Get out! Get out! It's spreading fast!' We didn't know what he was talking about, but he kept shouting that the fires were exploding like crazy upstairs and that we had to get out right away. So we all took off. I could see the blanket catching fire behind me as we were running out of the room. Once we were outside, we could see flames shooting out of the second floor windows, and in just a few minutes there was fire and smoke everywhere. I couldn't believe how fast it all happened.

"JJ didn't know that Katrina had changed her mind and that she wanted to stop it. He didn't know. He was upstairs. He thought we were all doing what he was doing. When he found out, he just kept telling Katrina how sorry he was over and over again. She wasn't mad at him. She was just as sorry as he was for the whole mess. I believe that if it had been a stranger's lodge, someone else's trophies, she would have wanted to go through with it with the rest of us regardless because she felt so strongly about it. Probably more so than the rest of us. Do you know what I mean?"

"I don't know, Audrey. It may be that she felt that strongly about it because it was her grandfather, someone she loved very much, who had killed all those animals. She might not have been as passionate about it if it were someone else who had done it. It might not have even occurred to her to burn down a stranger's lodge in the first place."

"I suppose so. Maybe that is why she changed her mind. Maybe she couldn't do to her grandfather what she wouldn't do to a stranger. But it didn't matter anymore. By that time, we could have either called for help and ended up in a lot of trouble for nothing, or we could stick to our original plan. And, you know, Professor, JJ would have gotten the worst of it if we had bailed. None of us wanted that, especially Katrina.

"Afterward, we were all afraid that JJ would confess, and we pleaded with him not to. We told him everything would turn out all right if we all just stuck together. It wasn't his fault. But you know, he actually forced us to follow through with what we had set out to do in the first place. If we were to tell the truth now, people would say we're lying to save our own skins, that we're blaming the one person who isn't here to deny it. You believe me, Professor, don't you?"

"Of course," he said.

For the first time, it was entirely clear to him. Every piece of the puzzle fit. His students had courted disaster and when they achieved it in spite of themselves, they sought redemption through the virtue of their intentions.

He believed Audrey and he was sure Janet would believe her as well if he could persuade Audrey to tell her. But what would be the point of that? The case was closed. Justice had been served. Moreover, he had to agree with Audrey that some people, though not Janet, might think it was a little too convenient to blame JJ. Jon Herriman would certainly think so, and there was no telling what he would do, or how someone like Audrey would fare against his wrath. On top of that, if she were to surface now, Audrey would certainly be the prime suspect in the raid on the animal shelter. No, there was no point in telling Janet.

"In a way," he said to Audrey, "it really was an accident wasn't it?"

"I guess so, but none of us said so publicly or on the witness stand, did we? If we had, we would have looked ridiculous for claiming credit for the fire in that email to the TV station. No one would have taken our message seriously after that. It would have all been for nothing. We let everybody draw their own conclusions."

Maggie appeared with the second plate of FlapJacks, though they had barely started on the first. Audrey slathered butter over hers and smothered them with syrup while Edward scooped strawberry jam out of a pod.

"Will you be going home now?" he asked her.

"Not right away. Maybe in a few weeks."

"What about college?"

"AnaLise said you were fired because of us. Is that true?"

"No, they just didn't extend my contract into the new year, and it wasn't because of you. They felt that my class didn't fit into their vision for the school. It's all right. I'm an adjunct professor; I'm used to moving around."

"I won't go back there. I might take a year off. Where will you go?"

"I have a couple of prospects. I haven't decided yet."

Audrey checked her watch and then quickly took two more large bites of the pancakes and drained her glass of orange juice.

"I have to go," she said. "AnaLise is picking me up at the park. She's going home to Denver and she asked me go with her. It'll be fun, and then from Denver, I can take a plane or bus to wherever I want to go."

He stood up as she was slipping her backpack over her shoulders.

Noticing his cane for the first time, she said, "Oh, God, I'm sorry, professor, I've had so much on my mind, I completely forgot about that. Riley told me you were run over by JJ's crazy little brother. If he knew how much JJ respected you, he'd be begging for your forgiveness."

"That's all been settled," he replied. "I'm doing okay, and like you, I'm ready to move on with my life. Take care of yourself, Audrey, and stay in touch."

Stepping around the table, she quickly hugged him and hurried away like a Joan of Arc striding boldly into battle.

As he sat alone finishing his lunch, he felt his earlier optimism, his great expectations for the future, begin to dissipate like a pleasant dream after the first few moments of wakefulness. He would be leaving behind a mess of his making for someone else to clean up. Havoc and disarray everywhere he turned ever since he had the temerity to adulterate Aristotle's anima. And ahead of him lay a job at any one of several colleges that was seeking his services not in spite of what he had done but rather because of it. They apparently expected him to replicate the passions he had inflamed at Gennesaret, though, please, if you will, without the attendant criminality. They needn't worry, he thought. The odds of lightning striking twice through him were astronomical. For it to have happened at Gennesaret an extraordinary convergence of elements had to have been in place: the perfect combination of students with the perfect catalysts (Katrina, JJ, AnaLise, Audrey) among them, the perfect inspiration, the perfect rabbit and billionaire, the perfect time and place. He could give the same lecture a hundred times at a hundred different colleges without achieving the same results. At his next class, his anima(l) shtick might very well be met with laughs or yawns, and a disappointed administration would soon send him packing. But what choice did he have?

Well, at least he could choose where he would go to test his theory of the singularity of Gennesaret, and he was determined to do just that when got back to his apartment. Reviewing his short list of job offers, he weighed the pros and cons of each until he settled once again on Upland Community College. It was the easiest choice to make because he had made it once before and he had already thought through all the trivial details of getting there and being there. He had already imagined himself there and could easily do so again, something that proved more difficult when considering the great sesquicentennial expectations of Joshua Forge. Shedding any lingering ambition, he gave no more thought at all to the Yale seminar. He just wasn't up to it.

That done, there was nothing left for him to do except pack the few belongings that he had bothered to unpack. He was especially grateful that his books were already boxed. Once he received confirmation that his application had been accepted, he'd load up his car and consign Gennesaret to memory, to the substratum of his being. First, though, there was his date with Janet, the only thing in his life right now that he was looking forward to.

Chapter 18

"I'm afraid I'm going to have to cancel on that dinner," Janet said.

He pressed his phone against his check and processed her words. Cancel, not put off. And yet something had probably just come up for that night. She was a police detective; things happened without notice.

"Oh, okay, I understand," he said, choosing to hear it that way. "I won't be leaving until Friday, so maybe tomorrow or the next day."

"No, Edward, you don't understand." Her voice was mild, even, constrained. "We've arrested Riley in connection with the raid on the animal shelter. Sergeant Marchant brought him in himself. Can you imagine how Don must have felt? He suspected his little brother was involved from the moment that flyer turned up. The shelter is right across the parking lot from our office, and the euthanasia unit in back isn't accessible to just anybody off the street. Riley took that picture, and then he and a couple of friends released the animals. He won't say who. But I bet you know, don't you?"

Oh, hell, he thought. Either Audrey had mentioned their meeting to Riley or someone had seen them together at the café.

"I'd like to explain, Janet, if I could," he said.

"It's too late for that," she replied, her voice rising. "I've given you every opportunity to be square with me, to trust me, and you've burned me every time. Did you think Maggie wouldn't recognize Audrey? Audrey was no stranger at the café, and neither were you. And unlike you, Maggie had enough respect for me to tell me."

"I've meant no disrespect, Janet. Audrey spoke to me in confidence. She trusted me as well. And if Audrey, like JJ, hadn't felt they could confide in me, if they had never spoken to me, the results would have been exactly the same. Don't you see, you would have gotten no information from me because I wouldn't have had any to give you? I know, it sounds like an absurd rationalization, but that's the trap I was in."

"No, the results might not have been the same. I might have been able to stop this from cascading the way it has. Now, Riley will probably spend time in jail. And there's a warrant out for Audrey's arrest. Where has she gone?"

"She left town with AnaLise. She said she didn't know where she'd be going."

"There's more. You'll be seeing this in the news pretty soon. The police in Ohio have arrested Peter Huelander for that drone stunt at the hunting preserve, and the police in San Diego are looking for Katrina Morrison and her friends. They had their chance, now they'll all go to jail this time and not even Franklin Scott can stop it. He can pay for the ruined tuxedos and gowns, but the charges this time include assault and terroristic acts."

"I warned Audrey. I didn't want to see this happen to her or the others."

Janet was silent for a moment before continuing. "It's lucky for you that you're leaving town because Sheriff Ortega is looking for any excuse to have you arrested. You better not even spit on the sidewalk or make a right turn without signaling while you're here. The raid on the animal shelter occurred right under his nose, and that doesn't look good in an election year."

"I don't care about the sheriff, Janet, but I care about what you think. I can't tell you how sorry I am. I wish there had been another way, a third choice that would have satisfied everybody. I wish I could have been more honest with you without being dishonest to myself."

She sighed audibly and said, "Edward, set down that philosophy book and slowly back away."

That was a good sign, right, her kidding?

He thought so and pressed. "If these kids had been stealing or intentionally injuring people, if they had been doing anything illegal out of self-interest or with malice, I wouldn't have hesitated to tell you. They believed that what they were doing was right and that it mattered, and I had no answer to that."

"I know, but that doesn't fix it, Edward. Good luck at your new job," she said, ending the call, ending any friendship they might have had.

Setting down his phone, he reached for his last bottle of oxycodone. That third bottle of 30 pills should have held him through most of September, and yet here it was late August and there were only four left. He had been taking them "as needed," just as Doc had prescribed, and he was sure that he hadn't been abusing them. He had just needed more than he thought he would. He would get these twinges of pain in his leg above the knee – as he had while talking to Janet – and whenever that happened, he felt the need. He popped one in his mouth and took a sip of water from the bottle on the end table beside the recliner.

He leaned back in the chair and turned his thoughts back to Janet.

He wasn't surprised by her reaction, and he couldn't blame her. When she caught him holding back on his identification of Angela Nieto at the bank she said she was getting used to his furtiveness, but clearly it had bothered her on a personal as well as professional level. That night, after the scolding, she must have assumed that they had cleared the air and that the trust between them had been re-established. He would come clean from then on, and so, she had forgiven him. If he weren't leaving so soon, he'd make every effort to better explain himself to her, to somehow made amends, to gain her forgiveness one more time.

Picking up his phone, he called the clinic hoping for an appointment with Doc so that he could refill his prescription and leave town the next day. There was no longer any reason to put it off until Friday. Except for some clothes, including the dress slacks and blazer that he had intended to wear for his dinner with Janet, and a few other necessities, his car was packed and ready to go. He was thwarted by the clinic, however, as Doc couldn't fit him into his schedule until Friday afternoon. If he took the offered appointment, he'd have to stay in town a day longer than he originally planned. If he passed on it, he could leave the next morning with maybe one pill left. Also, if he passed on it, he would prove to himself, and to Jerry, that he was not yet so dependent on the pain killers that he'd be willing to put off his departure for four days just to get his hands on more.

The following morning, he loaded up what was left of his belongings and stopped by the manager's office to pay his final month's rent. Though it was still an hour before sunrise, the pitch darkness was beginning to give way to a streak of lusterless gray along the bottom of the eastern horizon. He had intended to skip breakfast, but he felt invigorated by the freshness of the morning air and the first steps he had taken, with minimal reliance on his cane, toward what he told himself was another of life's adventures. For some reason, he had always found it more stimulating to leave one place than to arrive at another. He had said so to Jerry the night before.

"It's probably due to the latency between the two," Jerry offered. "You know what you're leaving behind and you have some idea of what awaits you. The mystery is in the middle."

"It's all about the journey, the road trip," Edward acknowledged, trying to keep it simple.

They were having a farewell beer on Jerry's balcony and had been talking mostly about the gastronomical spectrum from vegan to omnivore, with Jerry trying to determine exactly where to place someone like Edward, who would eat eggs, dairy, and an occasional salmon steak while clinging to his virtue. With prejudicial terminology – "pre-chicken," "mother's milk," "baby Nemo," and the like – Jerry succeeded in inching him farther up the spectrum toward the omnivores but Edward would not budge past the halfway mark.

"Jerry, you're the only friend I have here," he confessed as he was leaving.

Jerry hugged him and said, "Listen, Edward, you must want a friend to have one. Give people a chance and you might be surprised."

"Okay, I get it Jerry," he said, "you're channeling Mister Rogers."

"Don't ever give up, Edward, and remember, it's all in the delivery."

He had no trouble finding a parking spot between two pick-up trucks in front of the café. That early in the morning, the few customers there tended to hail from the industrial and agricultural sectors of the local economy. These were the early risers and harder workers with a taste for the greasy spoon fare. The business class and college crowd were usually later to bed and later to rise, saving themselves for the battered lunches and the after work and midnight noshing.

Taking a seat at the counter, he ordered his usual scrambled eggs, toast and coffee, all the while trying to shake "scrambled pre-chickens" from his mind. He glanced at the bearded customer sitting a couple of empty stools away. The man looked over at him at the same time and they instantly recognized each other.

"Hey," Cap said, "you're the professor who came up with the L. I saw you on TV."

"Yes, I saw you, too," Edward said. "I was impressed with what you had to say. I gave it a lot of thought afterward. It's Cap, isn't it? My name's Edward, Edward Stathakis."

"Capson, Frank Capson. I go by Cap." He slid his bowl of oatmeal down the counter and moved to the stool beside Edward. "I'm glad I ran into you, Ed. I wanted to ask you something. You seemed to hedge when the reporter asked you about souls. You seemed to prefer the word being or existence. What's wrong with just calling it a soul?"

"Nothing. I just think it's been co-opted and arbitrarily defined by organized religion, mostly Christian, as some kind of a being within a human being whose existence is dependent upon faith. If you want to call your experience of life your soul or an animal's experience of its life a soul, I don't have an argument against it."

"I get that, Ed," Cap said, peering at him through his round, wire rimmed glasses and raking his beard. "But the being dies, the existence ends, but souls don't."

"That's where faith enters the picture. I can believe that that is true, but I can't know that it is. I believe what I know. Do you see what I mean?"

"Sure," he said, pausing while the short-order cook placed Edward's breakfast on the counter and refilled both their coffee cups. "I know when my dog Ruby was dying a couple of months ago, I saw the same thing in her eyes that I saw in my dad's eyes when he was dying. There seemed to be something there deep inside them, something behind their eyes that was saying, 'It's okay, I'll take over from here.' I guess I know it and I believe it."

"As I said, Cap, I don't have an argument against it." In fact, he wished he could believe it as well, but he had given up trying long ago. "I think when it comes down to how we view life here and now, we're probably in agreement."

Cap shrugged, "Close enough, I guess."

Cap seemed younger in person, aged only by the gray, prospector's beard and a frailness of body.

"What kind of work do you do, Cap?"

"I work at that auto recycling place a few miles up the road. I'm a junkyard dog."

"Oh, yeah, I drive by there all the time. Today will be the last time."

"Leaving town? I thought you were teaching up at Gennesaret."

"My contract expired. I've got a job at a college down in Ogden."

"Hey, Ed, I hate to impose, but could you give me a lift? The clutch went out on the junker I was driving. It was fine yesterday, then this morning it was shot. I think it's the throw-out bearing. I was going to ask around the room here since probably half of these guys are going that way, so if you can't do it..."

"I'd be glad to." He'd have to shift the boxes on the front passenger seat into the already crammed rear seats, but he figured he could make room for someone who had just called him Ed.

The process proved a little more difficult than he anticipated and involved piling the boxes in back up to the headliner and placing a couple of shoe boxes and an overnight bag under Cap's feet. Cap, a fairly short man, did not mind, saying the make-shift foot rest was actually comfortable.

As he was about to back out of his parking spot, Edward discovered that boxes were now blocking his rearview mirror, but he decided he could just as easily watch Connor receding from his life in the sideview mirrors until they reached the junkyard.

"Are you from here, Cap?" he asked his passenger when they were on the highway.

Before Cap could answer, the car was bumped from behind, crunching metal and plastic and jerking their heads back against the headrests. The tires screeched but the car held to its lane.

"What the hell?" Edward said. "I didn't see anyone behind us."

Looking into the sideview mirror, Cap said, "No headlights, Ed. Looks like they're pulling over."

Edward slowed the car and he, too, began to pull over until Cap yelled, "Gun it, Ed, they're taking another run at you!"

Incredulous, he hesitated and checked his own sideview mirror and saw a shadow-like vehicle speeding toward them. He turned back into the highway and stepped on the gas not quite fast enough. They were bumped again, more violently than the first time. The tailgate window shattered and the rear of the car was thrown sideways. He maintained control, however, and pressed the pedal to the floor.

"That's it, you're pulling away from them now, Ed. Keep going."

"Cap, my cellphone's in the console there. Call 911, will you?"

As Cap was reaching for the phone, something ripped through some of the boxes behind them.

"They're shooting at us, Ed. That was a bullet. Don't slow down, and swerve a bit, will you?"

He didn't need to be told. He was soon doing eighty and weaving in and out of his lane. They were approaching the series of curves along the stretch of road that ran alongside the river, but he maintained the speed and came out of the first curve well ahead of their pursuer.

"It's an old pick-up, Ed. They can't keep up with you on the curves."

"I've got it, Cap, make the call!

Edward was struck by how calm Cap sounded as he was talking to the 911 operator, how calm, in fact, he had been all along. Some of it had rubbed off on him and he told himself he was lucky to have Cap there with him.

As they were coming out of the last curve, he was about to speed up again when up ahead a rabbit hopped out into the road and stopped dead in the headlights.

"Shit!" Edward screamed, swerving sharply to the right and slamming on his brakes as the car plowed into a steep berm.

An instant later, the speeding pickup swerved just as wildly but to the left, screeching across the opposite lane while doing a one-eighty. It flipped and rolled down an embankment and crashed against a utility pole. Flames shot out from under the exposed undercarriage of the truck and smoke billowed out of the engine compartment.

Edward and Cap climbed out of the car, and while Cap was reporting their location to the 911 dispatcher, Edward rushed as fast as his injured leg could carry him across the road and down to the wreck. The truck was lying on its passenger side. Edward couldn't see anyone inside the cab and thought the driver might have been thrown out of it when it rolled. But when he hoisted himself up over the cab to check, he spotted the driver crumbled down on the floorboard against the seats. By then, the fire was spreading from the engine compartment to the dashboard and the cab was filling with smoke. He tried to open the door, jerking at it with all his might, but it was crushed in place. Taking a deep breath, he leaned down through the window and grabbed the driver by his belt and pulled him up far enough to then take hold of his arms. As he was dragging him up and out the window, the sleeve of his own jacket caught fire, as did the driver's pant legs. With one final heave, he tumbled backward off the cab with the driver falling on top of him. Only then did he feel the fire searing the flesh of his arm and the sharp pain shooting through his leg.

Cap by then had reached them and began ripping off Edward's burning jacket. Tossing it aside, he then scooped up handfuls of dirt to douse the flames on the driver's trousers,

"Can you move, Ed?" Cap asked. "This truck's going to be a fireball in a few minutes."

Edward sat up and with Cap's help got to his feet. They then each took an arm and dragged the driver away from the truck. From the light of the exploding fire, Edward could see blood streaming over the driver's eyes from a gash in his forehead as well as from his nose and lips and from torn flesh beneath his jaw bone.

"Why, that's Luke Herriman!" Cap said. "He was sitting there in the café when we left."

CHAPTER 19

During his second ride in an ambulance that summer, he was conscious the whole way and remained conscious as he was wheeled into the clinic and received emergency treatment for the second-degree burns over much of his left hand and forearm. A young doctor who introduced himself as Dylan assured him that other than significant scarring, there would be no permanent damage.

"When it's completely healed in a couple of months, it will feel tight when you flex the involved area, but it shouldn't impact your range of motion."

Edward's more immediate concern was the excruciating pain, for which the doctor ordered a shot that promptly knocked him out. He awoke a few hours later to find a nurse gently applying a fresh coating of antibiotic cream over his arm. She informed him that he'd be there for several days at least to guard against infection.

Doc showed up a short time later with the results of an x-ray of his leg.

"You stressed it, but there's no new injury," Doc said. "Your burned arm is our main concern."

"How's Luke Herriman?" Focused on his pain, he hadn't thought to ask until now.

"I'm not sure," Doc answered. "You know I can't say much because of HIPA, Edward, but considering you saved that boy's life, I will tell you that when he left here, we had him listed in critical condition. You saw for yourself the burns over both his legs and that injury to his head."

"Where did he go?"

"An air ambulance flew him over to the University Medical Center. They can handle that kind of trauma."

Doc urged him to use a walker and move around as much as possible, to sit rather than lie down when resting and to not hesitate to request pain medication.

"Dylan's your attending physician, but I'll look in on you from time to time."

A few minutes after Doc left, the nurse returned with a walker that was designed to use with just one hand. He sighed at the sight of it and lowered the head of his bed, hoping to be overtaken once again by sleep. He was about to drift off when Cap walked in.

"Hey, Ed, I just stopped by to check on you. I've been down at the sheriff's office all this time giving a statement. I've lost a day's work."

"I'm sorry about that, Cap."

"Don't worry about it, Ed. It's my junkyard. I can come and go as I please. My dad left it to me, you see?"

He smiled at the always earnest expression on Cap's face and said, "I was lucky to have you with me today, Cap. It would have turned out a lot worse if you hadn't been there."

"Maybe, but who knows?" Cap replied. "You know, Ed, when he started ramming and shooting at us I thought for sure he was aiming for me. I thought, you know, someone's pissed off about what I said on TV or because of an impound that ended up in my yard. I didn't think a college professor would have the kind of an enemy who would want to kill him. It was the detective at the sheriff's office who set me straight about that."

"Detective Ellison? Janet Ellison?"

"Yeah, that's her. She's a nice woman. Her father was mayor here for a couple of terms, you know. Harry Ellison. He once tried to close down my dad's business. He thought it was an eyesore. I don't hold that against her, though, it's just politics. Matter of fact, she sometimes sends business my way."

"I met her. She is a nice woman."

"I hope she doesn't send me that burned out pickup; there's nothing there left to salvage."

"Do you happen to know what happened to my car?" he asked Cap.

"Yeah, after they took you and Luke away, one of the cops told me they'd tow your car to their lot for safekeeping. I told them it had all your belongings in it."

"Okay, good."

"Well, Ed, it's been a pleasure meeting you, believe it or not. When you drive out of town next time, stop in and say hello or goodbye as the case may be. I make a decent cup of coffee."

"I will, Cap, thanks."

Cap started to leave, but then stopped and turned around, saying, "One thing puzzles me, Ed. You took a risk to avoid killing that rabbit, and I'd like to think I would have done the same. I have more than once, you know. A lot of jackrabbits get hit along the road there. But Luke, he set out to kill us, or you, I guess, so why would he have a problem running over a jackrabbit? Does that make sense to you?"

"I don't think he had time to make a choice," he answered, recalling the theory propounded by Riley Marchant. "It's what one of my students referred to as a kneejerk reaction. Something jumps out at you on the road, you swerve. I think if Luke had had time to consider his options, he wouldn't have hesitated to hit the rabbit."

"Yeah, sure, that makes sense," Cap said, nodding as he left.

Doped up with the pain medication, Edward fell asleep soon thereafter and awoke a few hours later when the scorching pain in his arm flared up. Another shot tamped it down, and he then got up out of the bed and took the walker for a walk through the halls until the cart with the dinner trays appeared. His injury hadn't dampened his appetite, and he sat down to his tray of fish and chips, green salad and garlic bread with uncharacteristic relish. As luck would have it, Jerry arrived in time to cast an ironic glance at the bite of Nemo still left on his plate.

Helping himself to one of the fries, Jerry examined the flaming red patches of skin on Edward's arm and remarked, "I had buffalo wings with cayenne hot sauce for dinner."

"You're looking at my arm as if you're hungry for more."

Jerry laughed and filched another fry. "But seriously, Edward, what is it going to take to get rid of you. We've said goodbye, what two, three times, and you're still here."

"Believe me, Jerry, it's not for lack of trying."

"Doc told me all about it. That kid got the worst of it this time. He was like Wile E. Coyote going after the Roadrunner with a stick of dynamite in his hand."

"He was the stick of dynamite, Jerry. He had to explode. I think it was inevitable."

"I was up at Gennesaret this afternoon along with some of the other faculty for a meeting with Jon Herriman. When he didn't show, Mrs. Tidwell came into the office and told us what had happened and that Herriman was on his way to the UMC. She said before he left, he dictated a one sentence letter resigning from the board and also as acting dean."

"I feel sorry for the man, for all that's happened to his family," Edward said.

"You wouldn't wish it on your worst enemy."

"No, I wouldn't, Jerry, and I didn't think of him or his son as my enemy. I was theirs, though. They made that clear enough."

"Doc says they'll discharge you by the weekend. What are your plans? You can crash at my place if you like."

"Thanks, Jerry, but my plans haven't changed. I'm leaving town as soon as I get out of here."

"Okay, I'll come by to say goodbye all over again before you go, but absolutely, positively for the very last time, Edward."

"I promise." Then as Jerry was walking out, he called out to him, "Jerry, have you heard from Alice?"

"Not a thing. When I do, I'll have her call you."

He was left alone for the rest of the night and thought a lot about Alice and then Janet. He half expected Janet to show up, not necessarily on a personal visit, but maybe just to take his statement, but she didn't appear until the next morning.

She walked in briskly in her uniform, as expressionless and businesslike as the first time he met her. He had expected as much, but he was nevertheless disheartened, and yet at the same time relieved that she had come at all, having feared she might delegate the taking of his statement to someone else.

Smiling lamely, he got up out of the chair beside the bed and said, "Good morning," not daring to say her name and afraid that substituting it with "Detective" would strike her as hostile.

"I thought you Greek philosophers usually drank hemlock, but you seem intent on doing it the hard way," she said.

"This wasn't intentional," he said, raising his burned arm, cheered by her unexpected smile.

"No, Edward, but you brought it upon yourself," she said, dropping her tote bag on the bed. "If you had let us put Luke away for a while, you both would have been better off. What's it going to be this time? Are you going to have us charge him with an illegal lane change?"

He hadn't thought of that, of the responsibility he bore for this latest fiasco. His own choices had left the door open to Luke's irrational anger.

"I know, you're right…" he hesitated, "Janet, but I thought he had gotten it out of his system. I had no idea that his rage or pain or whatever it was had burrowed that deep into his psyche."

She stepped around the bed and took a closer look at the burns on his hand and arm.

"That's gotta hurt," she said.

Dwelling on the revelation of his guilt, he asked, "How is Luke? Have you heard anything?"

"I'm told he could lose one of his legs. It's too early to tell, but he might also have some brain damage."

"Oh, man!"

She looked at him, reading him, and said, "Look, Edward, I was just giving you a hard time. If we could see into the future, we'd all do some things differently. You did what you thought was right. You gave the boy another chance and he blew it. That's on him, not you."

"Yes, it's all in how the dominos fall."

"That's it, you have to look at it philosophically," she said, laughing,

"I'll give it a try."

"The kid owes his life to you, but I wouldn't hold your breath waiting for a thank you. When I told his old man what you had done, he just sat there stone-faced. Didn't say a word."

"It doesn't matter," he said.

"Okay," she said, pulling a clip board and her smartphone out of the bag. "Let's get your statement on the record."

"Wait, before you start recording, Janet, I want to ask you again to give me a chance to explain why I held back on you. It's a lot more complicated than a broken promise. I understand why you're fed up with me, but if you hear me out, we might part ways without rancor. I know that with you an apology won't cut it, but you have no idea how bad I feel about disappointing you."

She smiled as if she had already forgiven him. "When are you leaving?"

"Probably on Friday."

"That gives us a couple of days. I promised you a beer, and unlike you, I keep my promises."

Though he could not see into the future, he believed that the future is created in the moment, recreated in the next, and again in the next… From the day of his lecture on De Anima(L), the tipping of the first domino, he had acted according to the dictates of that moment, in accordance with his will and the sum of his experience, just as any animal would. He could not have done anything differently, including breaking his promise to Janet, including giving Luke a second chance. That's who he was, Edward Stathakis, and he was okay with it.

"I'll hang around a few days longer if necessary."

"Okay, you'll get your beer. Now let's get your statement."

"It could have been Jumpin' Jack."

"Let's stick to the facts."

The End234

About the Author

Joe (Giuseppe) Costanzo was born in Pedivigliano in the mountains of Calabria in Southern Italy, a town not unlike the fictional Roccamonti in his novel ***RESTORATION***. He emigrated to America with his family, arriving in New York City in 1954 aboard the ill-fated Andrea Doria.

From New York, the family headed west, settling in Salt Lake City, near the coal mines of Eastern Utah and Colorado, where his maternal grandfather, Felice, once worked. His paternal grandfather, Stefano, supported his family back in Calabria from the rails in Pennsylvania. Both of his grandfathers were so-called "birds of passage" who frequently traveled back and forth between Italy and America and were the inspiration for his novel ***THE GRAND JUNCTION***.

After graduating from the University of Utah, Joe was hired as a reporter for the Deseret News and received a national award his first year on the job for his coverage of an airline hijacking. Over the next three decades, he covered some of the biggest news stories in the Intermountain West, including the execution of Gary Gilmore, and he won numerous other regional and national awards, including recognition from the William Randolph Hearst Foundation, the Associated Press, and the Society of Professional Journalists.

His experiences reporting on the issues of crime and justice, natural calamities, the environment, religion, the Italian-American experience and animal rights served him well in the writing of his first novel, ***GRAPHIC TIMES***, as well his latest work, ***DE ANIMA(L)***.

CPSIA information can be obtained
at www.ICGtesting.com
Printed in the USA
BVHW071339210219
540838BV00001B/15/P